A FATEFUL BETRAYAL MUST COME TO PASS . . .

"You're concerned about him, aren't you?" Andre said.

Travers glanced at her and grimaced. "Yes, I suppose I am. Funny, isn't it?"

"You got too close," said Delaney. "You allowed yourself to get involved."

"Listen, you study a man for half your life and then live with him, go through several wars with him, especially a charismatic man like Caesar, and you try not to get involved," said Travers. "The man's become my friend. You understand that? It's hard not to like a man like Caesar. Yes, he's ambitious and he's arrogant, but great men always are. He's larger than life . . . one of the greatest men who ever lived. And I have to make sure that he gets murdered."

Travers took out his Roman dagger and stared at the foot-long, lethal blade. "Can you imagine what it's like to be stabbed with something like this? Twenty-three times. Twenty-three times, they're going to plunge daggers like this into his body. And not only am I helpless to do anything about it, I've got to make certain it gets done."

"No, Travers," Lucas said. "*We've* got to make certain it gets done."

11 TIMEWARS

THE CLEOPATRA CRISIS

SIMON HAWKE

ACE BOOKS, NEW YORK

For Claude and Linda

This book is an Ace original edition,
and has never been previously published.

THE CLEOPATRA CRISIS

An Ace Book / published by arrangement with
the author

PRINTING HISTORY
Ace edition / September 1990

ISBN: 0-441-81263-5

Ace Books are published by The Berkley Publishing Group,
200 Madison Avenue, New York, New York 10016.
The name "ACE" and the "A" logo
are trademarks belonging to Charter Communications, Inc.

PRINTED IN THE UNITED STATES OF AMERICA

10 9 8 7 6 5 4 3 2 1

A CHRONOLOGICAL HISTORY OF THE TIME WARS

April 1, 2425:	Dr. Wolfgang Mensinger invents the chronoplate at the age of 115, discovering time travel. Later, he would construct a small-scale working prototype for use in laboratory experiments specifically designed to avoid any possible creation of a temporal paradox. He is hailed as the "Father of Temporal Physics."
July 14, 2430:	Mensinger publishes "There is No Future," in which he redefines relativity, proving there is no such thing as *the* future, but an infinite number of potential scenarios, which are absolute relative only to their present. He also announces the discovery of "non-specific time," or temporal limbo, later known as "the dead zone."
October 21, 2440:	Wolfgang Mensinger dies. His son, Albrecht, perfects the chronoplate and carries on the work, but loses control of the discovery to political interests.
June 15, 2460:	Formation of the international Committee for Temporal Intelligence, with Albrecht Mensinger as director. Specially trained and conditioned "agents" of the committee begin to travel back through time in order to conduct research and field test the chronoplate apparatus. Many become lost in transition,

trapped in the limbo of non-specific time known as "the dead zone." Those who return from successful temporal voyages often bring back startling information necessitating the revision of historical records.

March 22, 2461: *The Consorti Affair*—Cardinal Ludovico Consorti is excommunicated from the Roman Catholic Church for proposing that agents travel back through time to obtain empirical evidence that Christ arose following his crucifixion. The Consorti Affair sparks extensive international negotiations amidst a volatile climate of public opinion concerning the proper uses for the new technology. Temporal excursions are severely curtailed. Concurrently, espionage operatives of several nations infiltrate the Committee for Temporal Intelligence.

May 1, 2461: Dr. Albrecht Mensinger appears before a special international conference in Geneva, composed of political leaders and members of the scientific community. He attempts to alleviate fears about the possible misuses of time travel. He further refuses to cooperate with any attempts to militarize his father's discovery.

February 3, 2485: The research facilities of the Committee for Temporal Intelligence are seized by troops of the TransAtlantic Treaty Organization.

January 25, 2492: The Council of Nations meets in Buenos Aires, capital of the United

Socialist States of South America, to discuss increasing international tensions and economic instability. A proposal for "an end to war in our time" is put forth by the chairman of the Nippon Conglomerate Empire. Dr. Albrecht Mensinger, appearing before the body as the nominal director of the Committee for Temporal Intelligence, argues passionately against using temporal technology to resolve international conflicts, but cannot present proof that the past can be affected by temporal voyagers. Prevailing scientific testimony reinforces the conventional wisdom that the past is an immutable absolute.

December 24, 2492: Formation of the Referee Corps, brought into being by the Council of Nations as an extranational arbitrating body with sole control over temporal technology and authority to stage temporal conflicts as "limited warfare" to resolve international disputes.

April 21, 2493: On the recommendation of the Referee Corps, a subordinate body named the Observer Corps is formed, taking over most of the functions of the Committee for Temporal Intelligence, which is redesignated as the Temporal Intelligence Agency. Under the aegis of the Council of Nations and the Referee Corps, the T.I.A. absorbs the intelligence agencies of the world's governments and is made solely answerable to the Referee Corps. Dr.

Mensinger resigns his post to found the Temporal Preservation League, a group dedicated to the abolition of temporal conflict.

*June, 2497—
March, 2502:*

Referee Corps presides over initial temporal confrontation campaigns, accepting "grievances" from disputing nations, selecting historical conflicts of the past as "staging grounds" and supervising the infiltration of modern troops into the so-called "cannon fodder" ranks of ancient warring armies. Initial numbers of temporal combatants are kept small, with infiltration facilitated by cosmetic surgery and implant conditioning of soldiers. The results are calculated based upon successful return rate and a complicated "point spread." Soldiers are monitored via cerebral implants, enabling Search and Retrieve teams to follow their movements and monitor mortality rate. The media dubs temporal conflicts the "Time Wars."

2500–2510:

Extremely rapid growth of massive support industry catering to the exacting art and science of temporal conflict. Rapid improvement in the international economic climate follows, with significant growth in productivity and rapid decline in unemployment and inflation rate. There is a gradual escalation of the Time Wars, with a majority of the world's armed services converting to temporal duty status.

Growth of the Temporal Preservation League as a peace movement with an intensive lobby effort and mass demonstrations against the Time Wars. Mensinger cautions against an imbalance in temporal continuity due to the increasing activity of the Time Wars.

September 2, 2514: Mensinger publishes his "Theories of Temporal Relativity," incorporating his solution to the Grandfather Paradox and calling once again for a ceasefire in the Time Wars. The result is an upheaval in the scientific community and a hastily reconvened Council of Nations to discuss his findings, leading to the Temporal Strategic Arms Limitations Talks of 2515.

March 15, 2515—
June 1, 2515: T-SALT held in New York City. Mensinger appears before the representatives at the sessions and petitions for an end to the Time Wars. A ceasefire resolution is framed, but tabled due to lack of agreement among the members of the Council of Nations. Mensinger leaves the T-SALT a broken man.

November 18, 2516: Dr. Albrecht Mensinger experiences total nervous collapse shortly after being awarded the Benford Prize.

December 25, 2516: Dr. Albrecht Mensinger commits suicide. Violent demonstrations by members of the Temporal Preservation League.

January 1, 2517: Militant members of the Temporal Preservation League band together to form the Timekeepers, a terrorist offshoot of the League, dedicated to the complete destruction of the war machine. They announce their presence to the world by assassinating three members of the Referee Corps and bombing the Council of Nations meeting in Buenos Aires, killing several heads of state and injuring many others.

September 17, 2613:   Formation of the First Division of the U.S. Army Temporal Corps as a crack commando unit following the successful completion of a "temporal adjustment" involving the first serious threat of a timestream split. The First Division, assigned exclusively to deal with threats to temporal continuity, is designated as "the Time Commandos."

October 10, 2615:   Temporal physicist Dr. Robert Darkness disappears without a trace shortly after turning over to the army his new invention, the "warp grenade," a combination time machine and nuclear device. Establishing a secret research installation somewhere off Earth, Darkness experiments with temporal translocation based on the transmutation principle. He experiments upon himself and succeeds in translating his own body into tachyons, but an error in his calculations causes an irreversible change in his subatomic structure, rendering it unstable. Darkness becomes "the man who is faster than light."

November 3, 2620:   The chronoplate is superseded by the temporal transponder. Dubbed the "warp disc," the temporal transponder was developed from work begun by Dr. Darkness and it drew on power tapped by Einstein-Rosen Generators (developed by Bell Laboratories in 2545) bridging to neutron stars.

March 15, 2625:   *The Temporal Crisis:* The discovery of an alternate universe following an unsuccessful invasion by troops of the Special Operations Group, counterparts of the time commandos. Whether as a result of chronophysical instability caused by clocking tremendous amounts of energy through Einstein-Rosen Bridges or the cumulative effect of temporal disruptions, an alternate universe comes into congruence with our own, causing an instability in the timeflow of both universes and resulting in a "confluence effect," wherein the timestreams of both universes ripple and occasionally intersect, creating "confluence points" where crossover from one universe to another becomes possible.

Massive amounts of energy clocked through Einstein-Rosen Bridges has resulted in unintentional "warp bombardment" of the alternate universe, causing untold destruction. The Time Wars escalate into a temporal war between two universes.

May 13, 2626:   Gen. Moses Forrester, director of the Temporal Intelligence Agency (which has absorbed the First Division), becomes aware of a super secret organization within the T.I.A. known as "The Network." Comprised of corrupt T.I.A. section chiefs and renegade deep cover agents, the Network has formed a vast trans-temporal economic empire, entailing extensive involvement in both legitimate businesses and organized crime. Forrester vows to break the Network and becomes a marked man.

PROLOGUE ═══════════

Rome, January 10, 49 B.C.

The house of Gaius Cassius Longinus was surrounded by a wall, as were the homes of all wealthy Romans, for the city had been growing at an alarming rate. Every day, more and more refugees arrived from the provinces. It was no longer safe to travel alone at night. The streets were choked with thieves and cutthroats who wouldn't hesitate to kill for a few measly denarii. The gatekeeper opened the heavy wooden door, admitting Marcus Brutus and his slaves, whom he had brought along for protection. Each of them was armed with a *gladius*, the Roman short sword, and Brutus himself wore a *parazonium*, the bottle-shaped, foot-long dagger that no Roman male went without these days. The times had grown perilous. He took off his cloak and handed it to the gatekeeper.

"See to it that my slaves are fed," he told the gatekeeper. "Have the others arrived yet?"

"They are dining in the *peristylum*, Master Brutus," said the gatekeeper. "I was told to bid you join them as soon as you arrived."

"Thank you," Brutus said. He shivered in his toga,

despite several layers of tunics that he wore beneath it. Unlike Cassius, who never seemed to feel the chill and took cold baths every day to inure himself to it, Brutus always felt the cold. Roman houses were never very warm in winter. They had no fireplaces or chimneys. What little heat there was came from a system of central heating called a hypocaust, which consisted of spaces underneath the floors and in the walls where smoke and heat from a roaring fire stoked in the cellar could circulate. However, the courtyards of the houses were open to the elements and the cold always managed to get in. All Romans suffered in the winter, huddling at night beneath their bedclothes of tapestries and carpets, with open charcoal braziers burning in their rooms, rendering the air smoky and oppressive.

In winter, they suffered from cold. In summer, there was the stench. Slops and sewage were simply thrown out into the streets, where their stink mingled with the smells coming from the cook shops and the bakeries, many of which kept hogs to eat their refuse and the hogs, of course, left their own. It all mingled to produce an atmosphere that choked the lungs and drove wealthy Romans out of the city, to their country estates. Winter was a time of chills; summer was a time of fevers. Brutus sometimes wondered why he bothered staying in Rome. Being governor of a province would have seemed more preferable, but then Rome was Rome and the provinces provided no society, no stimulation for the intellect. Rome was the center of the world, and these days, the center of the world was turbulent.

Brutus strolled through the atrium, with its marble columns, exquisite mosaic floors, its curtains and elegant furnishings in ivory, bronze, and rare woods. Cassius had spared no expense in the construction of his house, and every year, he refurbished a part of it. There was always some kind of construction going on in Rome. There was a shortage of housing and most of the tenements were shoddily and hastily built. There was a constant danger now from fire, or from falling buildings. But Cassius was able to employ the finest architects and builders. The atrium, a large courtyard surrounded by a series of rooms, was open

to the air, with a large pool in the center that collected
rainwater and which, from time to time, Cassius had
stocked with carp. There were bedrooms on the second
floor, but Cassius lived primarily in the second building, the
peristylum. It was built around another courtyard, a metic-
ulously landscaped garden surrounded by columns, with
fruit trees, flowering shrubs, and fish ponds. In the warm
months, Cassius kept an aviary. He was particularly fond of
peacocks, though Brutus couldn't stand the strutting birds.
They were beautiful to look at, but their ceaseless, raucous
cawing was annoying in the extreme. Now, however, all the
birds had died, as they did every winter, and the garden
looked bleak, matching the disposition of the city.

Cassius and the others had already started their dinner.
They were reclining on their stomachs or their sides on
couches placed around the table, attended to by the slaves of
the household. The stove was putting out some welcome
heat and there were several braziers burning, as well as a
number of oil lamps, with wicks of flax that could provide
up to forty hours of light on a pint of oil. No candles were
in sight. Candles were used only by the poor, who could not
afford the oil. They used them very sparingly, since the
tallow was often eaten when times grew lean.

Cassius, though lean himself, had never known lean
times. He was fond of surrounding himself with luxuries.
The sideboards were adorned with gold and silver cups and
dishes, silver spoons and knives—though most food was
eaten with the fingers—and elaborately carved drinking
horns covered with gems and mounted in gold and silver.
The money Cassius spent on murals, on tables of rare
woods, or chairs of carved ivory could have kept an average
Roman family fed for several years. And, as usual, he set an
elegant table.

In the city, the staple food of the masses was wheat and
corn, which most people ate boiled, as a sort of porridge.
Few could afford meat. For most Romans, variety in diet
was provided primarily by vegetables, sometimes fish or
wild fowl. But Cassius dined like the aristocrat he was.
Dinner began with salads, radishes and mushrooms, eggs

and oysters, washed down with generous amounts of
mulsum, a sweet brew of warm wine mixed with honey.
The main course consisted of six or seven dishes—
mackerel, eels or prawns, boar, venison, wild goat, suck-
ling pig, hare, stuffed dormice, geese, ostriches, pheasants,
doves and peacocks, honey-sweetened cakes and fruit, all
washed down with copious amounts of Greek Chian wine
that was heated and mixed with water, then served in horns
and bowls so that bread could be dunked into it.

Frequently, Cassius' guests would gorge themselves until
they were so full, they couldn't eat another bite. Then they
would stick feathers down their throats, vomit on the floor,
and, while slaves cleaned up the mess, eagerly reapply
themselves to the feast spread out before them. Often,
Cassius staged lavish entertainments during dinner. Musicians played while his guests ate, or perhaps some popular
poet recited his latest works. Sometimes there were dancing
girls—Cassius was especially fond of dancing girls—and
dwarf acrobats and conjurers. But there was no entertainment on this night. The mood of the diners was grim,
conspiratorial.

"Ah, Brutus!" said Cassius, greeting him with a wave.
"Come in, come in, we've been waiting for you."

"It seems you have begun without me," Brutus said.

"Here, take a place by me," said Cassius, moving over
on the couch. "Don't worry, there is plenty more. Here,
have some wine. You look cold."

"I *am* cold," said Brutus, gratefully accepting the steam-
ing cup.

"You should immerse yourself in the *frigidarium*," said
Cassius. "I've told you time and time again, one must fight
the cold with its own weapons."

"I prefer to fight it with steam, thank you," Brutus said.

"You know everyone, of course."

"Of course," said Brutus, nodding to Casca, Cimber,
Ligarius, and Labeo. They were all influential citizens of
Rome. Powerful and ambitious men. He sipped the wine
and was gratified to feel its warmth spreading through him.
A good night to get drunk, he thought.

"We were discussing Caesar," Cassius told him. He picked up a radish and popped it into his mouth, crunching on it noisily.

"What else?" said Brutus, allowing the heat of the wine cup to warm his hands. "All Rome is discussing Caesar. One hears of little else."

"The man's a dangerous rebel against the traditions of Rome," said Ligarius, a portly, balding man who always spoke as if he were uttering grave pronouncements. He was known as "the soporific of the Senate."

"Caesar's entire life has been a history of rebellion," Brutus replied wryly.

"Yes, that is true enough," said Cimber, a young man with dark, curly hair and deep-set eyes that gave him something of a haunted look. "They still talk about how, as a boy, after he was nominated to a priesthood at the temple of Jupiter, he flouted convention by breaking his engagement so that he could wed a young woman of more noble birth. And when Sulla ordered him to divorce and honor his original engagement, Caesar refused! Can you imagine refusing Sulla?"

"I can well imagine Caesar doing it," said Brutus with a smile.

"I recall that story," Labeo said as he licked his fingers and wiped them on his tunic. "He was stripped of his priesthood, his wife's dowry, and his own inheritance. Sulla was so angry with him that Caesar was forced to go into hiding."

"Yes, but Sulla pardoned him," said Brutus.

"Only because Caesar had influential friends who interceded for him," said Casca with disgust. Casca had never been a man who troubled to conceal his feelings. Wiry, dark, and foxlike, his sharply chisled features gave him a predatory look. He was one of Caesar's most vocal critics. Perhaps too vocal. His friends frequently cautioned him, yet he paid them no mind.

"Caesar has always had influential friends," said Brutus. "He goes to a great deal of trouble to secure them."

"I hear he sometimes secures them in the bedchamber,"

said Labeo with a grimace of distaste. "Be careful, you oaf!" he shouted, hurling a piece of venison at the slave who had leaned over to refill his goblet. "You almost spilled that on me!"

"I had heard that, too," said Cimber, adjusting his tunic and getting grease stains on it in the process. He wiped at them absently, spreading them still farther. "During his assignment as aide to the governor of Bithynia, weren't there rumors of a homosexual relationship between Caesar and King Nicomedes?"

"Malicious gossip," Brutus said.

"Perhaps, but where there's smoke, there's fire," Cassius said, giving them all a knowing look. "And there has always been such gossip about Caesar. He swims in a veritable ocean of scandalous rumor. When the revolt broke out following Sulla's death, did he not immediately hurry home, anxious to take opportunity of any chances to advance himself?"

"Are you speaking of the alleged conspiracy with Lepidus?" said Brutus, reaching across the table for some fruit. "The way I heard it, he chose to stay well out of it."

"Only because he knew that Lepidus would fail," said Casca. "He was afraid to take the chance of throwing in with him."

"Afraid?" said Brutus. *"Caesar?"* He chuckled. "The man is absolutely fearless."

"Yes, that is true enough," Cassius conceded. "He is courageous to the point of foolishness. Such as that time when he was captured by Cilician pirates while en route to Rhodes. They held him for ransom for over a month, during which time it's said he often told his amused captors that he would pay them back by crucifying them. They doubtless found his youthful braggadocio vastly entertaining. However, they were not quite so entertained after the ransom money had been borrowed and Caesar was released. He raised a fleet to pursue them, captured them, and did exactly as he'd promised. Then he seized their booty as his prize and used it to raise a force so he could join the campaign against King Mithridates, for which he was voted the rank of tribune on his return to Rome. No, Brutus is right. If there is one thing you cannot say about Caesar, it is that he has ever been afraid of anything."

"Have you heard the story of when he was sent to Spain, as quaestor?" Labeo asked. "Supposedly, he saw the statue of Alexander in the Temple of Hercules and became quite upset. The thought that by the time Alexander was his age, he had already conquered the world while Caesar himself had done nothing nearly so significant caused him to quit his post and return to Rome, from where, presumably, world-conquering could be more easily accomplished."

"And there followed rumors of Caesar being involved in several conspiracies for revolution, most notably with Crassus," Cimber added. "Even then, he lusted after power."

"I've heard those rumors, too," said Brutus, "but nothing ever came of such plots. If, indeed, they ever existed."

"Oh, they existed, you can be sure of that," said Cassius, tearing off a piece of bread and dunking it into his wine. As he chewed on it, some wine dribbled down his chin and he wiped it away with the back of his hand.

"If nothing came of those plots, it was only because the moment was not right or the other participants in the conspiracies were hesitant," said Labeo with his mouth full. "But did that stop Caesar? No, he went on angling for higher office and making a reputation for himself as a prosecutor, one who was not above bribing witnesses to bring charges against his enemies."

"He also shamelessly curried favor with the public by staging elaborate entertainments," Ligarius added between gulps of wine, "which placed him heavily in debt. Yet it paid off. Eventually, he managed to secure the office of Chief Priest. They say he bought the votes."

"What about when Catiline was brought up before the Senate on charges of conspiracy?" asked Cimber. "The entire House was in favor of the death penalty. Caesar alone argued against it. Perhaps he was mindful of his own aborted conspiracy with Crassus."

"If that isn't damning evidence, what is?" asked Casca

sourly. "I heard he so incensed the Senate with his obstinacy that the house guard went so far as to unsheath their swords. They would have killed him, too, if not for Cicero's intercession."

"Not that Cicero was ever fond of Caesar," Cassius said dryly. "He simply thought that killing someone in the Senate was bad form."

Brutus chuckled. Cicero might have phrased it exactly that way himself.

"You may laugh, Brutus, but it would have saved everyone a lot of trouble if they'd done away with him right there and then," said Casca. "I tell you, his luck is simply unbelievable."

"What about when the House voted to suspend him?" Labeo asked. His white tunic was spattered with food stains. "The people clamored for his reinstatment and the Senate buckled under, restoring him to office. Yet no sooner had they done so than his name was linked to the conspiracy of Catiline."

"The man he had so ardently defended," interjected Casca sarcastically. "Yet he not only managed to wriggle out of that one, but he also turned the tables on his accusers and had them sent to jail. Can you believe it?"

"He always was audacious," Cassius agreed. "It was not long after that, the Senate decided to send him off to Spain. Doubtless in the hope that some obliging savage would stick a spear between his ribs. Naturally, Caesar immediately saw this as yet another opportunity to distinguish himself. However, he was worried that his creditors would seek his impeachment, so they could keep him in Rome until he could pay off his debts. Which, of course, he could not do. So what was his solution? He rushed off to Spain at once, without waiting for his appointment to be officially confirmed or even for the House to vote him the necessary funds. After all, why should such small matters of legality bother the great Caesar?"

"But you must admit that he did bring things back under control in Spain by the following summer," Brutus pointed out. He held out his cup to be refilled.

"True, but then he returned to Rome without waiting to be properly relieved and demanded, *demanded*, to be awarded a triumph," Cassius replied scornfully. "Not only that, but at the same time, he announced his intention to run for a consulship. Now everyone knows that a commander who petitions to enter the city in triumph is supposed to wait outside the city until he receives his answer, whereas a man who wants to run for consul must be present in Rome to file his candidacy. Clearly, Caesar could not legally do both, but did that dissuade him? Not Caesar! He tried to get himself exempted from the election regulations, so that his friends could file his candidacy for him. Talk about audacity! The resulting protests in the Senate forced him to either give up running for consul or forgo the triumph. He decided that being elected consul was more important, so he gave up the triumph, entered Rome, filed his candidacy, and, running true to form, proceeded to bribe the voters."

"The way I heard it, his enemies bribed the voters themselves to cast their lot for Bibulus," Brutus said.

"With the result that both men were elected," Casca said with disgust. "The whole thing was a farce!"

"And after his election, Caesar embarked upon still *more* intrigues," said Cassius. "He somehow managed to work his charm on Pompey, who was still angry with the Senate for the difficulties they had given him in pursuing the war against Mithridates. Caesar managed to patch things up between him and his old fellow coconspirator, Crassus, who was still smarting over being eclipsed by Pompey in their defeat of that rebel gladiator, what was his name? The surly-looking bastard with the dimple in his chin."

"Spartacus," said Brutus, popping a stuffed dormouse in his mouth.

"Yes, that's the one. Caesar brought Pompey and Crassus together and arranged for them to agree upon a pact. All three of them swore to oppose any actions of the Senate that any one of them might disapprove of."

"If you ask me, *that* was the turning point for him," Ligarius pronounced. "Crassus had the money, Pompey had influence and his soldiers. After that, Caesar began to make his presence in the Senate felt with a vengeance."

"Wasn't his first act a rule that all daily proceedings of the Senate and the courts be published, insuring that the people would know about everything he said and did?" asked Cimber. He turned. "You! Yes, *you*, the ugly one! More wine!"

"Yes, and he quickly turned that to his advantage," Cassius said. "When he proposed some agrarian reform and his old opponent, Bibulus, took a stand against it, Caesar actually had him driven from the Forum at sword point! The idea, one supposes, was to prove to all those who would read of the proceedings that the great Caesar would stop at nothing to champion any cause that would benefit the Roman people."

"And at the same time, demonstrate to the members of the Senate what would happen to anyone who dared oppose him," added Ligarius. He shifted his position on the couch and broke wind prodigiously.

"By the gods, Ligarius!" said Cimber with a grimace. "You could empty out the Circus with that one! *Phew!*"

"When was it that he married Calpurnia?" Labeo asked.

"About the same time Bibulus decided it was more prudent for him to retire from public life," said Cassius. He ate an olive and spat the pit out on the floor. A slave immediately picked it up. "Marrying Calpurnia gave him access to her father's money. At the same time, he broke his daughter's engagement so she could marry Pompey, thereby cementing his relationship with the most famous general in Rome."

"You tell me that was not ambition?" Casca asked angrily. "Nor was that enough for him! He then decided that being appointed provincial governor of Gaul would present him with the most opportunities to secure wealth and triumphs, so he used his influence to make sure that he got it."

"Well, that's not quite true," said Brutus. "The Senate was only too glad to give it to him. No sooner had he left his office than they began an inquiry into his conduct during his term as consul. The moment Caesar left the city, his *quaestor* was charged with malfeasance, laying the groundwork for charges against Caesar himself. But nothing ever came of it."

"Only because Caesar had contributed generously to all of the chief magistrates and supported candidates for office who would look after his interests," Cassius said. "He has always been a corrupt intriguer. I cannot understand why you defend him, Brutus."

"It is not my intention to defend Caesar," Brutus replied. "Nor does he require my defense. Can you deny the good he did for Rome? In Gaul, he expanded his army with legions raised at his own expense. He even went so far as to recruit and train an entire legion from the province. In the nine years of his military governorship, he subjugated all of Gaul to Roman authority. His legions took over eight hundred towns, conquered three hundred states, and killed over a million enemy barbarians, taking as many prisoner. If you are going to point out the man's faults, then do not neglect his virtues."

"Virtues! *What* virtues?" Casca asked, raising his voice. "You speak as if Caesar gained nothing for himself! Gaul has made him rich! And he was lavish in his gifts of slaves to anyone who could be of benefit to him. Any man who looks at Caesar's history with a clear eye can come away with but one conclusion! All Caesar ever wanted was *power*! His ambition simply knows no bounds. I tell you, he intends to seize Rome itself! He plans to depose Pompey and make himself dictator!"

"I have seen no proof of that," said Brutus.

"No? Then why did he refuse to be relieved?" countered Casca. "The Gallic Wars are over! The province has been pacified. Why does he refuse to disband his legions? I'll tell you why! Because he still faces charges of malfeasance during his term as consul! Because he still has debts that he does not wish to pay! Because he had made wild promises that he knows he cannot keep! And most of all, because he has acquired a taste for power and he does not wish to give it up. Even his old friend, Pompey, considers him a threat!"

"Perhaps," Brutus replied, "but there are those, present company included, who have gone to great lengths to make a breach between Pompey and Caesar. And frankly, while Pompey may be a great general, as a statesman he leaves much to be desired."

"Your feelings about Pompey are well known," said Casca, dismissing his comment with a wave of his hand. "He did execute your father, after all. Or was it *really* your father that he killed? Perhaps there is another reason for your reluctance to condemn Caesar. It is well known that your mother was once his mistress."

Brutus gave Casca a long, hard look. "Caesar is *not* my father," he said stiffly.

"Then why does he bear so much affection for you?" Casca asked.

"Was I invited here to be called a bastard and insulted?" Brutus shouted, throwing his wine cup to the floor. The slaves hastened to mop up the spill. Brutus started to rise, but Cassius took him by the arm.

"No, no, Brutus, stay, please! It was merely the wine speaking, wasn't it, Casca? It is just that we are all inflamed with passion and concern about our future. We meant to share our feelings with you. We had believed that you were with us, but it seems that you cannot forget your father's fate at Pompey's hands and therefore lean toward Caesar. Well, that is regrettable, but we love you none the less for it."

"You judge me wrongly," Brutus said. "I despise Pompey, that is true, but neither do I favor Caesar. Politics must be dispassionate. A lesson some of us have yet to learn," he added with a pointed glance at Casca. "I may not share the vehemence of your feelings against Caesar, but I do not believe that he is the man to govern Rome."

"Then you are with us?" asked Cassius.

"If it must come to a choice between Pompey and Caesar, then for the good of the republic, I must put aside my own feelings and stand for Pompey," Brutus replied. "Caesar has accomplished great things, but I believe that Cicero is right. His chief concern is for himself, not Rome."

"Cicero is wise," said Ligarius, nodding. He belched loudly.

"The gods have spoken," Cimber said, raising his cup and draining it.

"Then why have you not invited him tonight, so that you could partake of his wisdom?" Brutus asked.

"Cicero is wise, but he is also old," Cassius replied. "It is for young men such as ourselves to plan the future."

"To plan conspiracies, you mean," said Brutus.

"Against whom do we conspire?" asked Cassius, raising his eyebrows in surprise. "Against Caesar? He is not the power in Rome, thank the gods, yet he is a threat not to be taken lightly. All here are loyal citizens of the republic, merely expressing their concerns about the future. Is that conspiracy?"

"Perhaps not," said Brutus. "Yet it has the flavor of one."

"Come now, Brutus," Cassius said, putting his arm around him, "you are among friends. Set aside your worries. There are many flavors here to tempt you. Such as this excellent Greek wine, for instance."

Cassius gestured for a slave to pour Brutus another cup.

"Let us have no more talk about conspiracies." He winked. "At least, not for tonight."

Brutus drained the cup and held it out to be refilled. The wine was filling him with pleasant warmth. A warmth that seemed to banish the chill of an uncertain future. Yes, indeed, he thought, it was a good night to get drunk.

Capt. Jonathan Travers of the United States Temporal Army Observer Corps, alias "Lucius Septimus," personal secretary and aide to the commander of the legions, stood outside his tent and gazed out at the troops camped all around him. The legionaries were relaxing around their cook fires, but there was a tension of anticipation in the air. Each of them knew that in the morning, they would take part in a historic event that had no precedent.

The camp had been situated on the slope of a hill. The entrance gates were on the downslope and the rear gates

were at the crest. The legions had camped out in the open,
away from wooded areas that could provide an enemy with
an opportunity to make a sudden attack from concealment.
The earthworks had been thrown up around the camp, the
soil taken from a twelve-foot-wide ditch dug around them to
a depth of nine feet. The earthen wall itself was ten feet high
and six feet wide, enough room for defenders to stand on
top and hurl their javelins in the event of an assault. Timber
and brush had been used to reinforce the earthworks and the
ramparts. When occasion demanded it, wooden towers
could be placed atop the wall, but this was only a temporary
camp and there was no need for them.

The camp was laid out in a large rectangle, divided into
three roughly equal parts. These divisions were marked off
by two broad "streets" that ran the width of the entire camp.
The *praetorium* was the headquarters section, where
Travers had his tent. It occupied a wide space in the exact
center. Directly behind the *praetorium* and separated from it
by the second of the two main streets, the *via quintana*, was
the *quaestorium*. It was a similar space situated at the
middle of the camp, where hostages, prisoners, booty,
forage, and supplies were kept. The *praetentura* was the
front section of the camp, separated from headquarters
section by the first of the two main streets, the *via
principalis*. One fourth of the cohorts were encamped there,
in tents facing the wall, on either side of the *via praetoria*,
which was the street leading from the center of the camp to
the front gates. Half the cavalry was camped there too, as
well as the archers and the slingers, situated so that they
could quickly move out the front gate to form an advance
guard in the event of an attack.

The remainder of the cohorts and the cavalry were
disposed on either side of the *praetorium* and in the rear of
the camp. Running around the entire perimeter, just inside
the wall, was a broad street one hundred and twenty feet
wide, meant to allow movement for the troops defending
the walls and to prevent hostile missiles coming over the
wall from reaching the tents. There were smaller streets
running lengthwise and widthwise throughout the camp,

separating each cohort from the one beside it. Everything was laid out with practiced, logical precision. There was a specific allotment of space for the tents, the pack animals, the servants, and the stacking of weapons. The plan never varied from this basic layout. The soldiers were so well drilled at setting up the camp that they had begun digging the fortifications at noon and the entire task had been completed shortly before sunset. Each man had worked for one hour before he was relieved, while other troops formed a protective front to cover the work while details of cavalry scouted the area to provide security. Everything was done with an efficiency and a precision that an elite 27th-century military unit would have envied, but then again, these were no ordinary troops. The Romans had fielded some of the finest armies in all of history and these were the finest troops ever fielded by Rome, led by the greatest general the republic had ever seen—Gaius Julius Caesar.

As a career officer in the Observer Crops, Travers would spend most of his adult life stationed in this time period, in the 1st century before the birth of Christ. Volunteers for Long Term Observer posts did not receive antiagathic treatments to retard the aging process. (Had Travers come from a family that could have afforded buying those treatments for him at an early age, he would not have qualified for L.T.O. posting, otherwise how could he explain remaining youthful while everyone around him aged normally?) The hazardous nature of his assignment meant that he could easily lose his life at any time. Few people would have volunteered for such a post, but Travers was one of a unique group of scholar adventurers who eagerly accepted such risks and hardships in return for the opportunity to spend their lives in intensive, close-up study of important historical figures—observing history as it was being made and safeguarding it, as well.

Though he would be an old man when Travers returned to the 27th century, he would not have traded this opportunity for anything. When he clocked back to Plus Time, assuming he survived to complete his tour of duty, Travers would receive his antiagathic treatments. (Though they would not then be as effective as they would have been had he received them as a younger man.) They would not return his lost youth, but they would nevertheless extend his life beyond the normal span. He would be able to retire on a government pension, with all of its attendant perks, to either teach or write about his experiences. Travers hoped to produce the definitive life of Julius Caesar, as written by a man who had witnessed most of it firsthand.

The preparations for his assignment had been exhaustive. Qualification as an L.T.O. placed him among the elite of the Temporal Corps, second only to the agents of Temporal Intelligence. Only those with the very best educational backgrounds were selected and they had to be in peak physical condition, as well. (Once they graduated from the grueling training course, they were given implant conditioning, programmed through a biochip surgically implanted in the cerebral cortex with the knowledge and the behavior modification patterns that would enable them to blend in with the time period and the society within which they would have to function.) Cosmetic surgery was performed when necessary. They had to look the parts they were to play.

Travers had an outstanding classical education and a gift for languages. He was fluent in Greek and Latin, but that was not enough. He had to be conditioned not only to speak, but to *think* in Latin and behave as a Roman would. Being well versed in history could also be a liability. It would hardly do for him to quote Cicero in casual conversation before Cicero had actually said what he was quoting! The Time Wars had rendered the continuity of history fragile enough without endangering it further, especially now that insurgents from the parallel universe were seeking to disrupt the timestream. Not only did Travers have to pass as a Roman and survive long enough to complete his dangerous assignment, he had to be on the alert for temporal anomalies. He also had to watch his step, to make sure he did not cause any himself.

It had been necessary for him to have become an expert on the life and times of Julius Caesar, but even that was not enough. There was no escaping the Principle of Temporal Uncertainty. It was impossible to determine absolutely any degree of deviation from the original historical scenario because of the lack of total historical documentation. There was always room for error. No one could possibly document any historical period down to the most minute detail. In any given period of time, things had occurred that history had no knowledge of. It was also possible that the mere fact of Travers' presence could affect events in some way. Every moment Travers spent in Minus Time was dangerous. Yet that was part of the intoxicating thrill. To Travers, the risk was worth it. He already knew more about Julius Caesar than anyone living in his own time period. With each moment he spent in Minus Time, he was learning more.

He found Caesar to be brilliant, innovative, an extremely versatile commander. He was completely fearless and his opponents found him totally unpredictable. A skillful swordsman and horseman, he often led his legions on foot, marching like an ordinary soldier rather than riding like a general. He lived life at a much faster pace than those around him. His tremendous powers of endurance allowed him to cover over a hundred miles a day in light carriages, traveling over the worst of roads at twice the pace of the average traveler. He often dictated letters and reports to his secretaries en route, sometimes as many as four or five simultaneously. He also composed scholarly works or poems while he traveled, or worked on his famous *Commentaries*, in which he dispassionately, even modestly, but clearly with a thought for history, chronicled his military campaigns in Gaul.

He possessed great personal charm and a wit that infuriated his rivals in Rome when he turned it against them. Yet, for all his gifts, he looked incredibly ordinary. He was tall and very fair, with a broad, scholar's face and melancholy dark brown eyes. He was also very vain. He kept his face and head carefully trimmed and often depilated his body hair with tweezers. He had started balding at a very early age and was in the habit of trying to disguise it by combing what little hair he had forward over his high forehead.

Later, when the Senate voted him the privilege of wearing
a laurel wreath on all occasions, he was almost never seen
without it. He was somewhat eccentric in his dress. He had
added fringed sleeves to his purple-striped senatorial tunic,
an affectation that caused his enemies to refer to him as a
woman behind his back and added fuel to the numerous
rumors of his alleged bisexuality. He suffered from bouts of
epilepsy, but sought to fight them off with exercise and
moderate diet.

His legions loved him. A naturally gifted speaker who
had studied rhetoric in the school of Apollonius of Rhodes,
he would often address them in the field, and always on the
eve of any action, speaking to them warmly and with great
emotion, man to men. He always saw to their welfare first
and had forged a unique and powerful bond with his troops.
They would have followed him to hell.

In the morning, when they crossed the Rubicon, they
would follow Caesar where no commander had ever taken
his troops before—to Rome itself.

The Senate was alarmed at his successes, terrified of his
legions. They were well aware of his immense popularity.
He had staged gladiatorial shows for the people and
sponsored lavish public banquets. He distributed grain to
his troops at the slightest excuse and gifted them with Gallic
slaves. He sent slaves and presents to prominent aristocrats,
made loans to people who found themselves in debt,
collected vast amounts of tribute from conquered territories,
and sought favor with kings and allied tribes by sending
them prisoners or lending them troops, all without even
bothering to seek authorization from the Senate. He helped
people with legal difficulties and sympathized with those he
could not help. It had been reported that he told them,
"What you need is a civil war."

Even his old ally, Pompey, had grown apprehensive
about Caesar. The ties between the two men had been
weakened by the death of Caesar's daughter, Julia, who had
been Pompey's wife, and of Crassus, who was killed in
Parthia. As a newly elected consul, Pompey had become the
most powerful man in Rome. He saw Caesar as a threat. His

legions seemed invincible, their loyalty to him was absolute.

On his return to Rome, Caesar still faced charges of irregular conduct from when he had served as consul. He had incurred tremendous debts and made many promises that would be difficult, if not impossible, to keep. In his time as governor-general of Gaul, he had acquired a taste for power, and nobody believed that he would easily give it up. Consequently, as "a matter of public interest," the Senate had decided that since the Gallic Wars had ended and peace had been restored, Caesar should be relieved of his post before his term expired. They had also directed him to disband his legions. Caesar's response was to march on Rome.

Travers alone knew what would happen when Caesar crossed the Rubicon. He would wage a bloody civil war, crush Pompey's forces, and seize absolute power, bringing to an end the days of the republic. His name would become synonymous with the title that he would assume—*imperator*. But on the night before he was to cross the Rubicon—a phrase that would go down in history as signifying facing the greatest trial and passing the point of no return—Caesar was keyed up and nervous.

He always looked for omens and was in the habit of consulting soothsayers. Word had reached him of a local "oracle," with great spiritual powers, who was said to have the ability to see into the future. He had sent for this oracle and was anxiously awaiting his arrival. He had grown impatient and sent a messenger to Travers, ordering him to have the oracle brought to him as soon as he arrived. And as Travers stood outside the entrance to the *praetorium* and waited, he saw the detachment of men that Caesar had sent out approaching down the *via praetoria*. With them was a tall and slender figure carrying a staff and dressed in a hooded black cloak.

Travers hurried to meet them. The centurion in charge gave him a salute.

"You are the oracle?" Travers asked the hooded figure. He could not make out the man's face.

"I am."

"The general is expecting you. He is most anxious to hear your prophecy."

As, in fact, was Travers. He hoped that he would be allowed to stay and listen. He did not really expect to hear anything surprising. Oracles and soothsayers knew what was expected of them when they were brought into the presence of a famous general and found themselves surrounded by an army. Under such circumstances, it would not be wise to read "unfavorable portents." The man would doubtless give a reassuring reading in the most general terms, promising success and power and the favor of the gods, pocket his "offering" and hurry home. However, Travers thought it might make for an interesting scene in his book.

"You've searched him, of course?" Travers said to the centurion.

"Of course, Praetor. The man was carrying no weapons."

"Good. Come with me."

Travers led the way to Caesar's tent, with the *vexillum*, the general's standard, a white banner inscribed with red letters giving Caesar's name and identifying his army, placed outside it. The tent was made of leather, with two upright poles and one ridge pole. When on the march, Caesar did not avail himself of any luxuries, which endeared him to his men. He lived as they did, ate as they ate. He was pacing back and forth, nervously, attired simply in his tunic and sandals. He looked up eagerly as they entered.

"Ah, Septimus! You have brought the oracle?"

"This is the man, Caesar."

Travers beckoned the hooded figure forward.

"Pull back your cowl," he said.

The man pulled back his hood. He was completely bald, with a prominent, hooked nose and deep-set dark eyes that gave him a sepulchral look. His face was long, with a pointed chin and pronounced cheekbones.

"What is your name?" asked Caesar.

"I am called Lucan, General," the man said softly.

"You know who I am?"

A brief nod.

"They tell me that you can see into the future."

"I have that gift."

"I would have you look into my future and tell me what you see."

Lucan nodded. "Please, sit down," he said.

They sat down at the table.

"Do you require an augury?" asked Caesar.

"No. That is not the nature of my gift. Give me your right hand," said Lucan.

Caesar held out his right hand, palm up. Lucan took it in his own right hand and covered it with his left, then closed his eyes. Nothing terribly dramatic, so far, Travers thought. An oracle without much imagination. Caesar looked slightly disappointed.

"You are a man of great ambition," Lucan said without opening his eyes. "You have made many enemies. Some who were once your friends."

A safe assumption to make about a famous general, thought Travers, though not the sort of flattering beginning that he had expected.

"That is true," said Caesar.

"Please," said Lucan, opening his eyes. "I do not wish to offend, but I must ask you to remain silent until I have finished."

Caesar nodded.

Lucan shut his eyes once more and remained silent for almost thirty seconds. He was frowning slightly.

"I see that you are about to embark upon undertaking a great risk. Old friends will become your bitter enemies. There shall be great conflict, yet you shall succeed, though not without cost."

Caesar smiled.

"But this undertaking . . . this war . . . will be only the beginning for you. I see that you aspire to greatness and you shall achieve it, as did Alexander, whom you so much admire."

Travers raised his eyebrows. The man must have been briefed by someone. Probably he had asked questions about

Caesar from the men who had been sent to fetch him. Caesar's admiration of Alexander was hardly a secret.

"I see great power in your future," the oracle continued, speaking softly. "Absolute power. And your fame shall last throughout the ages. You shall have many conquests, both martial and romantic. I see that you will fall in love with a wise and ambitious foreign woman who will smite you with her beauty. A young queen who shall bear you a son."

Travers stared at the oracle intently. This was unusually specific. And also uncannily true. He was talking about Cleopatra. No, he thought, don't be ridiculous. How could he possibly know that? It was just flattery that happened to be coincidence. Caesar had several queens as mistresses at one time or another. It was not an unusual assumption to make about a famous Roman general and a provincial governor who had regular contact with local royalty.

"I also see violent death in your future," Lucan said. "There will be portents and warnings. You must not ignore them. For if you do, I see the image of your body bleeding, pierced with many wounds. You will not fall in battle, but at the hands of those you think your friends. Beware the Ides of March, Caesar. Beware the names of Casca, Brutus, Cassius, Cimber . . ." His eyes fluttered open. "I am sorry. I can see no more."

Caesar was frowning. Travers held his breath. He could scarcely believe what he had just heard. The oracle had just named Caesar's assassins!

"This violent death you see upon the Ides of March," said Caesar. "It will occur soon?"

"In five years' time."

Travers almost gasped. He had pinpointed the time precisely!

"And is there nothing I can do to alter this fate?" asked Caesar.

"Perhaps. To a man who takes his fate into his own hands," said Lucan, "nothing is impossible."

"What must I do, then, to avoid this violent death?"

"Give me your left hand," said the oracle.

Caesar held it out and Lucan took it in both of his, as he

had done before. For a moment, he said nothing, concentrating. Then . . .

"There is a chance that you might be able to avoid the fate your destiny has in store for you," Lucan said. "But you must be mindful of the omens. One in particular, above all others. I have but a dim perception of it. You will know it when that which was concealed shall stand revealed."

Lucan released Caesar's hand. "I can tell you no more. Only that when you recognize that omen, you must hearken to its counsel."

"And that is all that you can tell me?" Caesar asked.

"That is all. And now, General, I must beg leave to retire. The sight has wearied me."

"My men shall escort you from the camp," said Caesar. "I thank you, Lucan, for your prophecy." Caesar picked up several gold coins and gave them to the oracle. "Septimus, see to it that he is safely conducted from the camp."

His mind in a turmoil, Travers went with the soldiers to escort Lucan through the gates. Outside, it was dark and the oracle looked ghostly as he walked silently toward the gates with the hood over his head.

"How did you know those things?" asked Travers.

"I have the sight."

"But you named names, you gave an exact date!"

"It was what I saw."

"But you told Caesar that it was possible for him to change his fate," said Travers. "How? How can any man alter his own destiny?"

"A man's destiny is but the result of his actions in the present and the past," said Lucan. "Those actions set his feet upon a path that will lead him to his destiny. When I look into a man's future, my sight travels along the path that man has chosen by his actions. If that man were to choose a different path, it would lead him to a different destiny. However, it is my experience that most men never change."

There is no future, Travers thought, his mind racing. There is only an infinite number of possible futures. What Lucan had just told him was an almost perfect paraphrase of the Principle of Temporal Inertia.

"Can you look into my future?" asked Travers.

"No," said Lucan.

"Why not?"

"Because the sight has wearied me. I need time to recover."

"Perhaps later, then?"

"I fear not. I am leaving upon a long journey in the morning. And your general shall take you with him upon his."

They had reached the gates.

"I doubt that we shall meet again, Praetor Septimus," said Lucan. "But perhaps that is for the best. Believe me, most men are better off not knowing what their future holds in store for them. Good fortune to you."

He passed through the gate.

"The oracle is right," said the centurion. "If it is my fate to die tomorrow, or soon thereafter, I would prefer not to know of it tonight." He clasped the hilt of his sword. "And I would sooner trust my fate to this than to the prophecies of oracles and soothsayers. Good night to you, Praetor Septimus."

He turned and went back toward the tents with his soldiers.

Travers turned to the guard at the gate. "I must speak further with that man. Let me through."

They passed him through the gates and Travers hurried after Lucan, but after running no more than a few steps, he stopped. The slope of the hill fell away from the camp, leading to a meadow. The open country was gently illuminated by the moonlight.

There was no sign of the oracle. It was as if he had simply disappeared.

1 ═══════════════════════════════

TAC-HQ, Pendleton Base, California, June 13, A.D. 2627

The penthouse of the headquarters building of the Temporal Army Command had originally been the personal quarters of the Pendleton Base commander, but since General Moses Forrester had assumed that post, as well as the directorship of the Temporal Intelligence Agency, it was hardly ever used. Forrester, a bull of a man, completely bald with a face like a pugnacious bulldog and a powerful, bodybuilder's physique that belied his advanced age, lived on the floor immediately beneath it, where his offices were located. They were the same quarters he had resided in when he was the commander of the elite First Division, better known as the Time Commandos.

Forrester had spent his entire life in the service, which had entailed, as life in the service always had, a great deal of moving around. Now that he had reached a point in his career where he didn't have to move, he bloody well wasn't going to, not even if it was just upstairs. He had grown accustomed to his quarters, and even if they were not as spacious and luxurious as the penthouse, they suited his needs. He merely had to step outside his door to reach his suite of offices, the heart of TAC-HQ, and he had his secret room there, concealed behind a wall, a small private sanctum that only a few people knew about where he kept his prized and highly unauthorized mementos of the past. Occasionally, he had used the penthouse to hold parties or house visiting dignitaries, but it was now a highly restricted area.

Aside from Forrester himself, only three people were authorized access to it. Those three were Capt. Finn Delaney, Lt. Andre Cross, and Col. Creed Steiger of the Temporal Intelligence Agency. And one other man, who had no official authorization, because he did not need one. Dr. Robert Darkness, the man who was faster than light.

The sole tenant of the penthouse was the reason for the maximum security. He was Col. Lucas Priest, whose name was listed on the Wall of Honor in the lobby of the building, along with the names of all the other members of the First Division, now merged with Temporal Intelligence, who had been killed in action in Minus Time. Lucas Priest was, with the possible exceptions of Lazarus and Christ, the only man in history to have come back from the dead.

He had died saving the life of Winston Churchill, but the enigmatic Dr. Darkness had interceded with his fate. The story was as complex as it was baffling. It pivoted around the mysterious, brilliant, and eccentric scientist and the nature of what he had become.

Darkness had once been an obscure research scientist working in the field of temporal physics. In the course of his work, which was centered on temporal translocation, he had invented the most devastating weapon ever devised by man—the warp grenade, a combination nuclear device and time machine. It was small enough to be carried in one hand and its built-in chronocircuitry allowed for pinpoint adjustment of its nuclear explosion. It could be "fine-tuned" to use all or any part of the tremendous energy that was released. The surplus energy was then clocked through an Einstein-Rosen Bridge, a "wormhole" in the fabric of space and time, to explode harmlessly in the farthest reaches of the cosmos. Or so it was believed.

No one knew exactly what had happened. The prevailing theory was that such incredible amounts of energy clocked through Einstein-Rosen Bridges, perhaps combined with the strain already placed upon the timestream by the actions of the Time Wars, had somehow shifted the chronophysical alignment of the universe. The result was that a parallel timeline, a mirror-image universe, had been brought into congruence with our own. Each time a warp grenade was detonated, the parallel universe was nuked. Space colonies that they had established were utterly destroyed, with catastrophic loss of life. And now the two parallel timelines were at war.

It was a "limited" war, but it was still the most dangerous war humanity had ever fought. Both sides refrained from the use of strategic weapons, because each of their time-streams had become perilously unstable. Both timelines were "rippling," intertwining like a double helix. The result was the "confluence phenomenon." At various points in space and time, the two timelines intersected and the parallel universes met. At those points, it was possible to cross over from one universe into the other. The resulting potential for the disruption of either timestream was staggering.

People simply disappeared. A man could be walking down the street, turn a corner, and suddenly find himself in another universe. And these confluence points did not necessarily correspond in space and time. That same man might turn a corner and suddenly find himself not only in another universe, but in another country, in a different time period. If he kept his head about him and was able to retrace his steps exactly, there was a chance he could get back to his own time and universe, assuming he was lucky. Confluence points were invisible. Their focal points varied in size and they were incredibly unstable. There was no telling how long they would last.

The timestreams would ripple and a confluence point would come into existence, a "window" into another time

and another universe. The ripple effect would move on and
the confluence point would disappear. It could last for
hours, days, weeks, or only seconds. It could lead to a point
in the middle of an ocean or a desert in the other universe,
or even to deep space, in which case death was instantaneous and horrible.

In the face of such a threat, international conflicts had
become utterly meaningless. The Time Wars as they had
once been fought had ceased, escalating into a far more
frightening conflict. Each universe was now threatened by
the very existence of the other. Each was now faced with
three prime necessities.

The first was to map as many confluence points as
possible. If a confluence point could be located, it could be
used to cross over from one universe into another, to stage
temporal disruptions in the opposite timeline. Ranger Pathfinder units whose job was to map confluences and the
territory on the other side had the most hazardous duty in
the entire Temporal Corps. They had no idea what they
might find on the other end of the confluence and they could
never be sure that they would be able to get back. If the
scouts did come back, with detailed accounts of what they
had encountered in the parallel universe, further action
could be contemplated. If they did not return, the worst was
assumed and no one else was sent through that confluence
point. In either case, the confluence was secured for its
duration, to make sure no one blundered into it and that no
one or nothing came through from the other side. In some
cases, it was to no avail. Occasionally, something could
come through that nobody could stop, as had happened at
Tanguska, in Siberia, where a meteor came through a
confluence point and caused incredible destruction.

The second imperative both universes were confronted
with was the Time War that they waged between themselves. Each attempted to locate safe confluence points that
the other had not yet managed to discover, so they could
send agents through to disrupt the continuity of the opposing timeline. Apparently, temporal physicists in the parallel
universe believed that a temporal disruption of a magnitude

sufficient to bring about a timestream split in the opposing universe would work to overwhelm the confluence effect and separate the two timelines once and for all. Consequently, they were sending across agents and temporal strike teams from their Special Operations Group to gather intelligence and stage temporal disruptions in an attempt to split the timestream. There was a chance that their thinking was scientifically sound; however, temporal physics—or zen physics, as it was often called—was a nebulous and elusive area of science. It was where scientific logic merged with metaphysics. Temporal relativity was never absolute. There was also a chance that a timestream split in either universe, aside from the potentially devastating consequences in the universe in which it would occur, could result in the creation of yet another timeline that would compound the confluence effect and make it even worse, with *three* timelines intersecting. Or, worse still, it could set off a chain reaction, with the creation of another timeline disrupting the temporal continuity of the other two, creating further timestream splits and the creation of still more timelines, with no end in sight. It could end in ultimate entropy. No one knew for sure. Yet both universes continued to wage their Time Wars, on the principle that the more the opposing universe was occupied in trying to compensate for disruptions in its own timestream, the less time, energy, and manpower it could expend in trying to disrupt the timestream of the other.

The third problem faced by each universe was safeguarding the temporal continuity of their respective timelines. The confluence phenomenon dramatically increased the chances of temporal disruption. It was necessary to clock as many Observers as possible into the past, so that history could be preserved. In order to facilitate this seemingly impossible task, the majority of the temporal forces of all nations had been converted to Temporal Observer status, with the best and brightest assigned as L.T.O.'s, to keep watch on figures of historical significance. C.T.O.'s, or Chief Temporal Observers, functioned as field commanders, supervising the T.O. units in their respective sectors.

Any sign of a disruption was immediately reported to TAC-HQ, so that a team of Temporal Intelligence agents could be dispatched to Minus Time to deal with it. Yet, this task was akin to bailing a rapidly sinking rowboat with a thimble. No matter how many Observers were dispatched into the past—and thousands upon thousands were—they could not possibly cover all of human history. And the increased presence of people from the future in the past served by itself to increase the odds of temporal disruption.

Waging the war with strategic weapons would have been too dangerous, for there was no way of telling if a nuke launched at the opposing universe would actually explode there, or if it might become caught in a confluence and cause untold destruction, and possibly a timestream split, in the universe that had launched it in the first place. So the war was fought through the means of historical disruption. But there were more than just two sides.

The conflict was complicated further by the existence of the Temporal Underground, a loosely organized confeder-ation of deserters from the future who had fled into the past in order to escape the madness. No one was quite certain what to do about them. Technically, they were criminals, fugitives. It was up to the Temporal Intelligence Agency to track them down and apprehend them, but the T.I.A., particularly the covert field section, had never seriously considered them a priority. In fact, many of the old covert field agents had maintained contacts among the members of the Underground and sometimes called upon them for assistance in their missions. When Forrester had assumed the directorship of the agency, he had put a stop to such practices, as well as to the corruption in the T.I.A. He had discovered that many of the covert field agents, as well as their section chiefs, had been running an extensive trans-temporal black market operation to enrich themselves. The corruption went all the way up to the previous director.

Their immensely profitable and highly illegal sideline was referred to as "the Network" and it involved such things as using time travel to manipulate the stock and commodities markets, smuggle rare coins from the past to sell in future time periods, practice piracy on the Spanish Main and sell the booty in the 19th and 20th centuries. The Network had hijacked gold and works of art from the Nazis. They were involved in the East India Company. They used time travel to scam betting operations, and the list went on and on and on. They were the ultimate soldiers of fortune, less interested in their duties as temporal agents than in their crosstime financial ventures. Forrester had tried to put a stop to their dangerous and illegal activities, but he had not been entirely successful. He had disbanded the covert field section and put every agent he could get his hands on, from the lowliest records clerk to section chiefs and senior administrators, through a scanning procedure in an effort to ferret out the ones who were involved in the Network. However, word got out and many of them simply disappeared, going underground in time and becoming a transtemporal Mafia, the ultimate organized crime family. They had put a price on Forrester's head. There had already been several attempts on his life. He had no doubt there would be more.

And what of the man who had started it all? As he walked down the corridor from his quarters to the lift tubes, Forrester thought that perhaps it was unfair to blame it all on Robert Darkness. Darkness had not started the Time Wars. The Time Wars had come about when nations had decided to use time travel to settle their conflicts by having their troops do battle in the past, in order to protect the present from the ravages of war. There was no real evidence to support that it was the invention of the warp grenade, and not the actions of the Time Wars, that had brought about the confluence phenomenon. Yet, Darkness himself seemed to accept responsibility for what had come about.

He was not on Earth when the confluence phenomenon came into being. He had disappeared mysteriously and no one had any idea what had become of him. Forrester later learned that Darkness had established a research laboratory on some far-off, desolate planet and had gone there to perfect his process of tachyon conversion. Darkness had discovered a way to focus a tachyon beam and send it through an Einstein-Rosen Bridge, which amounted to instantaneous transmission. No time lag whatsoever. Going from Point A to Point B without having to cover the distance in between. His next step was to start working on a process whereby the human body could become converted into tachyons, which would depart at six hundred times the speed of light along the direction of the tachyon beam, through an Einstein-Rosen Bridge. His main concern had been that tachyon conversion might violate the Law of Uncertainty. The beam was focused by means of gravitational lenses, but there was no receiver, so in order to insure that what would materialize at the other end would not be some kind of a blob, he had incorporated a timing mechanism into the conversion process, which would reassemble him in the proper order, at the proper time and place, based on the temporal coordinates of transition. What he was seeking was the ultimate form of transportation, something that would surpass even the chronoplate devised by Dr. Mensinger.

Unfortunately, when Darkness tried the process on himself, he had discovered that it was ultimately restrained by a little known law of physics called the Law of Baryon Conservation. When he had arrived at his point of destination, he discovered that he could not move from the spot on which he stood. Something had happened to his subatomic structure. He took on the appearance of a hologram. He had become a ghost with substance. His body had been permanently "tachyonized." He had become faster than the speed of light. He could move from place to place, traveling through time and space at will, but only by translocating or, as he called it, "taching." He could not walk so much as one step. He could appear to "walk," after a fashion, but it was only a series of incredibly rapid translocations, having the multiple-image effect of high-speed photography.

Quite possibly, thought Forrester, the tachyonization had had an effect upon his mind as well, although with Darkness, it was difficult to tell. The man was incredibly brilliant, light-years ahead of all his peers (both figuratively *and* literally). They could not even begin to understand his work. His personality was, to say the least, idiosyncratic. He was a man of immense wealth, holding the controlling interest in Amalgamated Techtronics and a number of other large multinational corporations. He felt himself accountable to no one. What he had done with Lucas Priest was a perfect example.

Lucas should have died, thought Forrester, despite the fact that Col. Priest was his closest friend. He should have died and he should have stayed dead. What Darkness had done was inexcusable. Ever since he'd done it, Forrester had spent many sleepless nights, worrying about the possible consequences. As had Lucas Priest himself, on whom the strain was obvious.

It had happened in the year 1897, while Priest, Cross, and Delaney were clocked out on a mission to Afghanistan, during the Pathan revolt against the British. A strike team of the S.O.G., from the parallel universe, had come through a confluence in the Khyber Pass and was working to change the course of history. Priest and Cross had been standing on a bluff with the British command staff, watching the fighting that was taking place below them, between the Ghazis and the Bengal Lancers. A lone Ghazi sniper who had concealed himself in the rocks had drawn a bead on the battalion surgeon, mistaking him for the British general. Priest had spotted the sniper and, without thinking about the possible consequences of his interference, had shouted out a warning. The surgeon, his instincts honed by combat, had immediately dropped to the ground, but by doing so, he had left the young Winston Churchill, who was present as a war correspondent, directly in the line of fire. Churchill was too slow to respond and Priest, in his cover as a missionary, had not been carrying a weapon. He had done the only thing that he could do—he flung himself at Churchill, knocked him out of the way, and took the bullet meant for him. Or, more accurately, meant for the surgeon with whose destiny Priest had interfered.

Lucas was killed instantly. They had even buried him. But Dr. Darkness changed all that in a manner that Forrester still could not completely comprehend. During a prior

mission, Darkness had implanted each of the three commandos, as well as temporal agent Steiger, with a particle-
level tracer device of his own design, one that bonded itself
to their molecular structure. It allowed him to find them no
matter where they were in space and time. What Darkness
had not revealed to them was the fact that these tracer
devices were also prototypes of a new invention he was
trying to perfect—a new generation warp disc. The original
warp disc, the one now issued to all temporal personnel,
functioned on the same principle as the warp grenade and
had superseded the more cumbersome, obsolete chronoplate
of Dr. Mensinger. The new model Darkness had designed
was not worn on the person, but was integrated on the
particle level, actually bonding itself with the individual.
Moreover, it was thought-controlled, an idea that still
scared the hell out of Forrester.

The prototypes had all malfunctioned. The tracer functions worked perfectly, but the bonding process had damaged the temporal transponders, rendering them useless—
all except Priest's. Rather than lose his only working
prototype, Darkness had elected to bring Lucas Priest back
from the dead.

How he had done it was a zen physics puzzle. The leader
of the S.O.G. strike team from the opposing timeline had
been Priest's twin from the parallel universe. A man whose
personal history was apparently somewhat different from
the Priest that Forrester knew, but who was identical to him
in every other respect, right down to his genetic code. After
Priest had died, Finn Delaney had killed the "twin Priest."
Darkness had tached through time and taken the body of the
twin Priest, then tached back and, moving faster than the
speed of light, had substituted it for their Lucas Priest,
snatching him out of the bullet's path at the last nanosecond,
pulling him into his tachyon field and taking him back to his
headquarters on that unknown planet. There, he had activated the dormant, tachyon-based, thought-controlled transponder Priest had been implanted with. And now Priest
had returned, to see his own name listed on the Wall of
Honor, among those killed in action. There still remained

the question—what had actually become of him? And what had he become?"

Darkness had gone back into the past and changed something that had already happened. Or had he? Had he actually altered the past or had his actions in fact restored the past to the way it had originally happened? It seemed to Forrester, and to Priest as well, that there had to exist a point in time, *somewhere*, a moment in which Lucas Priest had actually died. Logic would seem to dictate that for Darkness to have gone back and saved him from death, he would have had to have died in the first place, otherwise there would have been no necessity for Darkness to do what he had done. However, when it came to zen physics, logic frequently broke down.

After the mission was completed, an S & R team was clocked back to retrieve Lucas Priest's remains. But had Search & Retrieve brought back his body, or that of his twin? Even if the remains had not been cremated, how would it have been possible to tell, since both were identical, right down to their DNA? Had Priest actually died, or had the corpse of his twin taken the bullet? Had Darkness merely caused a temporary "skip" in the timestream's continuity, or had what he had done in saving Priest become a temporal disruption that could have unforeseen consequences further down the timestream? Those questions plagued not only Forrester, but Lucas Priest, as well. And there were still more problems that Priest had to contend with, beyond the metaphysical riddle of his own existence.

By experimenting on himself, Darkness had created an instability in his own subatomic structure, an instability that seemed to be increasing with the passage of time. Darkness believed that, eventually, his tachyonized state would decay into discorporation and he would depart at multiples of light speed in all directions of the universe.

Forrester shuddered at the thought as he stepped into the lift tube and punched out the restricted code for the penthouse. Knowing that something like that would inevitably happen to you had to have an effect upon your mind.

He stepped in front of the scanner and a beam of light played on his right eye, reading his retinal pattern. Then the tube started to ascend. Priest could be facing the same thing. Although the process he had been exposed to via the particle-level implant in his body was different from that which had tachyonized Darkness, it was based on similar principles. Priest had no idea whether or not it would eventually do the same thing to him. Moreover, he had to contend with the problem of having been turned into a living time machine. It had become necessary for him to learn an entirely new level of mental discipline, because now any stray thought could launch him on a trip through time. It had already happened on a number of occasions. The thought-controlled temporal transponder was unable to differentiate between when he was awake and when he was asleep. Consequently, a dream could launch him on a trip through time as well. As Darkness had typically understated it, the device still "had a few bugs" in it.

The trouble was, since the transponder had become permanently bonded to Lucas, fused with his atomic structure, there was no way to remove it. Priest would simply "have to adapt," as Darkness had put it. Forrester would have dearly loved to take a swing at Darkness and lay the bastard out, then throw his ass in jail, but how could you hit someone who was faster than the speed of light, much less hope to incarcerate him?

The tube arrived at the penthouse floor and revolved to let Forrester out. Priest had called him the moment Darkness arrived. He "dropped in" from time to time to check on the progress of his living prototype. Forrester had asked Priest to prevail on Darkness to stay long enough to talk to him, but he had no idea if the man would still be there. Darkness did not wait on generals, or anybody else, for that matter. He could already have left, thought Forrester, and arrived back where he had started from before he had departed.

However, when he entered the penthouse, he saw that Darkness was still there. The scientist was standing behind the bar, helping himself to Forrester's twelve-year-old

Scotch. Andre Cross was there, as well, along with Finn Delaney and Creed Steiger.

Delaney, a brawny, powerfully built man with a face like an overaged delinquent's, looked, as usual, as if he'd slept in his black base fatigues. His dark red hair was uncombed, his beard scruffy, and his boots unshined, a stark contrast to Steiger, who always looked like a smartly turned-out member of a S.W.A.T. team. Col. Steiger's hair was dusty blond. He was clean-shaven and his hooked nose and cruel mouth gave him a predatory look. Andre Cross sat beside Priest. Her long, ash-blond hair fell to her shoulders and her fatigues were neatly pressed. Her movements denoted a finely honed, athletic muscular control. Her sharp features were striking and attractive. Sitting next to her, Priest looked, as always, like a model military officer. Slim, dark-haired, and handsome, he would have made a perfect model for a recruiting poster. The very vision of an officer and a gentleman.

They had all been trying to spend as much time with Priest as possible. Priest needed the support of his friends just now. He was under a great deal of strain. Forrester visited as often as he could, but the duties of command left him with little spare time.

They all got to their feet as he entered.

"As you were," he said.

Darkness glanced up at him from behind the bar. "You wanted to see me, Moses?"

He was tall and slender, a gaunt-looking man, with dark, unruly hair, deep-set eyes, a sharp, prominent nose, and a neatly trimmed moustache. He was wearing a Norfolk tweed shooting jacket in dark brown herringbone, with rust-colored suede leather elbow patches and a matching, quilted shooter's pad on the right shoulder. He had on a dark brown vest with a gold watch chain, a white Oxford shirt and maroon silk paisley ascot, dark brown tropical wool slacks and light brown calfskin jodphurs. He looked like the ghost of an English country gentleman. Forrester could see the back of the bar right through him.

"I have a few questions and I'd like some straight answers, Robert, if you don't mind," Forrester said.

Everybody else called him "Doc" or "Doctor," but Forrester and Darkness were on a first name basis, based upon a curious blend of mutual respect and cordial dislike.

"Ask," said Darkness, suddenly appearing about two feet in front of Forrester, holding a glass of whiskey. Instinctively, Forrester backed off a step and grimaced, annoyed with himself for doing so. Darkness smiled.

"I'll never get used to the way you pop around all over the damn place," Forrester grumbled.

"You said you had some questions," Darkness said. His voice sounded cultured, vaguely Continental. There was nothing about the way he spoke that was overtly arrogant or condescending, but that effect came across just the same. He was, thought Forrester, an irritating bastard.

"What's the long-term prognosis on Priest's condition?"

"We were just discussing that," said Lucas.

"Yes," said Darkness. "Unfortunately, it would appear that the long-term prognosis is not very favorable. There's been a dramatically measurable decay. It's apparently irreversible."

Forrester glanced at Priest with alarm. "You mean—"

"He means his particle gizmo," Lucas said, "not me."

"Particle gizmo, indeed!" said Darkness, rolling his eyes.

"Well, whatever you want to call the damn thing," Lucas said. "It seems the good doctor hasn't quite got it figured out yet. It's failing. Looks like it's eventually going to stop working altogether." He grinned. "Ain't that a damn shame?"

"What does that mean in terms of his health?" asked Forrester.

"His health?" said Darkness. "His health is excellent and will undoubtedly continue to remain so, unless he manages to get himself in the way of another bullet. I cannot be held responsible for his propensity for foolish heroics."

"He means I'm going to be all right," said Lucas, smiling. He looked better than he had in weeks, as if an enormous burden had been lifted from him. "But the doc's going to have to go back to the drawing board. Looks like his thought-controlled transponder is a long way from being perfected."

"You needn't sound so damned smug about it," Darkness said irritably.

Forrester felt enormously relieved. "You mean there's no chance of his experiencing discorporation?"

"None whatsoever," Darkness replied. "There was very little chance of that to begin with. I was reasonably certain that I had the problem solved, but it seems that the transponder itself is still unstable. It simply won't hold up. I can't imagine why." He grimaced. "It's really quite annoying."

"So you mean to say he's going to be the same way that he was before?" asked Forrester, his hopes rising. "Completely normal?"

"Yes, yes, yes," said Darkness with a sigh of exasperation. "Given the rate of decay, I would say within a week or two, at most. Perhaps only in a matter of days. Then he can once more revel in being the same, depressingly ordinary clod he always was."

"Thanks," said Lucas wryly.

"Don't mention it."

"That brings up my next question," said Forrester. "With the exception of the people in this room, nobody knows that Priest is still alive. Or perhaps I should say, alive *again*. That presents us with a problem. I should have informed Director General Vargas of what you've done, only I've done as you asked and I haven't. At least, not yet. I'm not at all sure I've done the right thing in not telling him at once, but I was more concerned about Priest's health and emotional well-being. Now that that issue seems to have been settled, there are a few things I need to know. Is there any reason why I shouldn't tell Director Vargas about what's happened?"

"I suppose not," Darkness said, "although I really can't see what purpose that would serve. They'd only bury you in official inquiries. It would cause them to start running about like chickens with their heads cut off, trying to figure out if there's been a temporal disruption."

"*Has* there been a temporal disruption?"

"I wouldn't concern myself with that."

"Perhaps *you* wouldn't, but I'm afraid *I* have to," Forrester replied.

"The world isn't going to end merely because Priest is sitting there, grinning like a Cheshire cat over the fact that my transponder is decaying," Darkness said.

"How can you know that for certain?" Forrester asked.

"Take my word for it," said Darkness.

"I'd like to, Robert, but how can you know that for sure?" Forrester persisted. "Unless, of course, you're from the future?"

The others stared at him.

"You are, aren't you?" Forrester said quietly.

Darkness regarded him with a steady gaze. "Very good, Moses. Very good, indeed. I see I've underestimated you."

"Jesus Christ," said Finn Delaney. "Now it all suddenly makes sense!"

"When did you first suspect?" asked Darkness.

"I'm not sure when the idea first occurred to me," said Forrester. "I'm just amazed that it didn't occur to me sooner. I've been doing a lot of digging, trying to check you out. I didn't get very far. Everything about your background is classified. Even *I* can't get to it. It's restricted to an access code that no one seems to know."

"I know you couldn't have cracked the code," said Darkness.

"No, I wasn't able to," Forrester admitted. "But I have a feeling that if I had, I would have discovered that the records had somehow been erased. Or something like that, right? There would have been some sort of malfunction that would have rendered them inaccessible, because past a certain point, your background would either be a forgery or it would simply stop. So, frustrated in that endeavor, I decided to do the next best thing. Find out who had the clearance to access your file."

"Only you could not discover that, either," said Darkness, smiling.

"No, I couldn't. However, I'm not the sort of man to give up on a problem. So I began to trace the authorization for the file's being classified."

"And you couldn't find it," Darkness said.

"That's right," said Forrester. "I couldn't find it. Only I *should* have been able to find it. You see, that's the trouble with covering your tracks, Robert. Sooner or later, it becomes obvious that they were covered. And that's when I knew. You were worried that someone might get curious, find the authorization order, and clock back to the date that it was issued to investigate. So you buried the order. If there even was an order to begin with. The whole thing was a sham. But I wanted to be absolutely certain, so I put a research team from Archives Section on the project and had them do it the hard way. They clocked back as far as we could trace you and started digging. And the trail just ran out. Past a certain point, you simply ceased to exist. That's why none of your peers in the scientific community can understand your work. It's why you've always been so far ahead of them. Because you were, quite literally, *ahead* of them. Years ahead." He paused. "How many years, Robert?"

"As you people in Temporal Intelligence are so fond of saying," Darkness replied laconically, "you have no need to know."

"I think I do," said Forrester. "I think we all do."

"What you think is really of no consequence," Darkness replied. "It is what you do that matters. And as you should know, better than anyone else, what you do must not be affected by your knowledge of what *will* be done."

"Just tell me one thing, Robert. Are you a temporal agent from the future or are you doing whatever it is you're doing on your own?"

"I think I've answered enough questions," Darkness said. "You already know a great deal more than you should."

"The one thing I don't understand is, why the warp

grenade?" asked Forrester. "You had to know what it would do. Didn't you? So *why*?"

"There is a reason for everything I've done, Moses," Darkness said. "And everything that I *will* do. At the proper time. That is really all that I can tell you."

"God damn it, Robert, don't you—"

Suddenly he simply wasn't there anymore.

"Jesus Christ," said Steiger.

"It's a strange feeling, isn't it?" Delaney said. "We think of ourselves as being the ones who go back into the past to adjust things and here we are, being adjusted ourselves. Sort of like the big fish eating the small fish eating the smaller fish."

"It does explain a lot," said Andre. "What do you think happened where he came from? You think it all finally fell apart and now he's trying to fix it?"

"We have, unfortunately, no way of knowing," Forrester said. "And, though I don't like it, we may well be better off not knowing. However, we do know at least one thing. What we're doing, or what we *will* do, is significant enough from the standpoint of the future for Darkness to have taken as much time as he has to involve himself with us."

"Swell," said Lucas. "So not only is the past messed up, but something's screwed up in the future, too. It figures. I knew it had to hit the fan one of these days. Well, at least there's a bright side to all of this. With that particle gizmo of his going on the fritz, pretty soon I won't have to guard my thoughts so carefully. No more dreaming of ancient Rome and waking up there."

"Funny you should say that," said Forrester.

2 ⎯⎯⎯⎯⎯⎯⎯⎯⎯⎯⎯⎯⎯⎯⎯⎯

"We've received a report of what appears to be a temporal anomaly from one of our L.T.O.'s," said Forrester.

"That sounds serious," said Steiger. "L.T.O.'s don't generally jump to conclusions."

"No, they don't," said Forrester. "The man's name is Travers. Capt. Jonathan Travers. I've had his file pulled. He's one of our best people. He's assigned to Julius Caesar."

Lucas exhaled heavily and shook his head. "A temporal anomaly involving Caesar could pose all sorts of problems. He didn't exactly lead an uneventful life. When did Travers make his report?"

"This morning. He clocked in with it personally, leaving Caesar's camp on the night before he crossed the Rubicon and started the civil war in Rome," Forrester said. "He clocked back out so he'd arrive just after he left, so he was only gone from Minus Time for a matter of minutes. Therefore, the risk was minimal and he felt justified in taking it. Under the circumstances, I'm inclined to agree. At first, he wasn't sure that what he had on his hands was an anomaly. Caesar, like other people of his time, was in the habit of consulting soothsayers and it seems that word had reached him of an oracle of some sort, a man named Lucan, who could see into the future. He had sent for this oracle to give him a reading on the night before he crossed the Rubicon. There's no historical record of any such event, but as we all know, that doesn't necessarily mean it didn't happen. Still, Travers found it curious, since both Caesar and his classical biographers had mentioned most of the occasions when he had received significant prophecies or omens. To receive a prophecy on the night of one of the most important events in his life would certainly seem significant, yet it was possible that history might have overlooked it.

"In any event," Forrester continued, "Travers didn't think much of it at first. He thought it might make for an interesting incident in his book. He plans to write a biography of Caesar when he returns to Plus Time. He managed to be present during the reading, which turned out to be rather unusual, to say the least. The oracle told Caesar that he would be successful in his civil war, that his fame would live for generations, and that he would fall in love with a beautiful young queen, an apparent reference to Cleopatra."

"Well, with all due respect, sir," said Delaney, "that sounds more like a generalized bit of fortune-telling than an anomaly. None of those so-called predictions would seem particularly farfetched for a Roman general with Caesar's reputation. Roman military governors often became involved with royalty. There were more kings and queens back then than you could shake a stick at. And flattering a general by promising him victory and fame would only be good business sense for an enterprising soothsayer."

"This soothsayer also told Caesar the exact date when he would be assassinated and to beware of men named Cassius, Brutus, Cimber, and Casca."

"Oh," said Delaney.

"Yeah, oh. What's more, he told Caesar there was a chance that he could change his fate if he paid attention to the omens, and one in particular, which he cited rather cryptically. 'That which was concealed shall stand revealed.' After the oracle went out the gates of Caesar's camp, Travers tried to follow him, only he had mysteriously disappeared."

"This was at night, wasn't it?" said Steiger. "Travers might have simply lost him in the darkness."

"The moon was out," said Forrester. "And the terrain around the camp was an unbroken slope that stretched down to a meadow, affording an unobstructed view for several miles.

"He might have gone around the camp, hugging the wall."

"Or he might have clocked out," said Andre. "I think Travers was right. It definitely sounds like a potential disruption. We can't afford to overlook it."

" 'That which was concealed shall stand revealed,' " said Lucas, frowning. "What does that mean?"

"I have no idea," said Forrester. "Travers is going to check back in as soon as something breaks. In the meantime, I want you all to report for mission programming and stand by to clock out on a moment's notice."

"That could pose a small problem, sir," asked Priest. "Officially, I'm still dead. If I report for mission programming, I'm liable give them one hell of a shock in Archives."

"Steiger can take care of that," said Forrester. "The T.I.A.'s always maintained its own programming facility for covert field agents. He can give you the coordinates and you can clock right in from here. I'll have the facility cleared, then Steiger can access the data from Archives and run the download himself."

"What about what Darkness said?" Steiger asked.

"That stays in this room," said Forrester. "I don't know what the hell he's up to, but there's little point in trying to second-guess him. You can't effect a temporal adjustment while you're worrying about whatever he might do. Or whether you're doing the right thing from the standpoint of the future. You can't try to second-guess yourselves, either. It'll only interfere with your mission. Just go in and do what you have to do. Forget about Darkness. There's not really anything that we can do about him, anyway."

"I'll need a warp disc," Lucas said. "With my transponder decaying, I don't want to take a chance on not being able to clock out if I have to."

"Good point," said Forrester. "I'll see that you get one."

"I wish we'd asked Darkness one more question," said Steiger.

"What's that?"

"What happens if that decaying transponder starts malfunctioning and causes Priest to translocate without being able to control it?"

Priest glanced at him. "Oh, thanks a lot. *Now* you bring that up!"

"Maybe you shouldn't go out on this one," Steiger said.

"Forget it," Lucas said firmly. "I *need* a mission. I've been going stir crazy cooped up in here. Besides, Darkness didn't say anything about the transponder's chronocircuitry running out of control. He just said it was decaying."

"As I recall, he also thought he had all the bugs ironed out of it in the first place," Steiger said.

"Look, if it's going to happen, it'll happen whether I'm here or on the mission," Lucas replied. "Staying behind won't change a thing."

"Maybe not, but it would keep you from jeopardizing the mission by clocking out suddenly at the wrong moment."

"I'm afraid he's got a point, Lucas," Forrester said.

Priest made a tight-lipped grimace. "All right, I'll concede that, but we still don't know it's going to happen. I think Darkness would've said something if there was a chance of that."

"But the point is that we still don't know for sure," said Steiger. "It means taking a risk."

"Like you've never taken risks?" Lucas countered. "Give me a break, Creed. Everything we do entails risk. And you've certainly taken more than your share." He turned to Forrester. "Sir, if you order me to stay behind on this one, I'll understand, but I'm asking you not to do that. I need this assignment. I'll start climbing the walls if I have to stay cooped up in here much longer."

Forrester glanced at the others. "You're the ones that'll be out there," he said. "It's your call."

"Lucas and I have taken our share of risks before," Delaney said. "I'd rather go out with him than without him. I vote yes."

Andre looked at Lucas and smiled. "So do I."

Steiger shrugged. "Well, it looks like I'm outvoted."

"If it's a problem for you, Creed, you can request to be relieved, without prejudice," said Forrester. "I don't want you going out on this mission if you haven't got complete confidence in every member of the team."

Steiger glanced at Lucas. "Priest, you understand, it's nothing personal."

"I understand," said Lucas. "I suppose if our positions were reversed, I might feel exactly the same way."

"But you're still not going to withdraw?" said Steiger.

"No."

"Well, in that case, I'd like to be relieved."

For a moment, there was an uncomfortable silence.

"Very well," said Forrester, breaking the tension. "You three report for mission programming in half an hour. Steiger, you want to set up that download for Priest?"

Steiger nodded. "I'll get right on it." He started to walk out with Forrester and paused at the door, looking back. "Priest?"

"Yeah?"

"Look . . . this isn't personal. No offense, huh?"

"None taken."

Steiger nodded and turned to follow Forrester out the door. The old man was waiting for him at the lift tube.

"This isn't like you, Creed," he said. "You've taken bigger risks before and you've never yet turned down a mission."

"That's right, sir. And I'm not about to start now. With your permission, I'd like to go along on this one, only undercover."

Forrester sighed and nodded. "Somehow I had a feeling that's what was on your mind."

"It's what I do best, sir," Steiger said. "Those three have

been working together for a long time. I've seen how they function in the field. They trust each other. Each of them has an instinct for how the others think. I'm the odd man out. I just don't fit in. I've always worked best on my own. It's what I was trained for."

"You're saying you want to go back on covert status?"

"Yes, sir, I do. I think I'd have much more to contribute that way."

"We've been over this before, Creed. My decision to shut down the covert field section wasn't arbitrary, you know."

"Yes, sir, I realize that. I know you don't approve of the methods we used in covert field section. And I know there were abuses, but that still——"

"Abuses is putting it mildly," Forrester interrupted. "The covert field section was nothing but a bunch of thrill-seeking cowboys who played fast and loose with regulations and had too much contact with the Underground. Part of our job is to *apprehend* those people, Steiger, not employ them as mission support. Or as functionaries in the Network."

"I understand that, sir, but it was a matter of priorities. Look, you know I was never involved with the Network. And the Underground is just as concerned as we are about temporal disruption. A disruption threatens them, too. They might be criminals from the purely legal standpoint, but they're not the real danger and they never have been. So when it came to a choice between busting some members of the Underground or enlisting them as sub rosa operatives, or trading information with them, okay, we didn't worry about the fine points of the law. There was a lot more than that at stake. I know you don't think there's a place for the way we used to do things, sir, but with all due respect, I think you're wrong."

The lift tube stopped at Forrester's floor, but he made no move to get out. Steiger wondered if he'd gone too far.

"All right," said Forrester. "Prove it."

"Sir? Does that mean you're authorizing——"

"I'm authorizing nothing, Colonel. All it means is that you're being placed on inactive status as soon as I can have the orders cut. You can consider yourself officially relieved of duty as of now. You've earned some R&R. What you do with it is entirely up to you."

"Thank you, sir. I promise you, you won't regret this."

"I hope not, Creed," said Forrester. "And I hope you won't regret it, either. Because if you fuck up, it's your ass."

Alexandria, the palace of the Ptolemys, 47 B.C.

"It is not the victory that I had hoped for," Caesar said as they rested in their apartments in the palace. "And a poor, ignoble death for a brave and noble soldier."

Travers thought that Caesar was being charitable, but he did not say it. Pompey the Great might once have been a brave and noble soldier, but in the end, his leadership and courage had both failed him.

When news of Caesar's crossing of the Rubicon reached Rome, the Senate was thrown into a panic. Caesar's army moved with their usual devastating efficiency and speed, immediately taking the town of Ariminum and marching ahead without encountering any opposition whatsoever.

People from the outlying towns began flooding into Rome, fleeing from the advancing legions, not having any idea what to expect. Their contagious fear began to spread throughout the city like a wildfire. Pompey declared Rome to be in a state of anarchy and, desperate to have enough time to marshal his forces, he left the city and went east, giving orders for the entire Senate to follow him. Many did, but most senators remained behind in Rome, concerned about their homes and their possessions. With so many refugees streaming into Rome, crime had increased dramatically and there was a lot of looting.

As Caesar's army approached the city, many of Pompey's troops joined with Caesar's forces and within sixty days of crossing the Rubicon, Caesar had effectively seized power without any bloodshed. But there still remained Pompey and his loyal legions, and though he was in command of the city, it was a threat that Caesar could not disregard.

He pursued Pompey to Brundisium, but as soon as he heard that Caesar was approaching, Pompey escaped to sea. Lacking the vessels to pursue him, Caesar then returned to Rome and appeared before the Senate. With the rank of praetor, Travis was entitled to attend and he sat in the Temple of Jupiter (the Curia, which would become the permanent home of the Senate, had not yet been built) and listened as Caesar addressed the House courteously, requesting that they send word to Pompey so that negotiations could be started toward a reasonable peace. However, the senators could not agree on what to do. Their position was precarious. To appear to give support to one general could prove disastrous if the other proved victorious, so the Senate did what politicians have been doing ever since. They procrastinated to avoid taking any stand.

Caesar left the temple in disgust. He did not have the patience to wait for their deliberations. His response to the Senate's stalling was to seize the public treasury, so that he could supply himself with the necessary funds to finish what he'd started. Then he left for Spain, where he engaged the forces of Afranius and Varro, Pompey's loyal generals, and after defeating them decisively, he returned once more to Rome, where the Senate, realizing the growing futility of Pompey's position, voted Caesar the title of dictator. In the event that Pompey still somehow managed to prevail, they could always claim that Caesar forced it on them. And with Caesar holding the position of dictator, it absolved them of the responsibility of making any choices.

Travers had remained at Caesar's side throughout it all and had observed firsthand that Caesar was not only a brilliant general, capable of inspiring fanatical devotion in his men, but also a skillful diplomat. His first act was to call back all those Romans who had gone into exile. He gave them back their rights as citizens and incurred the favor of many influential aristocrats by relieving them of their debts. He then made himself look better still by resigning the dictatorship that the fearful members of the Senate had conferred on him, having held the post for only eleven days, and declaring himself consul. That done, he immediately left Rome once more, on the trail of Pompey. The two armies met at Pharsalia in the largest and bloodiest battle ever fought between Romans. Caesar proved himself the better general and the man once hailed as Pompey the Great fled the scene of battle and retired to his tent, totally demoralized. When Caesar's troops had routed his army and started storming his camp, Pompey recovered his senses long enough to escape and flee to Egypt, where his fate awaited him. He had hoped to find an ally in the young King Ptolemy, who had backed him in the civil war, but the Egyptians had decided that they'd rather back a winner. As soon as he arrived, Pompey was put to death.

The war was over. More than six thousand of Pompey's troops had died. Gracious in victory, Caesar pardoned the prisoners and took them into his own legions. Then he pursued Pompey to Egypt, only to discover that the Egyptians had finished the job for him.

"At least now our men can rest awhile and recover," Travers said, "even if the best Egypt can do for them is that unwholesome corn that Pothinus has seen fit to distribute."

Caesar tightened his jaw muscles in anger. "He adds insult to injury by telling them to be content with it, since they are fed at another's cost. They deserve far better, Septimus, and by the gods, I shall see that they receive it! No general could hope for a more brave and loyal army."

"No army could hope for a better general than Caesar," said Travers, not intending it as mere flattery, but meaning every word of it.

"Thank you, my friend," said Caesar. "Nor shall I forget you, either. You have served me well through all these many years. But our work is not yet done. Egypt is a ripe fruit ready for the plucking. Tell me, what do you think of this oily eunuch, Pothinus? He seems to hold more influence with the king than do any of his ministers."

"Pothinus does seem to be the power behind the throne," said Travers. "The young king plainly defers to him. I have observed that the ministers take pains to ingratiate themselves with him. Or at least to avoid his displeasure."

"Yes, that is my opinion, too," said Caesar, frowning.

"It is Pothinus who rules here and not Ptolemy, who is little more than a child. And the ministers all fear him. I have been told that it was Pothinus himself who assassinated Pompey."

"You have been told?" asked Travers, instantly on guard. "By whom?"

Caesar smiled. "There are those here who are well disposed toward Rome, if only because they are ill disposed toward Pothinus. That crafty eunuch sees us as a threat to the power he has managed to accumulate through his manipulation of the king. We must have a care, Septimus, not to sleep too soundly so long as we remain here."

"You think that Pothinus would try to have us murdered? With our legions here?"

"He might well serve us as he did Pompey and then protest his innocence," Caesar said. "It would win him no small favor among our enemies in Rome. Although perhaps I worry needlessly. It is not yet the Ides of March." He smiled and Travers felt suddenly uneasy.

"Still," Caesar continued, "our influence in Egypt is not what it once was. Pompey has mismanaged things. I must take steps to remedy that situation. We must make the power of Rome felt here once again. Tomorrow, I will begin by demanding the tribute that is due to Rome, so that we might reward our army. And we must see to it that a more benign influence is set behind the throne. What do you know of the king's sister, the one who was exiled when Pompey was in power?"

Travers replied evasively. "Cleopatra? I fear that I know very little of her, Caesar. It is said that she is young and very beautiful. Also ambitious, which is why Pompey had banished her."

"I think perhaps we should recall her," Caesar said. "Let us arrange, through certain of these ministers who have no love for Pothinus, to send word to her to come and see me. I would like to speak with her myself and judge what manner of woman she is. Perhaps we can help her see that she would best serve her own interests by also serving Rome's. But I think it would not be wise to alert others of our plans before we have decided on a course of action. I will send word to her to come to me in secret."

Caesar smiled. "In the meantime, Septimus, my friend, we shall take full advantage of this grudging hospitality and send for wine. It shall probably be sour, but no matter. We shall only pour it out. Let them believe that we dissolute Romans are drinking through the night. So long as lights burn in our chambers, stealthy assassins might hesitate to enter." He clapped his hand to his sword hilt. "And if they do, we shall be sober and prepared for them."

Throughout the night, the palace servants brought them wine, which neither of them even tasted. The hours stretched toward dawn. Caesar had no need of Travers to help him stay awake. His hyper personality kept him going, dictating letters and portions of his memoirs until Travers was exhausted, and then Caesar, seeing he was tired, apologized for working him so hard and told him amusing anecdotes and stories of his childhood, which Travers wanted desperately to write down, but couldn't both because his wrist was sore from taking dictation and it was all that he could do to keep his eyes open. At some point, he dropped off, and when he awoke, it was morning and Caesar was still up, showing no signs of being tired. He chided Travers gently for falling asleep and when Travers apologized, assured him that it was perfectly all right, that he deserved his rest. *If I don't die on the battlefield,* Travers thought, *just trying to keep up with him will kill me.*

The morning was spent with Caesar visiting his troops and seeing to their comfort. Then he presented his demands to Ptolemy for payment of the tribute. The boy king simply sat there, looking at them sullenly, while Pothinus stood at his side and spoke for him. He was, thought Travers, a decidedly unpleasant man. He was large and fat and jowly, with a shaved head and a mannered, effeminate voice. His pudgy hands had rings on every finger but the thumbs and they gestured languidly when he spoke, making Travers think of pale and bloated slugs.

"Your petition has been noted," the eunuch replied pompously. "It would seem now, Caesar, that your business here has been concluded. The man you came here seeking has been dealt with, your soldiers have been fed and rested. We have done our best to be hospitable hosts. But the time has come when you should leave Egypt and go back to Rome. There are, no doubt, affairs of greater consequence you should attend to. You should not concern yourself with minor matters such as collecting tribute. It can be sent to you in Rome."

Caesar stiffened and his cheeks flushed red. "I do not require Egyptians to be my counselors!" he snapped. "And Rome does not wait on Egypt's pleasure. The tribute will be paid in due course, and speedily, else I shall instruct my army to seize it for themselves in whatever manner they so choose! It is *I* who have been patient, Pothinus. But my patience has been sorely tried. I would advise you not to try it further."

He turned on his heel and stalked out of the chamber, with Travers hurrying to catch up with him.

"I will rid Egypt of this insolent eunuch if it is the last thing I ever do," stormed Caesar as they headed back to their rooms.

Afterward, several of Ptolemy's ministers came to speak with him discreetly and Travers wondered which of them would send word to Cleopatra. He was excited at the thought of actually meeting her face-to-face, a woman who was one of the most legendary beauties and seductresses in all of history.

Despite all the years he'd spent at Caesar's side, there were still times when he found himself looking at that handsome, scholarly profile and thinking, "My God, I'm actually sitting here with *Julius Caesar*!" At such times, it seemed almost like a dream. And at other times, the world he came from seemed unreal.

He had been born in Dallas, Texas and had acquired an interest in ancient history at a very early age, a result of a typical boyhood fascination with the glamor of the Time Wars. Childhood play had led him to the library, to look up certain historical details so that he could settle arguments among his playmates about what sort of armor was worn by medieval knights and how ancient Romans fought. He was able to point out historical flaws in the design of the toy weapons that their parents purchased for them and was soon making his own from wood in his father's workshop. He sold them to his friends, who found that they held up to rough use far better than the flimsy plastic swords they bought in stores and made a far more satisfying sound when they were stuck together.

He became the local "armorer," constructing wooden swords and shields and daggers for his friends, and with practice, he became more skillful at it. Determined to be authentic at all costs, he did his research carefully and the more he read about ancient times, the more fascinated he became and the more he wanted to know. His interest in research helped him to acquire better study habits and his grades in school improved dramatically. His father, pleased with this development, as well as with his growing skill in craftsmanship, encouraged him and bought him better tools and books. While still in his early teens, Travers had graduated to working in metal. He started small, with handmade knives, but soon moved on to larger blades. By the time he was ready to enter college, he had made quite a bit of money selling replicas of Spanish swords, medieval maces, Viking blades and battle axes, Sinclair-hilted sabers, French rapiers and Scottish basket-hilted claymores to collectors and would-be Time Commandos who were happy to pay hundreds of dollars for authentic, exquisitely crafted "souvenirs of campaigns in Minus Time."

Travers entered Harvard on a scholarship and it was there that his area of interest narrowed to a specialization in classical times. He studied Greek and Latin and took graduate degrees in history, now certain of how he planned to spend his life. He intended to apply to the Observer Corps and be commissioned as an L.T.O., with hopes of a long-term posting in ancient Rome. His timing could not have been more perfect. He completed his Observer training at the head of his class, just as the Temporal Crisis struck and the focus of the Time Wars shifted from the settling of international disputes to dealing with the new and greater threat from the parallel universe. The majority of the world's temporal forces were being converted to Temporal Observer status, to function under the senior officers of the Observer Corps, and there was a drastic need for personnel with the sort of qualifications Travers had, especially as L.T.O.'s. They were as anxious to get Travers as Travers was to join them and he was able to write his own ticket. Without hesitation, he requested to be assigned to Gaius Julius Caesar.

Now, the future that he came from seemed less real to him than the time in which he lived. He had become a Roman in almost all respects, except for that certain distance that he always had to keep, to remind himself of who and what he really was and what his task entailed. For over a decade, he had lived the dream. Caesar had become his friend and it was difficult for him to think that in a couple of years, he would be murdered in the Senate, beneath the statue of the very man whom he had driven out of Rome and to his death in Egypt.

He thought of Casca, striking the first blow, and Brutus, delivering the last. Travers felt the blade of the *parazonium* he wore at his side. Of Macedonian origin, it was the knife worn by almost every male Roman and the secondary weapon of the soldier, a lethal, bottle-shaped blade with a strong central rib, three inches wide at the hilt, narrowing slightly at the midsection and then flaring out once more and tapering to a sharp point. He had seen the horrifying wounds the foot-long blade could make and he shuddered at the thought of having something like that plunged into his body. Caesar would be stabbed a total of twenty-three times by the conspirators, from the neck down to the groin, and he would fall at the foot of Pompey's statue, which he himself had ordered put back up after the mob had torn it down. His blood would splatter on the pedestal, causing all of Rome to talk for years thereafter about the supernatural influence at work in the assassination, as if the spirit of Pompey himself had presided over it in revenge. And part of Travers' job was to see that it happened exactly that way.

He had come to have a great deal of respect and affection

for Caesar, not only as a scholar studying his subject, but as a man and as a friend. It was hard to think that he would have to stand by and watch him die, and in such an awful manner, without being able to do anything to prevent it. But that was precisely what he had to do. If necessary, he would even have to get involved himself to make sure that history wasn't changed. As much as that thought disturbed him, the thought that forces from the parallel universe could be at work to change that disturbed him even more.

Over the next few days, Caesar grew more tense and irritable. He avoided Pothinus and the king as much as possible, which seemed to suit the two of them just fine. He took long walks in the gardens, always armed and always with Travers at his side and several soldiers close by. It was in the gardens that several of Ptolemy's ministers contrived to meet with him, or to send informers, to keep him advised of what Pothinus was doing. The longer they remained in Egypt, in the midst of palace intrigues, the more danger they were in. If Pothinus found out about Caesar's plan to reinstate Cleopatra, he would waste no time in having them removed. Travers would have felt much better staying with the army, but Caesar insisted upon staying in the palace, both to claim the treatment due Rome's emissary and to keep an eye on things.

They were dining in their chambers one evening when one of the ministers arrived, along with a servant carrying a rolled-up carpet over his shoulder.

"I have brought the additional bedclothing you requested, Caesar," said the minister, shutting the door behind him as the servant carried it in.

"Bedclothing?" said Caesar with a frown. "I did not ask for bedclothing."

"Perhaps Caesar does not recall," said the minister with a smile. "Lay it down upon the floor, Apollodorus."

Caesar got up from his chair. "What is this? I am quite certain that I asked for no—"

Apollodorus unrolled the carpet and stood back. A young woman had been rolled up inside it. She was lying on her stomach. She pushed herself up slightly from the floor and bent one lovely leg, tossed her head, getting the hair back out of her eyes, and looked up at Caesar with a smile.

"You did ask that I come to you discreetly," she said.

Caesar stood back with surprise.

"I am Cleopatra."

She stood and faced them. Travers stared at her, stunned. She was the most beautiful woman he had ever seen. Her hair was jet-black, long and straight. Her striking features were sharp and graceful. There was a proud nobility to her bearing. Her eyes were a deep brown, with a smoldering, penetrating gaze; her complexion dark; her mouth full and sensuous. Her figure was voluptuous, with large, firm breasts that were clearly outlined in the simple, thin, white linen shift she wore, her narrow waist and flaring hips accentuated by the gold girdle encircling it. Her legs were long and shapely, her small feet gracefully shod in thin, delicate sandals. She wore no jewelry except for an amulet around her neck. She was breathtakingly lovely. Travers recalled that at the time of meeting Caesar, this very meeting, she was twenty-one years old.

"That which was concealed shall stand revealed," Caesar murmured. Travers glanced at him sharply.

Cleopatra cocked her head, gazing at Caesar with puzzlement.

Caesar shook his head. "I was merely recalling something someone told me once," he said. He glanced at the minister and servant. "Leave us."

They went out and shut the door behind them. Caesar gestured toward his chair. "Please. Be seated."

She chose the couch rather than the chair and reclined upon it gracefully.

Caesar watched her appreciatively. "Allow me to present my friend, Praetor Lucius Septimus."

She inclined her head slightly toward Travers. Travers stood and gave her a slight bow. "I am honored, Queen Cleopatra."

"I am not a queen now, Praetor Septimus, merely an exiled princess. My brother is still king," she said.

"For the moment," Caesar said. He smiled. "I must

admit that I had not expected your arrival in so bold a manner. It was very clever of you."

"Our nights are cool," she said. "A Roman could be expected to feel the chill. No one would remark upon his asking for another coverlet."

"Had I known they made such coverlets in Egypt, I would have sent for one much sooner," Caesar replied with a smile. "I merely regret that I had to ask you to resort to stealth in order to arrive in your own palace."

"I understood the need," she said. "Pothinus would hardly welcome my arrival. Since I was sent to live in exile, he has made a breach between my younger brother and myself."

"A breach can be repaired," said Caesar. "It wants only a craftsman who knows what he's about."

Cleopatra smiled. "You do not have the look of a craftsman," she said.

"Neither have I the look of a general," Caesar replied, "or at least so I am told. And yet I lead Rome's finest legions. Legions that can assure your future as the queen of Egypt."

"You plan to depose my brother?"

"Only if it should prove necessary," Caesar replied. "I have no wish to harm him. I would be satisfied to have him rule with you to guide him."

"I see," she said. "Then it is Pothinus you wish to have removed."

"Rome needs an ally, not a scheming, unctuous eunuch who looks only after his own interests."

"And you think that I will not look after *my* own interests?" she asked coyly, arching a graceful eyebrow.

Caesar smiled. "It is in your interest to consider mine."

"Not Rome's?"

"I *am* Rome."

"So. And once I am queen, what would Rome have me do?"

"Merely be a friend to Rome," said Caesar, gazing at her steadily.

She gave him a knowing smile. "Then I am at Rome's pleasure."

3 ⎯⎯⎯⎯⎯⎯⎯⎯⎯⎯⎯⎯

The outskirts of Rome, April 30, 44 B.C.

The transition coordinates Travers had selected clocked them in on a wooded hillside a few miles outside of Rome. It was dark when they arrived, two-thirty in the morning by local temporal reckoning, though the Romans kept time in only an approximate manner. They based it on sunrise and sunset. They divided the day into twelve hours, with the first six hours being *ante meridiem* (before the middle of the day) and the second six *post meridiem* (after the middle of the day), but they did not divide hours into minutes, and their water clocks and sundials were never accurate in any sense of the term, so no one in Rome was ever really certain of the time.

Travers was waiting for them at the transition point, along with four other men. Travers, who had spent most of his adult life in Minus Time, did not know anything about what had happened to Lucas, so he naturally showed no surprise on seeing him. All he really knew about them was that they were an adjustment team from Temporal Intelligence. They, on the other hand, knew a great deal about Travers, having read his file, though the man who met them hardly resembled the photo they had studied. Travers had aged since that photo had been taken. The hard life he had led had taken its toll.

He was a small man, well built, with dark hair that had started thinning. He was in his late forties, deeply tanned and his face had lines in it that age alone was not responsible for. He had a weather-beaten look about him. His forehead was high, his features looked Mediterranean (partly a result of cosmetic surgery), and his eyes were dark and alert. He was wearing a simple tunic and sandals, with a cloak thrown over his shoulders. A short distance behind him, they saw a covered carriage drawn by two horses, which would be their transportation to Rome. There were three horses tied up by carriage and a small fire was burning in the clearing.

"You've studied the identities that I prepared for you?" asked Travers, after they had introduced themselves.

"My cover is Marcus Septimus," said Lucas. "I'm your younger brother, from Cumae. Our parents are both dead and we have no other living relatives. It's been a long time since we've seen each other, so now that you've returned from the wars, I've come to visit with you in Rome and I've brought my wife, Antonia, with me." He nodded at Andre, then indicated Delaney, whose beard had been shaved and whose hair had been dyed black for this mission. "And this is our friend, Fabius Quintullus, also from Cumae. We all grew up together and we're very close."

Travers nodded. "Good." He introduced the four men who were with him. "These are your slaves, whom you have brought with you from our family estate. This is Capt. Castelli, C.T.O. in this sector."

Castelli, the Chief Temporal Observer, stepped forward and greeted them. He was slim and very fit, with dark brown hair and blue eyes. He looked to be in his mid-twenties, though he was actually far older. "My cover name is Demetrius," he said. "I was a Greek soldier, from Sparta, captured in the wars."

"And this is Lt. Corwin," Travers said, indicating one of the other men. "His name here is Corac."

"I'm a Gaul," said Corwin. He was short and stocky, with fair skin and light brown hair. "One of the many prisoners captured in the Gallic Wars and sent back to Rome to be sold on the block. You bought me from a slave merchant in Ostia."

"Sgt. Andell," said Travers, introducing the next man.

"Antoninus," said Andell, giving his cover name, "also a Greek, from Athens. I've been your tutor since you were children."

He was of average height and dark complected, with thick, curly black hair and a wiry, compact build. He looked older than the others, perhaps in his late forties, which meant that he was easily three times that age, a veteran soldier of the Temporal Corps. The fact that he was still only a sergeant suggested that he must have been reduced in grade a number of times during his long career. Delaney, whose own record for reductions in grade was unsurpassed, glanced at Andell with interest. He was either a maverick, a chronic screwup (which seemed unlikely, given his posting and the fact that he was still alive), or somewhere along the line, he had pissed off the wrong person and messed up his chances for promotion.

"And Cpl. Drummond," Travers finished, introducing the last man.

"Drusus," said Drummond, the youngest of the four, blond and slim, with a boyish face and green eyes. "I'm the son of slaves, born on your family estate."

He looked about seventeen or eighteen, which meant that his actual age could be anywhere from late teens to early forties. The antiagathics made it impossible to tell with any accuracy. They were all regular T.O. Corps, which meant that unlike Travers, they had received the antiagathic treatments and were on short-term posting. A few years, at most, before they'd be turned around and transferred to another sector or another time period.

They sat down around the campfire. Lucas turned to Castelli. "What's the strength of your T.O. unit in this sector?"

"A platoon," Castelli said.

"That's all?"

"We're spread kind of thin," said Castelli, "but we can send for reinforcements if we run into trouble. It'll be your call."

"All right," said Lucas, turning to Travers. "What's the current situation?"

"Well, a great deal has happened since we left Egypt and I made my last report," said Travers. "The moment Caesar laid eyes on Cleopatra, he wanted her. And I certainly can't blame him. She's enough to take your breath away. After she came to visit him secretly in his apartment, they became lovers and he kept her with him in the palace. That was too much for Pothinus and Ptolemy to bear. It brought all the factions out into the open. Achillas, Ptolemy's general, raised a force against Caesar's legions and Pothinus made plans to assassinate us. Caesar got wind of it and killed Pothinus, then set out to destroy the army of Achillas. He engaged them and wiped out the entire force. Ptolemy died in the battle and Caesar set Cleopatra on the throne. By the time we left Egypt, she was pregnant with his son. Then Caesar marched against Pharnaces, son of Rome's old enemy, King Mithridates, and drove him out of Pontus in only five days. His legions rolled right over them. It was the occasion of his uttering the famous words, 'I came, I saw, I conquered.' Next, he led his legions into battle against the armies of Cato and Scipio, the last of Pompey's loyalists. He defeated them in North Africa and returned to Rome to celebrate triumphs for his victories. But he wasn't finished yet. Pompey's two young sons, Cnaeus and Sextus, had raised an army in Spain, intending to avenge their father. We immediately set off for Spain in order to engage them. We met their army at Munda. It was bloody. Over thirty thousand of the enemy were killed. We lost a thousand men. I had several close calls, myself. Pompey's youngest son, Sextus, managed to escape, but Cnaeus was killed and his head was brought to Caesar. That marked the end of the civil war. It was also the last war that Caesar would engage in. At least, it was the last war that he was *supposed* to engage in."

"What do you mean by that?" asked Lucas.

"I'm coming to that," said Travers. "Caesar didn't want to revive the ancient Roman kingship, because the people equated that with tyranny, so the title he chose for himself was dictator, like Sulla before him. This way, he could be periodically reappointed to the post, which at least gave the semblance of senatorial control in a republican government. But recently, he's had himself made dictator for life, with the title of *Imperator*. That was almost the same thing as naming himself king. A lot of people didn't take it well.

"Back when we first returned to Rome and he celebrated a triumph honoring his victory over Pompey's sons, it made him more than a few enemies," continued Travers as they warmed themselves around the fire. "It's one thing to celebrate victory over barbarians or foreign kings, but when you destroy the children of one of the greatest men of Rome and honor it with a triumph, you're going to upset a few people. He realized that and tried to make up for it by ordering Pompey's statues put back up after some of the pro-Caesar mobs, mostly comprised of Caesar's soldiers, tore them down. He held public feasts, distributed corn to the masses, and staged chariot races and gladiatorial combats. His old bread and circuses routine, playing to the masses. It worked for him before and it worked for him again. The only difference was, now he could afford it.

"He established a number of new colonies, in Italy as well as in Carthage and in Corinth. He settled thousands of the soldiers who'd served with him during all those years, rewarding them with land in their retirement, as well as many of the city's unemployed. Which means that if he ever has to raise an army quickly, all he needs to do is call on the colonies. Men who once had nothing but are now landowners, thanks to him, will remain unquestioningly loyal. He gave out consulships and praetorships left and right and increased the Senate rolls from six hundred to nine hundred, installing his supporters so now he virtually controls the Senate. He even pardoned some of his enemies, notably Brutus and Cassius. He gave them praetorships, despite their opposition to him in the civil war. He told me he did it so he could keep an eye on them. After all, the oracle told him to beware of them. The way he said it, I couldn't tell if he was joking or if he was serious. He tends to have mood swings and he can be hard to read sometimes. He's also used some of the wealth he acquired from the wars to construct the Basilica Julia and the Julian Forum, as well as the Temple of Venus Genetrix, the goddess of his family. And beside the statue of Venus, he's set up a gilded bronze statue of Cleopatra, which has raised more than a few eyebrows. She's in Rome now, with her son, Caesarion. He's set her up in her own house, complete with slaves and all the luxuries. He visits her every day. He's talking about divorcing Calpurnia and marrying her."

"But I thought Caesar never married Cleopatra," Andre said.

"No, he didn't," Travers replied. "But he's mentioned it to me several times now and I think he's serious. The people will overlook his keeping her as his mistress, but if he divorces a woman of a wealthy and influential Roman family in order to marry a foreigner, they'll turn against him. But Caesar doesn't seem to care. Cleopatra exerts a powerful influence on him. She's the one who was behind a lot of the autocratic changes that he's made and she caters to his ego, feeding it and his ambition. Why not surpass Alexander? Why not become a monarch, the ruler of the world? Busts of Caesar are being distributed all over Rome and throughout the provinces. He's had coins struck with his own image on them and the slogan, *'DICT. PERPETUO'*—perpetual dictator—the first time the portrait of a living Roman has ever appeared on the coinage. And now he's talking about raising legions once again to invade Parthia and avenge Crassus, then pressing on into the Orient, as Alexander did."

"Only he was assassinated before he could accomplish all that," said Delaney.

"Yes," Travers replied somberly, as if the thought disturbed him. "He was. History says that he grew careless and disregarded all the signs. Some historians have even ventured the opinion that he actually *wanted* to die, because his health was failing and he couldn't bear the thought of growing old. But I've lived with him for years now and I know that man as well as I know myself. He suffers periodic fits of epilepsy, but he's lived with that for years. He doesn't want to die. He wants to be immortal. He's fifty-six years old and he wants one last hurrah. The only reason he ignored the rumors of conspiracies against his life was because his ego simply wouldn't allow him to believe that anyone would seriously want to kill him. He had restored peace and prosperity to Rome and introduced a stable government. Without him, he was convinced that it would all fall apart. As he once said to Cleopatra, 'I *am* Rome.' And so he didn't take proper precautions. Only now, all that is changing. And Cleopatra is responsible."

"How?" asked Lucas.

"In about two weeks, it will be the Ides of March and Caesar is supposed to be assassinated," Travers said. "According to history, a soothsayer was supposed to have warned him to 'Beware the Ides of March,' but Caesar never took him seriously. But now, all he talks about is Lucan's prophecy. He's well aware that the fateful day is drawing near. He told Cleopatra about what Lucan said to him. 'That which was concealed shall stand revealed.' He believes that statement referred to Cleopatra. She was concealed in a roll of carpet that they use for bedding when she was smuggled into his apartment at the palace, and when her slave Apollodorus unrolled it, she stood revealed. Caesar told her that he knew she was his 'guiding omen' the moment he saw her, and she's done nothing to disabuse him of that notion. Not only has she been encouraging him in his plans for new conquests and greater glory, she's prevailed upon him to employ a bodyguard, as well. An *Egyptian* bodyguard, made up of soldiers she's brought with her, because the oracle had told him that he would die at the hands of those he thought his friends. Caesar had once employed a personal guard of Spaniards, but he dismissed them because he thought it wasn't good for appearances to have a bodyguard, much less one made up of foreigners. Now he's got an Egyptian one. That's an anomaly. They don't belong in this scenario. And there's something very strange about those Egyptians."

"You think they might be agents from the parallel universe?" asked Delaney.

Travers shook his head. "I don't know. Either they are, or *she* is."

"Cleopatra?" said Lucas.

"I think it's possible," said Travers, gazing at them seriously. "She has a tremendous amount of influence over Caesar. I've been giving it a lot of thought. What if she's my counterpart from the parallel universe? A sort of L.T.O., a mole infiltrated into this timeline with the specific purpose of creating a temporal disruption. Her mission could have been to seduce Caesar and bear his son. Maybe Caesarion isn't even his son. She might have been already impregnated with a male fetus when she met Caesar. Possibly one that's been genetically tailored. What would happen if Caesar *didn't* die? What would happen if he added to Rome's conquests and dramatically increased its territories? What would happen if Cleopatra prevailed on him to name Caesarion instead of Octavian as his heir? And Caesarion was someone the S.O.G. could control? It would completely change the course of history. Octavian would never become Caesar Augustus. Tiberius would never become Emperor, nor would Caligula or Claudius or Nero. It could change the entire course of civilization!"

"Do you have anything solid to base your suspicions on or is this just a hunch?" asked Delaney.

Travers shook his head. "I tell you, I don't know, but something is very definitely *wrong*. Those Egyptians simply don't belong here. And their presence has not been taken well. Caesar even brings them into the Senate with him. It's increased the animosity toward him, which on one hand is all to the good, I suppose, but on the other hand, he's become more cautious, more aloof, and more determined than ever to do things his way, come hell or high water."

"You're concerned about him, aren't you?" Andre said.

Travers glanced at her and grimaced. "Yes, I suppose I am. Funny, isn't it?"

"You got too close," said Delaney. "You allowed yourself to get involved."

"Listen, you study a man for half your life and then live with him, go through several wars with him, especially a charismatic man like Caesar, and you try not to get involved," said Travers. "The man's become my friend. You understand that? I've made him the subject of my life's work and I've gotten to know him as well as anybody knows him. It's hard not to like a man like Caesar. Yes, he's ambitious and he's arrogant, but great men always are. He's also capable of kindness, and loyalty, and devotion. It's not for nothing that his legions idolize him. He's larger than life. Intelligent, incredibly courageous, inspirational. One of the greatest men who ever lived. And I have to make sure that he gets murdered."

Travers took out his Roman dagger and stared at the foot-long, lethal blade. "Can you imagine what it's like to be stabbed with something like this? Twenty-three times. Twenty-three times, they're going to plunge daggers like this into his body. And not only am I helpless to do anything about it, I've got to make certain it gets done."

"No, Travers," Lucas said. "*We've* got to make certain it gets done."

"Evening, John."

John Marshall froze as he entered the dark bedroom of his house near the east bank of the Tiber. The voice had spoken in English and it sounded vaguely familiar. He lifted the oil lamp he carried in his hand. He was able to make out a dark figure sitting on his bed.

"Who *are* you?" he asked tensely, coming closer. He did not recognize the man.

"Someone who once saved your ass from the Spanish Inquisition."

"My God. *Steiger?*"

"Long time no see, John. Sorry if I ruined your evening. I sent the girl away. Told her I was an old friend of yours and wanted to surprise you. Little young for you, wasn't she?"

"Jesus. What the hell are you doing here? I never would've recognized you. You changed your face."

Steiger's hair was dark now and cosmetic surgery had dramatically altered his appearance. Not even his own mother would have recognized him. "Yes, I got tired of the old one. Actually, the situation called for a different look."

"You're on the lam? I don't believe it. You tied up with the Network?"

"You know about the Network?"

"Of course I know about the Network. But I never thought you'd get yourself involved with them."

"I didn't. I'm still with the agency."

"You're on assignment? But I thought the covert field section was disbanded."

"For someone who's several thousand years out-of-date, you manage to keep up pretty well."

"Come on. We've got our channels, you know that."

"Yes, I know. That's how I found you. You've done pretty well for yourself since I last saw you. Nice place you've got here."

"What do you want, Steiger? You here to bust me, is that it?"

"Now is that any way to talk after all the years we've known each other?"

"Yeah, but like you said, it's been a long time and things change. Stop rattling my chain, Creed. What do you want?"

"I need your help, John. Just like old times, remember?"

"I'm out of it now, Creed. I turned my back on all that."

"You can never turn your back on it, John. You know that."

"Damn you. I'm just trying to live a quiet, peaceful life."

"Peaceful? Staging gladiator fights, beast baiting, and chariot races in the arena? But I guess that doesn't count, huh? What the hell, it's only show business, right? I gather it pays well. Lets the noble Marcian buy young teenaged girls like the one I just sent out of here."

"Where the hell do you get off, judging me? Especially after some of the shit you've pulled."

Steiger held up his hands. "Okay. Forget it. So my hands aren't exactly clean, either. I guess I'm still sore about you going over to the Underground. You were a damn good agent, John. We can't afford to lose people like you."

"Yeah, and I can't afford to die, either," Marshall said, setting down the lamp on a small table and sitting down in a chair next to it. "I was getting pressure from the Network. Either you're with us or against us. And you know what happened to people who tried to buck the Network."

"I bucked 'em and I'm still around."

"Yeah, well, you always were a cowboy. You and Carnehan. The super spooks. Me, I got old and tired. I got slow. So I took early retirement."

He pressed something on the table and a hidden drawer popped out. Steiger instantly had a laser pistol in his hand. "Hold it, John."

"Take it easy, for God's sake!"

"Whatever's in there, take it out slowly."

Marshall produced a pack of cigarettes. "Satisfied?"

Steiger grinned and lowered the pistol.

"You want one?"

"Don't mind if I do. What happens if one of your slaves comes in and catches us smoking?"

Marshall lit one up and tossed the pack to Creed. "My slaves know what's expected of them. They don't come up here unless they're told to. I'm still a careful man, Creed."

"Yeah, but you're slipping. I got in here with no sweat."

"How the hell did you get in?"

"Came down from the roof."

"You see? I told you I'm getting slow."

He held out the lamp for Creed to light his cigarette.

"So. You going to tell me what you're doing here?"

"I'm on a covert mission. We may have a potential temporal disruption on our hands."

"You part of an adjustment team?"

"No, but there's been one clocked back here. Delaney, Priest, and Cross. You know them?"

"I've heard of them. I also heard that Priest bought it in Afghanistan."

"Not exactly," Steiger said. "But that's a long story."

"So they sent in the first string, huh? Must be pretty big. Where do you fit in?"

"Sort of unofficial backup. Undercover."

"Meaning they don't know you're here." Marshall grinned. "You haven't changed. Still the same old cowboy. What's going down?"

"I'm not exactly sure, but it has to do with Caesar."

Marshall exhaled heavily. "That *is* big. What've you got?"

Steiger briefly told him what he knew. Marshall listened silently, not saying anything till he was finished.

"And this L.T.O., Travis?"

"Travers."

"Right. He thinks it's going to center around Caesar's assassination?"

"That's my guess."

"What do you mean, it's your *guess*?"

"I mean I haven't spoken to the man. All I've got is the first report he made of a possible anomaly involving Caesar."

"You mean the oracle."

"That's right. Travers sent up the balloon and the team went out, but I've had no contact with him, so I don't really know what the latest intelligence is. Caesar's supposed to die in about two weeks. That's got to be the focus of the disruption."

"You think the S.O.G. is going to try to prevent the assassination."

"It would make for a hell of a disruption," Steiger said. "It would probably bring about a timestream split. I think this is going to be a rough one. The old man didn't approve of contacts between the agency and the Underground, but I've been trying to convince him he was wrong about that. We're going to need all the help we can get from now on."

"What made Forrester change his mind?"

"He hasn't. At least, not yet."

"So what are you telling me? He doesn't know about what you're doing here?"

"Not officially. I'm supposed to be on R & R. He knows what I'm doing, but no one else does."

"I get it. You fall down on this one, your ass is wide open and his is covered."

"Something like that."

"And you wonder why I decided to get out."

"What can you tell me about Caesar?"

"That you don't already know? Probably nothing."

"What do you mean, probably nothing?"

"Just what I said. What do you think, I'm on his dinner invitation list?"

"But you're the local impresario around here," Steiger said. "Hasn't he been staging chariot races and fights?"

"Well, yeah, but you don't think I deal with the man directly, do you? He's the Emperor, for Christ's sake."

"Who do you deal with?"

"Lately, it's been mostly Antony."

"Marc Antony?"

"That's right," said Marshall. "It's not always him in person, though. Most of the time, I work through intermediaries. He's an important man."

"Can you get me an introduction?"

Marshall sighed. "I guess I could try. Damn it. I thought I was through with all of that. Why the hell couldn't you leave me alone? You're going to get me killed, you know that?"

"I'll try to keep you out of it as much as possible," said Steiger. "All I need is a connection. And a base of operations."

"Here?"

"Partly, but I'd also like to arrange a safehouse. What would you recommend?"

"I own some apartments in a tenement block in the Argiletum, a shopping district near the Subura district. Not exactly your luxury accommodations, but I could set you up in one of those."

"Oh, so you're a slumlord, too?"

"Give me a break, Steiger. I'm trying to cooperate because I owe you."

"What, not for old times' sake?"

"Well, maybe that, too. And I've also got a life-style to protect here. I don't want a temporal disruption any more than you do."

"Okay. An apartment will do fine."

"You'll need money, I suppose."

"I've got some, but a little more can't hurt."

Marshall nodded. "All right. Anything you need, just say the word. But there's one condition. This is strictly between you and me. I don't want that adjustment team involved. I don't want them knowing about me. Otherwise, all bets are off."

"That goes without saying, John."

"Okay. I just wanted to make sure we understand each other. What about your cover?"

"What would make me interesting to Antony?"

"He likes chariot racing."

"A betting man?"

"Obsessive."

"Good. Why not say I'm a breeder of racing horses? And I've trained charioteers. You've bought strings from me in the past. Where should I be from?"

Marshall thought a moment. "Ilerda, in Nearer Spain. That would make you a provincial and no one would be likely to ask you any detailed questions about where you're from. You could always say you've never ventured very far from your farm out in the country, by the Ebro."

"So what brings me to Rome? A business deal?"

"Let's say I'm contemplating purchasing your entire operation, leaving you to run it, of course, and I've invited you here in order to discuss it."

"That would work." Steiger grinned. "Almost like old times, isn't it?"

"Too much like old times, if you ask me," Marshall replied sourly.

"When's the next race coming up?"

"As a matter of fact, I've got several teams entered in one tomorrow."

"Will Antony be there?"

"He never misses a race if he can help it."

"Good. What are the chances of putting in a fix?"

"You want me to fix a chariot race?" said Marshall with disbelief. "You realize I could get the death penalty for that?"

"Only if you got caught," said Steiger.

Marshall sighed. "Hell. I suppose it could be arranged."

Steiger smiled. "You haven't changed much, either, have you?"

"A man does what he can. You're planning to take Antony?"

"For a bundle," Steiger said. "What better way to get to know a man than to have him owe you money?"

4 ─────────────────────

"I hadn't expected it to look so beautiful," said Andre as they approached the city. Andell drove the coach, while Castelli rode ahead of them, with Corwin and Drummond mounted on their horses, bringing up the rear. Travers had clocked back to his villa in the city, to await their arrival.

"It looks better from a distance. First time in Rome, eh?" Andell said.

"I've served a hitch in Rome before," said Lucas, "but for Finn and Andre, I think it's the first time. Still, Rome was very different then."

"Oh, yeah? When did you pull a tour here?"

"Second Punic War," said Lucas. "I was with Scipio in the war against Hannibal."

"No shit, really? The old arbitration wars. I was there, too."

"You're kidding," Lucas said. "Which cohort?"

"Wrong army," Andell said with a grin. "I was with Hannibal."

Lucas frowned. "You were with *Hannibal*? How can that be? The U.S. Temporal Corps contingent was infiltrated into Roman forces during that Time War."

"I wasn't with the U.S. Temporal Corps," Andell said. "I

was fighting for the Nippon Conglomerate Empire back then. Freelance mercenary."

"That explains it," said Delaney. "I was wondering why someone your age was still a sergeant."

"Yeah. Big black mark on my record," Andell said. "Ex-mercenaries are scum of the earth, far as TAC-HQ is concerned."

"But you're American, aren't you?" said Lucas. "So you had to start out regular Corps before you went merc. What happened?"

"I caught a real bad tour that made me want out in a big way," said Andell. "I served a hitch in the War Between the States. I was with the Union troops at Shiloh."

Delaney whistled. "That must've been a rough one."

"Tell me about it. It made the Punic Wars seem like a cakewalk. I got shot up pretty bad and wound up just lying there on the damn battlefield, wondering if I was going to die or if the damn hogs were going to get to me first. There was a bunch of 'em rutting around the corpses. And some of them weren't even corpses yet. Not too far off from me, this huge pig was chewing on a guy's exposed intestines and he was still alive. I can still hear the poor bastard screaming."

"My God," said Andre.

"It gets worse," Andell said. "Somehow, I got the strength up to crawl away and get into the woods. Packed my wounds with mud and then started trying to limp back to our lines. Only a rebel patrol found me first. I wound up in Andersonville."

"Jesus," said Delaney.

"Yeah. Maybe the worst prison in American history. But there was a Union doctor there and he managed to get me patched back up, sort of, and I eventually managed to escape with a small group of men. We made our way to Sherman's troops and then, boy, we sure got even. Eventually, S & R found me and clocked me back. I spent some time in the hospital and then took my discharge. I figured I'd had enough. Only a funny thing happened."

"You couldn't hack civilian life," said Lucas.

Andell nodded. "You know about it, huh?"

"Yeah. I quit once, too. But there was just no going back. It was either reenlist or go crazy."

"Then you understand," Andell said. "War does funny things to some people. I don't know, maybe it's that after you've danced on the edge of the sword blade, you can just never go back to ordinary life. Lot of people do, but me . . ." He shook his head. "I never would've figured it. I thought I'd never want to go back in the military again, but civilian life just drove me around the bend. I started drinking. Got into drugs. Got busted a few times."

"That's why you couldn't reenlist," said Delaney.

"Yeah, they don't take convicted felons in the service. So I wound up going merc. Ran into a corporate recruiter in Miami. Next thing I knew, I was on a shuttle to Tokyo. They processed me, put me through detox, then clocked me out to Spain with a merc unit they were using and we joined up with Hannibal there."

"So you were in on the crossing of the Alps?" said Lucas.

"That's right. Not exactly your average day hike. But I'll tell you something . . . you'll probably think I'm crazy, but I loved every minute of it."

"How'd you wind up with the Observers?" Andre asked.

"I re-upped after I completed my hitch for Nippon and got assigned to the T.O. Corps."

"But what about your record?" Andre said, puzzled.

"They didn't know I had a record."

"I don't understand," said Andre, frowning.

"The Nippon Conglomerate gave him a new identity," Delaney explained. "Some countries do that for mercs. It's sort of a recruiting inducement. Do a good job for them, complete your tour without getting yourself killed, and they'll give you a brand-new identity, fully documented. You get to start off with a clean slate."

"So Andell's not your real name?" asked Andre.

"It is now."

"Aren't you taking a chance on telling us all this?" she asked.

"No, not really. Even if you turned me in, which I don't

think you would, HQ wouldn't really care. They're kind of pressed for manpower these days. As long as my official record's clean, they're not going to care about who or what I was before."

"But they're not going to promote you, either," said Delaney.

"No, that's for sure. I'll never make it past sergeant. But that's okay. I never much liked officers, anyway." He grinned. "No offense."

"None taken," said Delaney. "I know exactly how you feel."

"You're talking to the man who actually holds the record for the most reductions in grade in the entire Temporal Corps," said Lucas, smiling.

"Seriously?"

"Seriously."

"And you still made captain?" Andell shook his head. "You must be a real hotshot. Sir."

"I just don't understand it," said Delaney. "I keep taking the damn bars off and they keep slapping them back on me."

Andell grinned. They were entering the outskirts of the city. "So, you want the orientation lecture or you just going to let the programming kick in?"

"No, go ahead," said Lucas. "We can always use the perspective of someone who's been in the field for a while."

"Well, like I said, the city looks better from a distance. Once you actually get in the city itself, as you'll notice in a little while, there are still a lot of truly beautiful buildings, especially the temples and the villas of some of the aristocrats, but the streets are choked with what are essentially your basic slum tenements. This time of year, it's not too bad, but in the summer, you wouldn't believe the stink. They just throw their garbage out into the streets. Lot of people die from fever in the summer.

"At this point, we're actually entering the city," he continued. "Passing through the gates of Rome has become sort of a misnomer. Rome has outgrown its walls and gates. The streets and houses are spread out well beyond them.

The citizens of the republic are so secure these days that they feel they have no need of protective walls. Except around the better houses in the city, to keep the riffraff out."

"What road is this we're on?" asked Lucas.

"The Via Flaminia," said Andell. "You'll notice that it's paved, but it's got two dirt roads running along on either side, like shoulders. The Roman method of building roads is to first excavate a ditch with sloping walls, then fill it with layers of gravel, stone, and mortar. After the ditch is built up in this fashion, the top layer of stones is laid and the road is crowned slightly so water runs off to the sides. The dirt roads running along either side are for the unimportant traffic, your farm carts, peasants, and slaves. The legions have the right of way over everybody else.

"The outlying areas of the city we just passed through are primarily farms, olive orchards and vineyards, with several roadside inns along the way. Right now, we're in the suburbs, which will get denser as we come closer to the old city walls built in the 4th century B.C.

"Here comes your basic geography lesson. Rome itself is built on seven hills: the Capitoline, the Palatine, the Caelian, the Esquiline, the Viminal, and the Quirinal, which ring a small valley that was probably once a swamp. The seventh hill, the Aventine, is slightly to our south. The River Tiber flows along the western borders of the city and beyond its opposite bank is a range of hills called the Janiculum.

"As for culture, the wars with Greece and the conquest of Sicily in the First Punic War brought Romans into contact with Greek architecture, which they've been copying ever since. The first statues in Rome were of Greek origin, brought to the city as spoils of war. Around the middle of the 2nd century B.C., the discovery of a new type of limestone called travertine allowed them to build larger and more solid buildings, as well as their famous arches."

He turned back toward Lucas. "You probably won't recognize the city from when you were here before. There's been lots more construction and they're always building or repairing something. They use a type of lime-mortar that sets up so hard, it can easily be mistaken for modern concrete. Over there is the first aqueduct to bring water to the city, the Marcian, constructed in 144 B.C. And the first stone bridge across the Tiber was built about two years later."

"How do they build the arches?" Andre asked, consulting her programmed "submemory" and not coming up with an answer. The mission programming was never totally complete. There were inevitable gaps.

"They're constructed on wooden scaffolding frames that function as forms on which the stones are laid and mortared," Andell explained. "Then when the mortar has set, the forms and scaffolding are taken down. Simple, but effective. The roads and paths in the city itself were originally gravel, but they've been relaid with stone and volcanic lava from the Alban Hills. The so-called 'Golden Age' of Rome won't really begin until the time of the Nerva and Trajan, around 96 A.D., when there's going to be a tremendous boom in some really impressive construction. However, Caesar's already started a lot of new projects, some of which won't be completed until the time of Augustus. He's bought up all the land on the north side of the Forum, which we'll be passing shortly, and pulled down all the houses to start construction of a new square and market, which will be called the Forum Augusti when it's completed. To the southwest, you'll probably be able to smell it in a few minutes, is the *forum boarium*, the cattle market. Right next to it is the *forum holitorium*, the main market for oil, fruit, and vegetables. So you can get your produce in an atmosphere scented with manure."

"Is that the Forum?" asked Delaney, pointing.

"That's it," Andell said. "The Forum Romano, the most famous city square in all of history. That black stone building over there is the tomb of Romulus. And there's the Sanctuary of Venus the Purifier. Across from the Basilica over there is the Temple of Castor and Pollux, the twin gods. And over there, the Temple of Saturn. You can't see it from here, but right next to it is the Golden Milestone, from which all miles on roads leading to Rome are measured. And there's the Rostra, where they conduct trials and, on occasion, the Senate meets there, as well, when it's warm enough. Otherwise, until they build the permanent Senate House, the Curia Julia, they usually meet in the Temple of Jupiter, which is just to the east of here. On a nice day, you can stand in the Forum and hear someone like Cicero speak. If the wind is right, you can also smell the fish market. So much for historical glamor."

They passed the Forum and entered a residential area.

"A lot of the buildings are more run-down than I expected," Andre said. "It's a bit like towns and cities in medieval times."

"Yeah, there's a similarity," said Andell. "Few Romans except wealthy aristocrats and merchants can afford to live in a townhouse or a villa. The majority of the city's population lives in blocks of tenements like this, no more than three or four stories high."

"The streets are narrower than I expected, too," said Andre.

"They won't be widened until Nero's time," Andell replied. "Most streets in the city, neighbors across the street from one another can reach out from their balconies and shake hands. When Augustus comes in, he'll put a height limit of seventy feet on houses because of the poor construction. Sometimes the tenements just collapse all of a sudden, so be careful when you walk the streets. The average apartments are made up of small rooms over street-level shops, with shuttered windows looking out over the street or out into an interior courtyard. Tenants can buy a room outright, so you've got your original condos, but most people can't afford it, so they rent. You can make a good income as a landlord. The rents in Rome are about four times higher than in the country, anywhere from two thousand to thirty thousand sesterces. For that kind of money, you can buy a small house within sixty miles of Rome. Water's available from lead pipes coming from the aqueducts, but it's a luxury only the wealthy can afford. They pay for it according to the size of their pipes. Most tenants have no water pipes and they have to bring water from a public fountain or a bath. They also have to go to commercial bake and cook shops for their food, because most apartments don't have kitchen facilities. So Romans tend to eat out a lot."

"I don't see many carts or wagons," Lucas said.

"Just coaches and light carriages during the day," Andell said. "That's something new. By Caesar's order, the heavy wheeled traffic is only allowed in the city at night, so nights in the city can get noisy, especially in the business districts. It's like trying to get a good night's sleep in New York, with sirens and shit going off all the time. Same thing. Carts and wagons going by all night, drivers shouting, cracking whips, oxen bellowing . . . not the best idea in the world, if you ask me, but it does cut down on traffic during the day."

"The buildings look like a real fire hazard," Andre said.

"That they are. Fires are real common, especially this time of year, when people leave open braziers burning all night to keep warm. They don't have anything like an organized fire department, at least they won't until Augustus' time, when he'll form a sort of combination police and fire brigade called the Cohortes Vigilum, recruited from freedmen who'll get full citizenship after six years' service. But right now, a lot of people die in fires. They usually just let the damn things burn, then knock down what's left and start all over. You get maps of the city in your programming?"

"Yes," said Lucas.

"Good. You'll need 'em. You'll notice that there aren't any street signs and the houses aren't numbered. It can be hard to find your way around."

They swung down another street, heading back toward the Tiber.

"Travers has himself a villa by the river," Andell said, "so you won't be staying in one of those rattraps. Being buddies with the *Imperator* has its perks. It's still early, but in a few hours, things'll really start picking up. They're holding chariot races in the Circus today. Maybe some gladiator combat, too. Eventually, that'll all move to the Colisseum, but it won't be built for years yet. If you want to get a good feel for what's going on, the place to go is the baths. You can meet everyone from senators down to the tinker, the baker, and the candlestick maker. One *quadrans* gets you in for the whole day, but don't look for soap. And most of the baths are for men only, I'm afraid," he said, glancing at Andre.

"So I'll stink," she said.

"I don't think you'll have to do that," Andell said with a grin. "Travers has a small bath at his villa. That's a bigtime status symbol these days. Just make sure you don't bathe yourself. Have the slaves do it, even if you don't like the idea. It's expected."

"Male slaves or female slaves?" asked Andre.

Andell shrugged. "That's up to you, I guess."

She grinned. "This mission might not be so bad, after all."

"How long have you been on this tour, Andell?" asked Delaney.

"About seven years now," Andell replied.

"All in Rome?"

"First four in Rome, last three in Alexandria. We're not liable to run into anyone who knows me or any of the others, if that's what you're concerned about. Nobody pays much attention to slaves, for one thing, and we've all kept a pretty low profile. Except for Travers, of course, but his case is different. He moves in more interesting circles and he gets to live in a nice villa, instead of the rattraps we've been living in."

"But then you didn't have to go to the Gallic Wars, either," Andre said.

"I wouldn't have minded that one bit. I reenlisted to be a soldier, not a damn Observer. I'm due for a transfer in another year and I'm looking forward to it. I'm hoping I can pull a combat assignment. And I miss wearing pants."

"Watch they transfer you to Scotland," said Delaney.

"If you spent three years in Alexandria, you know about Cleopatra," Lucas said.

"We didn't exactly do dinner and dancing, you know," Andell said. "L.T.O.'s are the ones who get to rub elbows with the rich and famous. But I know about her, yeah."

"What do you think of Travers' theory?"

"I don't know. I think it's possible. The S.O.G. might've pulled a switch while she was in exile. And she didn't have a great deal of contact with her brother, Ptolemy, after she came back. If there was any change in her, her becoming a queen could easily explain it. People in Egypt aren't exactly in the habit of questioning their monarchs. In any case, she's in Rome now, where nobody knew her from before. If it was me and I was going to pull a substitution, I would've done it while she was in exile, just before she met up with Caesar. There's only one thing about it I can't understand."

"What's that?" asked Lucas.

"Caesar's Egyptian guard. I mean, like that's a real obvious anomaly. It's a documented fact that Caesar made a point of refusing to have a bodyguard around him at this time. It stands to reason that the S.O.G. would figure we'd have Observers back here and that's like running up a flag. Again, if it was me, I wouldn't give my play away like that. That thought's occurred to Travers, too. It really bothers him. He just can't figure it."

"Unless, in their universe, Caesar *did* have a bodyguard," said Delaney.

"You think so?"

"It's possible. We know their history is different from ours in some respects. That's why the confluence phenomenon is so dangerous. They infiltrated Archives Section and managed to learn a lot about our history through other means, but their knowledge could be spotty."

"Maybe," Andell agreed. "But Rome is a reasonably well-documented period. They could have infiltrated agents into any future temporal scenario and picked up the works of Suetonius or Plutarch or Tacitus or any number of the more modern classical historians. It would be standard mission preparation and not that hard to do. Stands to reason, doesn't it?"

"Yes, it does," said Lucas, frowning. "It doesn't seem to make sense."

"Not unless they figure there's nothing we can do about it," Andell said. "And there really isn't, when it comes to that. I mean, what are you going to do, walk up to Caesar and say, 'Excuse me, you know you're not supposed to have a bodyguard? Better get rid of them or you might not get killed?' Now that they're there, the only ones who can get rid of them are Caesar and Cleopatra."

"It could also be a way of drawing attention to what they're doing," said Delaney.

"Why would they want to do that?"

"To smoke us out," Delaney said.

Andell nodded. "That's an idea. If you try to do anything about the Egyptians, you're liable to give yourself away. And if you don't do anything about them and they're still with Caesar on the Ides of March, the conspirators may not have a chance to kill him. What happens then?"

"Then we may have to kill him," Lucas said. "Even if it means getting killed ourselves."

They drove the rest of the way to Travers' villa in silence.

People had started arriving at the Circus Maximus before dawn, so the tiered stands were almost completely filled by the time Steiger and Marshall arrived. However, unlike the plebeians, their places were assured. They sat in the front rows, which were reserved for senators, aristocrats, and Vestal Virgins. Steiger decided that he didn't quite fit into any of those categories.

The sight of the Circus itself was awe-inspiring. Shaped like a long rectangle rounded off at one end in a semicircle, the Circus Maximus was six hundred yards long and two hundred yards wide, built to hold a quarter of a million spectators. Caesar had rebuilt it, making it even grander than it was before. He had surrounded the arena with a moat, the better to separate the animals from the spectators during shows that involved wild beasts. Marshall explained that Pompey had used an iron fence, but the bars had buckled under the weight of elephants that had been pitted against some hapless prisoners and the spectators had been somewhat upset when the pachyderms decided that they wanted out.

The *spina*, the built-up "spine" dividing the center of the arena between the turning posts (three on each end), had been adorned with gilt bronze statues of the gods looking down upon the games. It also held the *septem ova*, seven large wooden eggs that were moved to count the laps. Later, during the time of Augustus, seven bronze dolphins would be added to the eggs as lap counters. The triple-tiered stands facing each other across the arena were monstrous. The lowest tiers were made of marble, the second tiers had seats of wood, and the third offered standing room only. They were completely packed and the crowd was still streaming in.

Outside, beggars, wine merchants, pastry cooks, astrologers, and prostitutes vied for the attention of the crowd. The courts had all been closed. Marshall explained that no business would be transacted in the city while the games were on. Indeed, it seemed to Steiger as if all of Rome had packed itself into the Circus. The spectators were a sea of white togas. As they approached their seats, Marshall pointed out a handsome, dark-haired man with a high forehead, an aquiline nose, and a full beard.

"That's Antony," said Marshall.

"What's with the sword?" asked Steiger.

"Antony always wears his sword whenever he appears in public," Marshall replied. "It's part of the image. His family claims to be descended from Hercules, by his son, Anton, and Antony likes to play the part to the hilt. The big, macho warrior. Come on, I'll introduce you."

"Ah, Marcian!" Antony said boisterously as they approached. "Come! Sit with us! Who is your friend?"

"Greetings, Marc Antony," said Marshall. "Allow me to present Creon Sabinus, who has come to visit me from Ilerda. I've bought many fine strings of horses from him over the years."

"Indeed?" said Antony, turning to Steiger with interest. "And what brings you to Rome from the provinces, Sabinus?"

"A little business and a little pleasure," Steiger replied. "Marcian has decided that I've been charging him too dearly for the horses that he buys from me, so he proposes to purchase my entire farm, so that he can sell them more cheaply to himself."

"That sounds like our Marcian." Antony laughed. "Always counting his fortune and finding it wanting. Take care that you do not sell your farm to him too cheaply, Sabinus."

"He needs no advice from you, Antony," groused Marshall. "The price that he has named amounts to a king's ransom."

"Come now, Marcian, it is a fair price and you know it," Steiger protested.

"Fair? You've been cheating me for years, you scoundrel. As you have doubtless cheated others." He turned to Antony. "He knows that if I buy his farm, I must retain him on a salary as breeder, so it is all to his advantage. He has, I'm afraid, less need for my money than I have for his horses. I've brought him to the races in the hope that I can induce him to lose some of it. Perhaps then he will become more reasonable."

"What, you plan to bet against him?" Antony asked, surprised. "Marcian, I have never seen you wager so much as a denarius!"

"No, not I," said Marshall. "I have already lost enough money to this brigand through our business dealings. I will not risk losing more. However, knowing you to be a shrewd judge of horseflesh and charioteers, I thought perhaps you would be good enough to fleece him for me. I would appreciate it if you would take as much of his money as possible. He's been most insufferable."

Antony threw back his head and laughed. "Did you hear, my friends? Marcian brings me a sacrifice of a provincial!"

They all laughed.

Steiger stiffened, as if with affront.

"No, no, do not look so, Sabinus," said Flaminus, clapping him on the shoulder. "I assure you, Antony meant it merely as a joke."

"Yes, doubtless we provincials, being so backward and naive, provide you Romans with much amusement," Steiger said.

"Come now, Sabinus, I meant no offense," Antony said placatingly. "And to prove it, and as much to please my good friend, Marcian, I will offer you a small, friendly wager, if you like. Not so much as you can't afford to lose."

"Indeed? And what makes you think that I will lose?" asked Steiger.

"Oho!" said Antony. "You hear, Trebonius? It seems that we have pricked his pride!"

"Have a care, Antony," Trebonius said in mock warning. "He is a breeder and must know his horses well."

"Perhaps, but does he know his charioteers?" asked Antony. "It takes more than a good team to win a race."

"That is true enough," said Steiger. "But I have had an opportunity to watch them exercise and have formed a few opinions as to the skill of the various drivers. Perhaps they are not as educated as your own, Marc Antony, but I have observed enough to guide my wager."

"Very well, then," Antony said with a grin. "We shall see. Shall we make a wager on the first race?"

"If you like."

"How much would you care to risk?"

"I do not know what is customary," said Steiger. "Would ten thousand sesterces be appropriate?"

"Ten thousand sesterces!" Trebonius said.

"See here, Sabinus," said Antony condescendingly, "pride can be a costly thing. Despite what Marcian said, and I am certain he was only joking, I have no wish to see you lose so much."

"It is a sum that I could easily stand to lose," said Steiger. "However, if you could not, I would certainly understand."

Antony raised his eyebrows. "I could stand to lose a great deal more than that, my friend," he said with a smile. "Very well, then. Ten thousand it is."

The sound of trumpets rang out through the arena and the crowd cheered as the presiding consul entered in his chariot, followed by his lictors and attendants. After them in the procession came the legionaries and the cavalry, followed by the teams of chariots. The drivers were all attired in colored tunics that denoted their teams. They had the reins wrapped around their chests, leaving one hand free to manipulate them and the other to use the whip. Driving a chariot took great strength and dexterity, as well as skill, and by wrapping the reins around their chests, the charioteers were able to add their full body weight to the task, as well as using it to balance the light chariots. It made the driving very dangerous, because in the event of a spill, the charioteer had to draw a sharp dagger and quickly cut the reins, otherwise he would be dragged along behind his horses. Even if he could cut himself loose in time, there was still the danger of being trampled or crushed by the wheels of the following chariots.

After the chariots came the singers, followed by the priests and the incense-bearers. Then came the images of the gods carried on biers. The crowd cheered and applauded as they made their circuit of the arena to the pounding of the drums and the blaring of the trumpets, then the cheering grew still louder as the Emperor appeared in his box, just a short distance from where Steiger and Marshall sat with Antony and his friends.

Steiger turned to look at Julius Caesar. He stood in the imperial box, wearing a laurel wreath and a purple-trimmed toga with fringes on the sleeves, holding his arms out to the crowd.

"Is that your first sight of the Emperor?" asked Trebonius, raising his voice to be heard over the cheering of the crowd around them.

"Yes," Steiger replied. "I must admit, he looks different than I had expected. More like a philosopher than a conquering general."

"Do not be deceived by his appearance," Antony said. "He is the finest general that Rome has ever seen. And I am proud to have served with him in the campaigns."

"A singular honor," Steiger said.

Antony smiled. "Perhaps later, I will introduce you to him. To ease the pain of your loss."

"It would indeed be a great privilege to meet the Emperor," said Steiger. "But I have not lost yet."

Antony grinned. "We shall see. That first rank of chariots will compete in the first race. And the second rank will race

after them, and so forth. As a breeder of fine horses, which
team do you fancy?"

Steiger considered the teams as they rode by in the
procession. "Of the first rank, I think I like the greens," he
said. "The brown *trigae*."

He pointed to the team of three dark brown horses
drawing a light chariot driven by a man in a green tunic.

"A good choice," said Antony, nodding. "You *do* know
your horses. But I think the whites will take the first race."

"Perhaps," said Steiger. "However, I will stand by my
choice."

"And be the poorer for it," Antony replied with a grin.
"But who knows, fortune may smile upon you."

After the procession completed its circuit of the track, the
chariots for the first race lined up at the far end of the arena.
The horses were restive, pawing at the ground. The charioteers held them back, easing them into position. The
presiding consul gave the signal for the trumpets to sound.
He stood above the chariots, dressed in a scarlet tunic, an
embroidered toga, and a heavy gold wreath. In one hand, he
held out a white cloth. In his other hand, he held aloft an
ivory baton with a bronze eagle on it, the symbol of his
office.

The charioteers had previously drawn lots for their
positions at the start of the race. The tails of the horses were
bound tightly, their manes decorated with pearls and gems,
their breastplates adorned with gold and silver and trimmed
with jewels. Each horse wore a ribbon with the color of its
team. The drivers stood in their chariots, some wearing
leather helmets, others wearing metal ones, their thighs and
calves beneath their brief tunics wrapped in leather leg-
gings. Most of them were low born and some had once been
slaves, but as charioteers, they could rise far above their
stations. Winning charioteers often received substantial
gifts from magistrates and aristocrats, sometimes even from
the Emperor himself, and they were paid generous salaries
by the owners of their teams, as well. They were the star
athletes of Rome, often wined and dined by their rich
patrons, and some of them were able to become quite

wealthy in their own right. A hush fell over the crowd as the consul waited to give the starting signal. Steiger's brown *trigae* had drawn a position third from the inside. Antony's whites were on the pole. The consul dropped the white cloth and the crowd cheered as the race began.

The blue team took an early lead as the horses thundered down the straightaway, heading counterclockwise around the track, toward the first turn. The greens ran second, the whites a close third. The drivers lashed the horses with their whips as they passed the stands where Steiger and Antony sat, coming up to the first turn.

"The first turn is always crucial," Antony said loudly, speaking close to Steiger to be heard above the crowd. "And Tibulus, who races for the whites, always rides close upon the leader as they close for the turn. Watch now!"

The blue driver took the turn a little wide, anxious to give himself plenty of room so as not to be caught between the posts and the press of the other chariots closing in. Tibulus, the charioteer for the whites, hung close on the heels of the blues, slightly to the inside. The greens were right behind him, swinging wider. The driver of the red team suddenly swung for the inside, trying to ace the greens out of position, but as they rounded the turn, the whites also swung sharply to the inside, toward the post, cutting off the reds. Having nowhere else to go, the red driver had to swing in closer still and the wheels of his chariot caught the post as they went around.

The crowd gasped collectively as his chariot struck and bounced up into the air, teetering precariously on one wheel for an instant, and then crashing back down again, dislodging the driver. He drew his knife and slashed the reins, cutting himself free, then rolled wildly to avoid being trampled by the team behind him. He didn't make it. The crowd roared as the horses of the green team trampled him and the chariot jounced over his body. As soon as the chariots had all passed, attendants ran out with a litter to pick up the fallen driver, who was writhing on the ground with pain.

Meanwhile, the whites had taken the lead on the inside of

the turn. As they thundered down the opposite straightaway, they were all out of sight behind the *spina*, but in moments, they were coming around the far turn and Steiger saw that the whites had increased their lead, while the greens were close behind them. It remained that way for the first two laps as the chariots gradually spread out along the track. By the third lap, the greens had closed the distance. By the fourth, they were almost neck and neck with the whites, but Tibulus was clearly the better driver and he gained an increased lead once more going round the turn. By the fifth lap, the greens had once more closed the distance, but the whites kept gaining on the turns, practically shaving the posts.

"Your greens are putting up a game fight," said Antony. "Demos drives well, but he won't catch Tibulus! Watch as he gives them full head on the last turn!"

Indeed, Tibulus took the last turn at what seemed a very reckless speed, his chariot sliding around almost completely sideways, but the maneuver gained him even more ground and as they raced for the finish, the whites came in well ahead of the greens.

"I fear that you have lost your wager, Sabinus," said Antony. "I told you that the whites would win. You see, it takes more than a good eye for horses to judge who will be the winner. A good charioteer makes all the difference."

"It would seem so," Steiger agreed. "I congratulate you. But you must give me an opportunity to win back my money. Would you care to wager on the next race?"

Antony laughed. "Marcian, your friend seems determined to give away his money! It seems your plan was sound. Perhaps I should demand a fee for helping you conclude your business with him!"

"You have already won ten thousand sesterces," Marshall said. "Let that be your fee, Antony."

"Done!" laughed Antony.

"Shall we say another ten thousand on the second race?" asked Steiger.

"If you think you can afford it," Antony replied dubiously.

"Marcian will vouchsafe my credit."

"Sabinus may be unscrupulous in business," Marshall said, "but you may take him at his word."

"I never questioned it," said Antony magnanimously. "Another ten thousand it is."

Steiger lost the second race, too. And the third, as well. Trebonius won the fourth, with both Steiger and Antony losing, but Antony recouped his losses to Trebonius on the fifth race, which Steiger also lost.

"I think perhaps we should cease to wager now," Antony told Steiger after the fifth race. "You already owe me fifty thousand sesterces and I have no wish to ruin you completely."

"You cannot keep winning all the time," said Steiger.

"I rarely lose, my friend."

"Then you will not give me one more chance to make good my losses?"

Antony shook his head. "I have already won more than enough from you, Sabinus," he said. "You would be wise to stop now."

"One hundred thousand sesterces on the final race," said Steiger.

"By the gods!" said Flaminus.

"Marcian, I fear your friend is being dangerously reckless," said Antony.

"Is it your concern for me that causes you to hesitate or does the prospect of losing so much make you nervous?" Steiger asked.

"Creon, perhaps you'd better reconsider," Marshall said.

"One hundred thousand is my wager," Steiger repeated firmly, looking straight at Antony. "Do you dare accept it? Or are you afraid to lose to a backward provincial?"

Antony stared at him. "Your friend Marcian will have to buy your farm from me," he said. "Because after this last race, I fear that I will own it."

"Then you accept?"

"Choose your team."

"I'll take the blues. The black stallions second from the post." There were four factions—the whites, the reds, the blues, and the greens, but for this race, the teams were paired, so that there were two charioteers driving for each faction, a total of eight teams of four horses each.

"The blues?" said Antony. He chuckled. "Alas, you have made a poor choice, Sabinus. Young Cassinus drives that team. He has the least experience of any of the charioteers! He has never before driven a *quadrigae*!"

"Nevertheless, I choose the blues," repeated Steiger. "I watched him exercise the other day. He seems to have a natural ability with the *quadrigae*. And the blacks he's driving are fine horses. I am confident of my choice."

"I will not quarrel with the quality of the team," said Antony. "But are you so confident of your choice that you will risk your utter ruin?"

"I am confident that you cannot continue to win all the time," Steiger countered stubbornly. "Do you accept the wager? Or is it too rich for your blood?"

"Creon . . ." Marshall said, taking Steiger's arm.

"Stay out of it, Marcian," snapped Steiger, shaking him off. "I await your answer, Antony."

Antony sighed and shook his head sadly. "So be it. One hundred thousand sesterces on the bays driven by Clocillus, for the reds."

"I will take thirty thousand of that wager, if you have not overextended yourself, Sabinus," said Trebonius.

"And I will venture twenty," said Flaminus.

"Done," said Steiger.

"Creon, are you mad?" asked Marshall.

"Antony is not the only one who can judge a charioteer," Steiger replied. "Cassinus seemed most promising when I watched him practice."

"You did not watch him against Clocillus," Antony said with a smile. "Clocillus has no need of practice. He is the finest charioteer in Rome."

The trumpet sounded once again.

"They are about to start!" Trebonius said.

The white cloth fluttered to the ground and the chariots were off. Clocillus took an early lead going into the first turn. Cassinus was sixth, well behind him, but the crush of the first turn took out two of the other chariots, one white, one green. They crashed into each other as they went around the post, and though the drivers managed to retain control by reining in, they slowed up two other chariots behind them and caused another to swing wide around them as they skidded toward the outside of the turn. Cassinus took the opportunity to get inside them and move up.

"A good move on his part," Antony conceded. "But he was merely fortunate. Clocillus still holds a commanding lead."

Going into the second lap, Cassinus was running third, but Clocillus and one of the chariots driving for the greens were still well ahead of him. They maintained that distance for another lap, but as they swung around for the third time, Cassinus slowly began to close the gap. By the fourth lap, the second green team was hard on his heels, with the second driver for the blues running just behind them. Clocillus was still in a comfortable lead. On the fifth lap, as they went around the post, the green team that was closing in on Cassinus took the turn too wide and Cassinus' teammate cut sharply to the inside, getting ahead of the greens and cutting them off as they went down the straightaway. Cassinus continued to close the distance between himself and the two leaders, while the green team that was just behind him couldn't get around the blue team that had passed it. They maintained that position going into the sixth lap when the team that was running second tried to cut in on the inside of Clocillus and ran out of room. The chariot overturned and they could see the driver sawing frantically at the reins as the horses dragged him along behind them. He managed to cut himself free just as they reached the outside of the turn and he rolled safely out of harm's way. Cassinus was now running second.

On the last lap, Cassinus started closing the distance between himself and the red team driven by Clocillus, gaining rapidly. The crowd was on its feet, cheering the underdog. In moments, they were neck and neck.

"Come on, Clocillus!" shouted Antony. "Use your whip!"

Side by side, the two chariots careened toward the finish, but Cassinus started to edge ahead. Antony and his friends were shouting and shaking their fists. Clocillus started to close, but they crossed the finish line with Cassinus barely a nose ahead of him. The crowd went wild.

"Well, deducting my earlier losses to you," Steiger said to Antony, "that makes fifty thousand sesterces that you owe me. Plus the thirty thousand from Trebonius, and twenty from Flaminus, that brings my winnings to a total of one hundred thousand sesterces. I have both made good my losses and turned a tidy profit." He grinned at Antony. "It seems that I am not exactly ruined."

"I cannot believe it!" said Trebonius. "Clocillus *never* loses!"

"And I was tempted to wager thirty thousand, but I did not wish to take advantage of a reckless provincial," Flaminus said, shaking his head.

"Your charity has saved you ten thousand sesterces," Steiger said.

"Now I'll be forced to meet his price," said Marshall gloomily. "Antony, what happened? You were supposed to *win*!"

"I would never have thought that Cassinus could beat Clocillus," Antony said. "But . . . perhaps he is indeed more suited to the *quadrigae*. Whether by luck or by skill or a combination of the two, he did it. And you, Sabinus, are a wealthier man because of your sound judgment. I congratulate you."

"And I you, on your grace in losing," Steiger said. "You must grant me the honor of entertaining you and your friends."

"What, with our own money?" Antony said. He chuckled and clapped Steiger on the back. "Very well, then. I accept."

"Wait till Caesar hears that you have lost more in one day than you have won in the entire year!" said Trebonius.

"I expect he will be much amused," said Antony wryly. "And he will doubtless wish to meet the man who humbled me. Come, Sabinus. Would you like to meet the Emperor?"

5

"That last race was close," Lucas said. "Almost a photo finish." He smiled. "Or it might have been, if they had cameras in ancient Rome."

"It's the first time I've ever seen Clocillus lose," said Travers. "The young driver who beat him just made his reputation. Clocillus is the best charioteer in Rome."

"He also threw the race," said Andre.

Travers glanced at her sharply. "What?"

"I said, he threw the race," she repeated. "It was fixed."

"Are you serious? How can you possibly tell?"

"If anyone can tell, she can," said Delaney.

They were seated in the stands within less than a hundred feet of where Steiger sat with Antony, though they had no idea he was there. With his new face, they wouldn't have recognized him anyway. They spoke in low voices, holding their heads close so that no one could overhear them.

"Andre grew up in medieval England," Lucas explained. "For most of her life, she passed as a male and was a mercenary knight, what they called a 'free companion.' The first time we met, it was in the lists at the tournament of Ashby."

"You mean you were temporally displaced?" asked Travers, stunned.

"It's a long story," she said. "I inadvertently became part of a temporal disruption and wound up being taken into the future by a member of the Underground."

"We first encountered Andre on a mission to 12th-century England," said Delaney, "so you can imagine our surprise when we saw her again in 17th-century France. It's quite a story. She was instrumental in helping us effect a temporal adjustment and since she had already been displaced from her own time, we took her back to Plus Time with us so her case could be reviewed, to make sure it didn't result in any temporal contamination. Once the Referees were satisfied, she joined the First Division and we've been a team ever since."

"Incredible!" Travers said. "You must tell me the entire story later, but right now, I'm curious as to how you knew the race was fixed."

"I learned how to observe horsemanship from jousting tournaments," she said. "In a situation where your life often depended on knowing your opponents, you learned to watch for the slightest indication of any weak points. After a while, you'd get to where you'd easily spot subtle things that most people would miss. The charioteer for the red team held back slightly on the final stretch. As you said, he's an outstanding driver. Even a keen observer might have missed it, but I was watching very closely, out of habit, I suppose, and I noticed that on the last two laps, he was taking his turns just a little wider than he had on all the previous ones."

"I never would have spotted that," said Travers. "Clocillus always takes the turns so tightly, he's almost right up against the post."

"That's why he got away with it," she said. "He takes a much tighter line through the turns than the other drivers, so when he went just a little wider, it still looked like he was taking them pretty close. But he went a little wider every time coming out of the turns and he held back a little going into the turns, allowing the blue team to catch up. Aside from that, when those two chariots collided in the first turn, it was done on purpose. I saw both drivers brace themselves for the impact as they went into the turn. They were prepared for it, before they should have known that it was going to happen. And the driver whose chariot overturned in the last lap? That was purposely done, as well. He was standing a little lower in his chariot going into the turn because he had his knees flexed, ready to spring clear. He timed it just right, so that he'd be at the apex of the turn, where the inertia would carry him to the outside of the track, well away from the chariots behind him, who knew that he was going down and were prepared. He was already reaching for his dagger an instant before he went over. Not that it still wasn't pretty dangerous, but with everybody knowing what was going to happen, the risks were considerably reduced."

"But that would mean that every one of the charioteers were bribed!" exclaimed Travers with astonishment.

"That would seem to be the obvious explanation," Andre replied.

"That's an incredibly serious offense," said Travers. "They could all lose their lives for that. You're absolutely sure? There's no chance you could be mistaken?"

"If Andre says that's the way it happened, Travers, you can take it to the bank," Delaney said.

"Find out who was the big winner at the track today and you'll probably find your fixer," Andre said.

"There's only one man I can think of, short of the Emperor himself, who could have gotten all the charioteers to work together in order to throw the race," said Travers. "And that would be Marcian. But I simply can't imagine him doing something like that."

"Who's Marcian?" asked Lucas.

"He's the *aedile* who oversees the administration of the games," said Travers. "He's also an extremely wealthy merchant who provides most of the horses and wild beasts for the shows in the Circus. He also stages gladiatorial combats, sort of a private entertainment contractor. But he never bets on any of the races. For a man in his position, it wouldn't look good."

"Maybe somebody got to him," Delaney said.

"That's hard to believe," said Travers. "Marcian is one of the richest men in Rome. I can't imagine what anyone could offer him to make him take such a risk."

"Political power?" Lucas asked.

"Possible, I suppose, but unlikely. His post carries a nominal senatorial rank, yet Marcian has always steered clear of politics. He has the reputation of being a very prudent man."

"In any case, it probably doesn't concern us," Andre said. "Not unless it might have anything to do with Caesar. Is Marcian a friend of his?"

"No, not really, but he *is* a friend of Marc Antony's, who is Caesar's right-hand man."

"Maybe we should meet him," Lucas said.

"That wouldn't be difficult to arrange," said Travers. "You think he might be involved somehow?"

"I don't know," said Lucas. "Is he a native Roman?"

"No, as a matter of fact, he isn't. He arrived in Rome about nine years ago. I think from Baiae, but I'm not sure. In any case, he was already quite wealthy when he got here, which helped him make connections quickly. The post of *aedile* is an elective office and word is he bought enough votes to put himself over. He built a palatial villa on the banks of the Tiber near the Aventine and he's prospered considerably since."

"Interesting," said Delaney. "You know him well?"

"We've met on several occasions, but I can't say I really know him well."

"Can we arrange to meet him socially?"

"Yes, I suppose so. I could hold a dinner party in my home and invite him, but since we're not exactly friends, it would help if I had a particular reason."

"Why not invite him so he can bring along some of the charioteers who raced today?" asked Andre.

"Yes, that wouldn't be unusual. Aristocrats enjoy rubbing elbows with the charioteers. It makes them feel adventurous."

"Good," said Lucas. "Set it up as soon as possible. We haven't got much time. There's only two weeks until the Ides of March."

"Yes, I know," said Travers grimly. He glanced down at the arena. "The gladiators are starting to come in. If it's all the same with you, I'd rather not stay around to watch this. I've seen quite enough of death."

They left the Circus and went outside to their carriage, where their "slaves" were waiting for them.

"Can we take a look at Cleopatra's house?" asked Lucas.

"Certainly," said Travers. "It's not very far from mine."

The streets were practically deserted as they drove back toward the Tiber.

"What did you make of Caesar's Egyptian guard?" asked Andell as he drove their carriage.

"We couldn't get a very good look at them," Delaney said. "I counted a dozen."

Andell nodded. "They go everywhere with him. Quite impressive, aren't they?"

"They looked very fit and capable," said Lucas.

"What do you think?" asked Travers.

Lucas shook his head. "I don't know. I wish we had more to go on. Do they stay with him in the palace?"

"Yes," said Travers. "They have rooms in the same wing as his."

"They're going to present a problem," Lucas said, "regardless of whether they're S.O.G. troops or actually what they seem to be. In either case, they're an anomaly and we're going to have to get rid of them somehow. The question is, how?"

"You're close to Caesar," said Delaney. "Couldn't you convince him that it's bad P.R. to have them around?"

"It is, in fact," said Travers. "There's been talk about them ever since Caesar took them on. He knows it and he doesn't like it. He used to have a bodyguard of Spaniards, a tough and surly-looking bunch, but he dismissed them for the sake of appearances. And those Egyptians haven't exactly improved matters. He knows it makes him look as if he's being protected by his mistress. I'm not really sure if he's going along with it just to please Cleopatra or because he's getting nervous now that the Ides is approaching. If he is, he'll never admit it. He's far too proud."

"Could you work on him without making your position difficult?" asked Delaney.

"I could try," Travers replied. "We've gone through a great deal together. I could probably get away with more than most people could when it comes to Caesar. But you can only press him so far. Plus I'd undoubtedly alienate Cleopatra and she has a lot of influence with him."

"More than a comrade in arms from the wars?" asked Andre.

Travers snorted. "You haven't seen her."

"How does Caesar's wife react to his relationship with her?" she asked.

"Calpurnia? She doesn't say anything about it. And no one dares mention it in her presence. I don't really know what she thinks about it. She doesn't reveal her feelings much."

"She can't be very happy about it."

"Maybe not, but this is ancient Rome. And Rome is very much a man's world. It is not uncommon for Roman men to keep mistresses. Most wives accept it, though it's not as if they have a choice. And Caesar is no ordinary Roman. Calpurnia seems very devoted to him, but then I've spent more time with Caesar than she has. If you're thinking about using her to discourage Caesar in any way, I'd recommend that you forget about it. There's only one woman who ever wielded any effective power in Rome and that was—or will be—Livia, the wife of Augustus. However, everything she did was done behind the scenes, through ruthless political manipulation and even murder. Compared to her, Caterina Sforza and Lucretia Borgia were Girl Scouts. Calpurnia is not the type to go in for that sort of thing. She's rather self-effacing and I doubt there's a devious bone in her body."

"Well, then perhaps we'd better consider people who *are* devious," said Lucas.

"You mean the conspirators?" said Travers.

"Yes," said Lucas. "If we're going to make sure that Caesar gets assassinated on schedule, it would behoove us to keep tabs on his assassins. They might need some encouragement."

"Not very much, I should think," said Travers wryly.

"What can you tell us about them? Personally, I mean?"

"I've met most of the chief conspirators at one time or another, since they're all active in politics," said Travers. "I can't say it was a very pleasurable experience, knowing what they're going to do. Or perhaps I should say what we *hope* they'll do." He paused and shook his head. "Why do I feel like a traitor when I say that?"

"Because you're not a cold-blooded bastard, that's why," said Delaney. "We've all done things we wished we hadn't had to do, things we haven't exactly been proud of. But they were things that had to be done, because so much depended on them being done."

"In a sense, Travers, they were things that had already happened," Lucas said. "I know it's sometimes hard to realize it, especially for someone like you, who's spent so much of his life in Minus Time, but all of this has already happened. From our perspective, and yours too, it happened almost three thousand years ago. We've simply come back here to make sure that no one tries to change that."

"I know," said Travers. "Intellectually, I realize all that, of course, but emotionally, it's still hard to accept. The man's a friend of mine. Perhaps the closest friend I've ever had. And he's much more than that. He's someone I spent much of my life studying and admiring. Meeting him was like meeting a boyhood idol. After all the years we've spent together, fought together . . . hell, he's even saved my life on several occasions . . ." His voice trailed off.

"It must be very difficult for you," said Andre sympathetically.

"More than you could know," Travers replied. "Until that night before we crossed the Rubican together, Plus

Time seemed almost like a dream. Like another life, a life I'd left behind. Then I had to clock back and make my report and reality was like a hard slap in the face. I've been speaking and even thinking like a Roman for so long that even now, English seems like a foreign language. Would you believe I'm a good ole boy from Dallas, Texas? Crazy, isn't it?"

"No, it isn't crazy," Lucas said. "Believe me, I can understand exactly how you feel. But you were going to tell us about the conspirators."

"Yes, I'm sorry, I got sidetracked for a minute there. According to classical historians such as Suetonius and Plutarch, there were supposed to be some sixty men involved in the conspiracy, but most of their names aren't known to history. Some were apparently soldiers who had fought with Pompey. Others were people who had private grievances against Caesar, still others, such as Brutus, were politically motivated, meaning that they believed they were acting in the interests of the republic. The core group was composed of Gaius Cassius Longinus, known as Cassius; his brother-in-law, Marcus Brutus; Decimus Brutus Albinus, one of Caesar's officers; Gaius Trebonius, a friend of Marc Antony's; Tillius Cimber; and the Casca brothers, Publius and Servilius. Cassius was the number one conspirator, the leader. Of them all, he is the most dangerous. He's shrewd and quick-witted, a calculating type. As Caesar himself has said, he has a 'lean and hungry look.' Not much gets past him and he's a keen judge and observer of human nature. Trebonius seems much more shallow. He likes to gamble a great deal and he's useful to the conspiracy because he's close to Antony. I don't know him very well, but he seems to be more of a follower than a leader. Albinus I know pretty well. He served with us in Gaul."

Travers paused a moment, his jaw muscles tightening.

"I found it difficult to get along with him," he continued, "knowing what he would eventually do. Caesar was always good to him, as he was to most of his officers. He gave him a provincial command and later made him a consul. I have no idea what made him join the conspiracy. Perhaps he really believed, like Brutus, that it was for the good of Rome, an end to autocratic rule. Which is ironic, when you consider the men who followed Caesar. The days of the republic are finished, though the conspirators don't know it. I always found Albinus very hard to read. He's not someone you'd want to turn your back on. Cimber I don't know very well at all. He seems ambitious, but other than that, I can't tell you much about him. As a close friend of Caesar's, I'm hardly someone they'd admit into their inner circle. As for the Casca brothers, Servilius I know only superficially and I don't think he's as deeply involved as his brother, Publius, who is someone to watch out for. There's a real hard edge to him. He's violent and he's got a mean temper. Next to Cassius, he's probably the most significant. Brutus is also part of the inner circle, or soon will be, and he is the most interesting. Also the most likable, strangely enough."

"Why do you say that?" asked Delaney.

"Just that it's strange for me to find one of Caesar's assassins likable. Supposedly, he's the one who agonized the most about it. There have been rumors that he's the illegitimate son of Caesar, but there's nothing to support that. Except that according to Suetonius, when Brutus was about to strike his blow, Caesar said to him, 'You, too, my child?' But there's no way of knowing in what sense he meant that. Or even if it 's exactly what he said. So I suppose the rumors could be true. It's a fascinating possibility, because Caesar did once have an affair with Brutus' mother, Servilia. Caesar pardoned Brutus for allying himself with Pompey in the civil war, but then he also pardoned Lassius and many others. It's one of the few things I've never been able to find out for certain. Brutus is sensitive on the subject and flatly denies it. Caesar simply won't discuss it. The one time I broached the subject with him, he became angry at me for listening to rumors and idle gossip."

"So you think that Brutus would be the most approachable?" asked Lucas.

"Yes, he'd probably be the easiest to get to know, but if you're planning to infiltrate the conspiracy, Cassius and

Casca are the ones you'll need to convince. That won't be easy. They don't know you. You're only a visitor in Rome and your cover identity as my brother will practically guarantee that he won't trust you. Of course, we could still pass you off as someone else."

"No, you've already told Caesar about me and it could complicate things if we changed our story. Besides, I wasn't thinking of myself," said Lucas. "I was thinking of Delaney. True, we all supposedly grew up together, but he hasn't seen you in years and people grow apart. We could easily stage a public confrontation of some sort between you, an argument about Caesar's autocracy or something."

"Yes, I suppose that could work," said Travers.

"If possible, I'd also like to figure out some way to get Andre next to Cleopatra," Lucas said. "What do you think the chances of that are?"

Travers pursed his lips thoughtfully. "Probably much better than your chances of infiltrating the conspiracy. Cleopatra hasn't exactly been embraced by Roman society. She acts as if she doesn't seem to care, but I'm not sure if I buy that. It's not that anyone would actively speak out against her, because of Caesar, but she's been widely blamed for Caesar's autocratic tendencies. She's a daughter of the pharaohs, after all, and as such, she doesn't share the republican sensibilities of most Romans. She's a Ptolemy and she can't understand or appreciate the freedoms most Romans enjoy. Nor has she made any secret of her opinions on the subject."

"What's she like?" asked Andre.

"Well, the most obvious thing about her is her beauty," Travers said. Then he corrected himself. "No, that isn't really true. The most obvious thing about her is her sex appeal. She practically radiates sexuality. She knows the effect she has on men and she certainly uses it to her best advantage. She lives in relative isolation in the house that Caesar gave her, along with her son, whom she claims is Caesar's. She was married to young Ptolemy XIII when they ruled together, then after his death, she married his brother Ptolemy XIV. Hardly what I'd call a loving family.

They all hated one another. Ptolemy XIV was supposedly poisoned on her orders."

"Nice lady," said Delaney wryly.

"Merely a product of her time, her culture, and her position," Travers said. "She's a compelling woman. Sharp, intelligent, and very willful. Which is only to be expected from the Queen of Egypt. That's her house right there."

They slowly passed an elegant, white-faced villa behind a high stone wall. There were Roman guards stationed outside it and several Egyptians watched them carefully from just inside the gates as they drove by.

"The problem is how to arrange a meeting with her," Travers said. "I couldn't exactly invite her over for dinner."

"I'll figure something out," said Andre.

"Be careful," Travers cautioned her. "Once inside those walls, you might as well be in Egypt. And though she seems very personable, Cleopatra could have you killed instantly, merely on a whim."

"I'll keep that in mind," said Andre.

"All right, then," Lucas said, "for now, that'll be our plan of action. We'll try to get Delaney in with the conspirators. Andre's assignment will be Cleopatra. As your brother whom you haven't seen in years, I'll be introduced to Caesar and see if I can't make myself fascinating enough for him to want to socialize with me. How much have you told him about your imaginary brother?"

"Not very much, really," Travers said. "I wanted to leave room for you to improvise. All I've told him is that we were always very close and that you stayed behind to run the estate when I went off to the wars."

"So I was never a soldier?"

"No. Why?"

"Just thinking. Did you write to me regularly?"

"Yes, as part of my own cover and to give me an excuse for making extensive notes on the campaigns. Castelli actually received the letters and he's been keeping them for me, for my use when I clock back to Plus Time and start working on my book."

"Good," said Lucas. "I think I've just figured out how to make myself interesting to Caesar."

"What do you have in mind?"

"Let's say that your brother, Marcus, always had a scholarly bent. An interest in philosophy and so forth. I'll be an armchair strategist. We'll say that I became so fascinated with your detailed letters about the wars that I've decided to write a study of military strategy, using Caesar's campaigns for my model."

"But you've never read those letters," Travers said. "I've got them at the villa now, but I doubt there's enough time for you to go through all of them."

"I won't have to," Lucas said with a smile. "I can skim them quickly, but I've been a student of military history for years. One of my favorite books was Caesar's *Commentaries*. I've read it several times and I took an implant download on it before we left Plus Time, so I'll be able to discuss the Gallic Wars with Caesar from his own observations."

"My apologies," said Travers. "I should have known you'd come prepared."

"One can never prepare too well for an adjustment mission," Lucas said. "The only trouble is, more often than not, all the preparation in the world simply isn't enough. Those Egyptians worry me. If, as you suspect, they're undercover S.O.G. commandos, we're really going to have our hands full. And if they're not, it still won't be easy getting them out of the way. I hope you can convince Caesar to get rid of them."

"What if I can't?"

"Then we may have no other choice but to get rid of them ourselves. In order for Caesar to be assassinated, we might just have to assassinate his bodyguards."

"All twelve of them?"

"All twelve. That means timing will be absolutely crucial. If we take them out too soon, it will give the conspiracy away and Caesar will probably surround himself with legionaries. If we take them out too late . . ." He took a deep breath and exhaled heavily. "Either way, it's going to be real tricky."

"But if there are sixty conspirators," said Andre, "couldn't they simply overwhelm the bodyguard?"

"One would think so," Travers said, "except there weren't sixty men involved in the assassination itself. Only a handful of them did the actual killing. Besides, it's one thing to attack a single unarmed man, but it's something else entirely to go up against a dozen armed and well-trained soldiers. Even if the conspirators could get through them, the bodyguard would probably slow them down long enough for the Senate House Guard to intervene. What made the assassination possible was the speed with which it was accomplished. In the confusion that followed, the assassins were able to escape, though they were all condemned afterward and some took their own lives with the same daggers they had used to murder Caesar."

"Here's a thought," said Delaney. "What would happen if there was an attempt on Cleopatra's life? Wouldn't Caesar be concerned enough to insist that she take the bodyguard for herself?"

"He might," said Lucas. "On the other hand, he might simply assign Roman legionaries to protect her."

"Wouldn't it make more sense for her to be protected by her own people?" Delaney persisted. "I don't know, but from everything I've heard about Caesar, it makes sense that he'd want her to take them back, to guard her in the house, and maybe assign additional troops to protect the grounds. It would seem that she'd want her own people around her, rather than a bunch of Roman soldiers who wouldn't know how to treat her properly."

"Only what if Cleopatra isn't really Cleopatra?" Travers asked.

"The way she reacts to an attempt on her life might tell us whether she is or not," Delaney said.

"You may have a point," said Lucas. "It might be worth a try. Only if we're dealing with the S.O.G., that could tip our hand."

"Maybe," Delaney replied. "But it would also tell us what we need to know, wouldn't it?"

"That's like standing up in the trench to find out if the snipers on the other side are paying attention," Lucas said.

"So? Since when were you afraid of snipers?"

Lucas gave him a sour look.

"Sorry. Bad joke."

"Did I miss something?" Travers said.

"It's another long story," Lucas replied. "I'd tell you, except I still don't know how it's going to turn out."

"I'm hoping for a happy ending," Andre said.

"So am I," said Lucas with a tight grimace. "So am I."

Dinner in the Imperial Palace, Steiger thought. I'm moving up in the world. Caesar had been so amused at Antony losing a fortune to him at the races that he had invited "Creon Sabinus" to dine with him that evening. Being an excellent rider, Caesar was also interested in talking about horsemanship. Fortunately, Steiger was qualified to discuss the subject knowledgeably. Not only was he a member of the Pendleton Base Polo Club, but during various assignments in Minus Time, he had also served with some of the finest cavalry detachments in history, from the Mongol hordes of Genghis Khan to Jeb Stuart's 1st. Virginia Cavalry. The only thing that gave him any trouble was the Roman custom of eating in the prone position while lying on a couch. He kept wanting to sit up.

"You should have been a soldier, Sabinus," said Caesar, laughing as he watched him shift his position uncomfortably. "Like me, you have difficulty keeping still. I can see that you are not one who is accustomed to pampered luxury. A fit, strong man such as yourself, it is a pity that you never joined the legions. You understand a great deal about horses and you seem to have an instinctive grasp of cavalry maneuvers. I could have used a man like you in my campaigns."

"I would have been proud to serve with Caesar," Steiger said. "But my father died young and it fell to me to manage the estate. Besides, I am undoubtedly more useful as a breeder of fine horses for Rome's legions than I would have been as a ordinary soldier in the cavalry."

"I do not believe that you would have been merely an ordinary soldier," Caesar said. "You have intelligence and wit, all the makings of a fine officer."

"I thank Caesar for the compliment. However, my destiny took a different course. I could not change it now."

"I have heard it said that a man could change his destiny," said Caesar, smiling. "Now that Marcian is purchasing your estate perhaps you will have the chance to alter yours. I will soon be embarking upon new campaigns of conquest, adding to Rome's territories. I will require able men. Why not come with me? I promise you that you would not be an ordinary soldier. For your knowledge and ability, I would make you a tribune with my cavalry."

"I am indeed honored," Steiger said. "When do you intend to leave on your next campaign?"

"I have an old debt to pay the Parthians, to avenge the death of my old friend, Crassus. I plan to depart from Rome on the eighteenth of the month. That should give you sufficient time to conclude your business with Marcian."

"But I had planned to engage Sabinus to manage the estate," Marshall protested.

"I am certain that Sabinus has slaves and freedmen overseers who could manage it for you equally well, Marcian," said Caesar. "And doubtless you could pay them less. I have greater need of able men than you. What say you, Sabinus? You have already increased your fortune at my friend Marc Antony's expense, and you shall increase it further when your business with Marcian is concluded. Once that is done, you shall be relieved of your responsibilities and there will be nothing to prevent you from enlisting with my forces. You could arrange for your money to be invested wisely and when you return, you will be a rich man. And you shall have your choice of properties from the lands that we shall conquer. You may build a villa, start a farm and live there, or you could live in Rome and hire a freedman to manage your property for you, along with the slaves you shall receive from among our prisoners.

I treat my soldiers well and reward them for their service. A man such as yourself could do well in the wars."

"Such inducements would seem impossible to refuse," said Steiger. He smiled. "As it would be impossible to refuse Caesar."

"Splendid! Then let us drink a toast to your new destiny!"

"To Parthia?" said Steiger.

Caesar smiled and raised his goblet. "To Parthia!"

"What the hell was that all about?" asked Marshall, after the evening was concluded and they had left the palace. "There's no need for you to join the legions. By the eighteenth, Caesar will be dead."

"But what if he isn't?" Steiger countered. "Suppose this anomaly with the Egyptians turns into a disruption and the conspirators fail to kill him? Then there will be nothing to prevent him from leaving on his new campaign against Parthia."

"And you intend to be with him," Marshall said. "So that the first chance you get . . ."

"You got it."

Marshall snorted. "Just like old times, huh? Cloak-and-dagger wetwork."

"Yeah. A tribune's cloak and a Roman dagger," Steiger said.

"You're actually hoping it'll happen, aren't you? Christ, you really *want* the conspiracy to fail, so that you can take Caesar out yourself."

"I'll do whatever I have to do," said Steiger, "depending on how things turn out. But it would be a hell of a thing, wouldn't it?"

"Yes, I guess it would at that. You'd be the man who sanctioned Julius Caesar. Not even Mongoose ever pulled off anything that big."

"It would convince Forrester that there's a place for the covert field section," Steiger said.

"With you as senior section chief, no doubt," said Marshall.

Steiger glanced at him. "Why not? I'd be the logical choice. And I'll need good, experienced agents."

"Forget about it," Marshall said. "I told you, I'm all through with that. I've got a good thing going here. I'd like to keep it." He gave Steiger a long look. "I *am* going to get to keep it, aren't I?"

Steiger shrugged. "It's your choice, John."

"Is it?"

Steiger met his gaze. "What are you saying, John? You think I'd turn you in?"

"You'd only be doing your duty if you did," said Marshall flatly. "It would be another feather in your cap, wouldn't it? Busting a renegade agent and using him to nail all his Underground connections. Might even net you a promotion."

"I don't want to be general that badly," Steiger said.

"So you say."

They stared at each other for a long moment.

"Is that what it comes down to, John?" asked Steiger, his tone emotionless. "We can't trust each other anymore? Is that what being in the Underground has done to you?"

"It's made me very careful, Creed," Marshall said evenly. "Maybe we're both working toward the same end, but we're really not on the same side anymore, are we?"

"Aren't we?"

Marshall shook his head. "No, Creed. You're still on the inside. I've opted out. That makes me a criminal. You can drop the hammer on me anytime you feel like it. I'm not very comfortable with that idea."

"I'm sorry you feel that way," said Steiger. "But you could always leave Rome. Go deeper underground, in some other time period where I couldn't find you. Of course, you'd have to start all over, but that wouldn't be very hard for a resourceful man like you. If you really believe I'd turn you in, why take the chance of staying?"

"You don't really understand, do you?" Marshall said. "I've got a good life here. A pleasant, simple, comfortable life. For the first time, I've found a sense of permanence. I don't want to run, Creed. I don't want to spend the rest of my life looking over my shoulder."

"Then you shouldn't have deserted," Steiger said. "What do you want me to say, John? That after all this is over, I'll go back to Plus Time and forget all about you? Fine. You got it. Is that what you want to hear?"

"I wish it were that simple."

"Yeah, so do I, but it isn't, is it? Because you don't trust me. If that's the way you feel, then nothing I say will make any difference. You see, that's what happens when you run, John. Sooner or later, you always wind up looking over your shoulder. If it's not me back there, it could be someone else. You'll never really know for sure. So you can keep running. Or you can stop and face the music."

"I'm not going back, Creed. That part of my life is finished."

"Then I guess you'll have to live with your decision," Steiger said. "I'm sorry there's nothing I can say or do to make that easier for you, but that's the way it is."

"I'm sorry, too," said Marshall. He sighed. "Hell, let's go get drunk."

6 ———————————————————

The dinner Travers had planned was a large one and he had invited some of the most influential citizens of Rome. Though he had not invited Caesar. One did not simply invite the Emperor to dinner, even if one was a close friend of his. And there was a reason why they did not want to have Caesar present at this occasion. They wanted to be able to talk about him in a manner that his presence would not have allowed. It was to be the occasion for Delaney, in his identity as "Fabius Quintullus," to make his first move in trying to insinuate himself into the conspiracy against Caesar.

Cassius and Marcus Brutus had been invited, as Travers knew them and many of the others from the Senate, as well as Antony and a number of his friends, at least one of whom, Trebonius, was known to them to be involved in the conspiracy. By this point, less than two weeks before the Ides of March, the conspirators would be well advanced in their plans. The thing to do was see to it that nothing changed them.

It seemed difficult for Delaney to believe that a conspiracy with so many people in it could have been effectively kept a secret, but then such was the character of life in

Rome among the powerful. Everyone seemed to have two
faces. The public face, which was worn from day to day, in
the Senate and on social occasions, and the secret, private
face, which was glimpsed only during moments of clandes-
tine intriguing. Rome had seen many conspiracies and
would see many more.

Travers had organized an entertaining party. His kitchen
slaves had been at work throughout the day, preparing the
many dishes that were served, and he had hired musicians to
play throughout the evening, as well as dancers, wrestlers,
acrobatic dwarves, and several magicians. It was mixed
company, some of the men having brought their wives,
others having brought their mistresses, and there were
single women in attendance as well as a bevy of attractive
slaves. It wasn't quite the decadent "Roman orgy" of
legend, but as the evening wore on, things loosened up
considerably and people started to drift off together to
explore the house or "walk" in the gardens.

Marcian had come, as well, along with a number of the
charioteers who had raced the previous day. Clocillus
seemed quite comfortable rubbing elbows with Rome's
upper crust. He knew that he was a celebrity. Some of the
others, particularly the young Cassinus, seemed a little
awkward, though Cassinus gradually grew more and more
at ease as he was repeatedly complimented upon his win
over Clocillus, who took the attentions paid his rival with
good grace and added his own supportive sentiments to
those of the others.

There was another man who came with Marcian, not one
of the charioteers, whom Travers did not know. Marcian
had introduced him as Creon Sabinus, a horse breeder from
Ilerda whose farm and estate he was attempting to buy.
Antony seemed to be friends with him, as well. They had
dined with Caesar the previous evening. It turned out that
Antony, an inveterate gambler, had lost a fortune at the
races to Sabinus, who had been losing steadily until he had
placed a daring bet on Cassinus during the final race. That
made Lucas and Andre pay particular attention to him. It
turned out that Caesar had been impressed by Sabinus, as

well. He had offered him a commission in his cavalry for his campaign against Parthia. A campaign that, if history ran true to course, Caesar would not live to embark upon.

Talk of Caesar's upcoming campaigns gave Delaney the opening that he was looking for to turn the conversation toward politics.

"I had not heard that Caesar was leaving for the wars once again," he said.

"All Rome speaks of little else," said Trebonius. "He plans to set out first for Parthia, to avenge his old friend Crassus, and then to press on for the Orient, as his hero, Alexander, had once done. The army is already gathering in the provinces."

"Then he will be gone for a long time," Delaney said. "Who will govern Rome in his absence?"

"His aides and secretaries, Oppius and Balbus," said Cassius, "if you can believe it. And they are not even senators. We are to be dictated to by mere functionaries while our Emperor pursues his dreams of glory in the East."

"But it is for the glory of Rome that Caesar embarks on these new campaigns," protested Antony. "Think of the wealth the empire shall acquire."

"I am thinking of the wealth that Caesar will acquire," Cassius said dryly. "And I am thinking of the days when Rome was a republic, not an empire, governed by one man who appoints mere secretaries to carry out the duties of his office while he goes adventuring abroad in an attempt to recapture the faded glory of his youth."

"A sentiment one could expect from someone who supported Pompey," Antony said derisively.

"Pompey never had himself proclaimed emperor," said Cassius. "If a man wishes to be king, then it would seem that the least he could do was stay and rule his kingdom as wisely as he can, not chase off to the far ends of the earth in a pointless quest to rival the exploits of a long dead general."

"It is Rome's destiny to rule the world," said Antony.

"As it was Caesar's to rule Rome?" said Cassius. "Well, I think it may be safely said that both those destinies have been realized. Rome does rule the world and Caesar now rules Rome. What need have we of further territories of dubious value? Rome prospers. I tell you, it is not for Rome's sake that Caesar goes to war again, but for his own. His hunger for power is one that can never be appeased. Already, he is a king in all but name. What more can he want?"

"To extend Rome's glory," Antony persisted.

"More likely, to extend his own," Cassius replied.

"You would not speak so if Caesar were here himself," Antony said stiffly.

"Ah, but the Emperor does not mingle with us mere mortals, except to dictate to us from his throne in the Senate. Only queens are fit company for kings," said Cassius with a smile, referring obviously to Cleopatra.

"Are these secretaries to sit upon the throne in his place?" Delaney asked before Antony could reply. "It seems an incredible insult to the Senate."

"It *is* an insult, Quintullus," Cassius said. "Yet it is one that we are all expected to suffer."

"It is not Oppius and Balbus who will rule in Rome, but Caesar," Antony replied. "They will merely act for him in his absence."

"But why must they, Antony?" Brutus asked reasonably. "Is the Senate not capable of governing Rome, as it did in the days of the republic? Has Caesar not increased the House in order to enable it to better bear the burden? Or does he believe the House so incapable that it must be guided in its actions by his secretaries?"

"It would seem that he does not wish the House to govern in his absence because he fears that they might make decisions of which he will not approve," Delaney said.

"I think Quintullus has struck upon it," said Cassius. "It is not Rome's power that Caesar seeks to increase, but his own that he wishes to protect."

"How can you speak this way?" asked Travers. "Look at all the good Caesar has done for Rome! He has restored Rome to prosperity and peace, from which we have all benefitted."

"Caesar most of all," Delaney said.

"I'm surprised at you, Fabius," said Travers. "You do not know Caesar as I do. What you say is not only unfair, it is untrue."

"Is it untrue that he has become an autocrat?" Delaney asked. "As Cassius has said, a king in all but name? Never has one man ruled all of Rome as dictator for life. How can Rome preserve her freedoms if all power is vested in one man? It seems dangerous to me."

"You can't seriously believe that Caesar would deprive Romans of their freedom," Lucas said.

"I know this is a subject on which we do not agree, Marcus," said Delaney, "but I also know that your perceptions have been colored by your brother's correspondence over all these many years. You have studied Caesar's campaigns and fought them over in your mind until you know every step that every soldier took. Caesar has become a hero to you, as to many others. I do not dispute that Caesar is a great man, perhaps even a good man, but he is still a man and not a god. And men can be corrupted. Especially by power."

"Quintullus speaks the truth," said Brutus. "Power is seductive."

"And we all know that Caesar is easily seduced," added Cassius with a smile.

"You are merely envious," said Antony.

"Of Caesar's sharing Cleopatra's bed?" asked Cassius. "There is no shortage of beautiful women in Rome, Antony. I have no need of foreign diversions."

"That is still another matter," said Delaney. "I have heard it said that Cleopatra has great influence with Caesar. Is it right that a foreign queen should hold such influence in Rome? Especially a queen that holds no respect for Rome's traditions. Is Egypt Rome's possession or is Rome Egypt's? Why must Rome's ruler be protected by an Egyptian bodyguard? Are there no Romans suited to the task?"

"The bodyguard was a gift from Cleopatra," Antony replied. "Caesar keeps them merely to please her."

"Or perhaps he does not trust his fellow Romans?" said Delaney.

"You are speaking like a fool, Fabius!" said Lucas.

"I am only speaking as one who is concerned," Delaney replied. "Concerned about so much power invested in one man. Concerned that autocracy is not compatible with freedom. There is a danger here, Marcus. I sometimes fear for Rome."

"I think perhaps that what you fear is greatness," Antony said. "Most men are not capable of greatness. They are little men and they do not understand it. What little men do not understand, they fear. I do not fear greatness, Quintullus. And I have no use for fearful little men. Good night to you."

"Spoken like a true lackey," Cassius said wryly as Antony departed. "But it grows late and I am weary of the evening's entertainment. I would be interested to hear more of your views, Quintullus. We should continue this discussion. Will you be at the baths tomorrow?"

"Yes, I had planned to go sometime in the morning," said Delaney.

"Good. Then perhaps we shall see each other there. Good night to you, Quintullus."

"And to you," Delaney said. Most of the guests had already left. He waited till Cassius had left with Brutus and then turned to Lucas and Travers. "I think the fish just bit."

"Just be careful," Travers said. "Don't seem too eager. Cassius is nobody's fool."

"Neither am I," Delaney said.

"What did you think of Marcian and Sabinus?" asked Andre.

"I didn't get much chance to talk to them," Delaney said.

"Marcian didn't seem very interested in conversation," Lucas said. "He disappeared somewhere with a couple of the women. And Sabinus spent most of his time talking with the charioteers. Of course, him being a horse breeder, that's not really surprising."

"He was the big winner at the races the other day," said Andre. "He took Antony and his friends for over one hundred thousand sesterces." She turned to Travers. "You said that Marcian was probably the only one who could have fixed the race and Sabinus was with him."

Travers nodded. "It's possible that they were in collusion. Marcian said that he was trying to purchase Sabinus' farm and estate. Maybe he set up the win to help his business deal. I can't see where such a risk would have been justified, but some men will do almost anything to win when it comes to business dealings. However, if that's the case, I don't see any connection to our mission."

"No, neither do I," said Lucas. "They don't seem like men who are interested in politics. But I think we made good progress tonight with the conspirators. Delaney can follow up on that and tomorrow, when you take me to meet Caesar, I'll see what I can do to get into his confidence. That still leaves Cleopatra."

"I'll figure something out," said Andre. She frowned. "Still, there's something about that Sabinus that bothers me. I can't quite put my finger on it, but I'd swear there's something familiar about him."

At night, the streets of Rome were often noisy. Produce and supplies were brought into the city on heavy carts, fights broke out, thieves and cutthroats plied their trade. But some areas of the city were quiet. Marshall moved softly down the graveled paths of the gardens on the banks of the Tiber. It was about three o'clock in the morning and a cool breeze was blowing. He came to a sitting area where a large sundial had been set up and stopped, waiting. A moment later, someone said his name.

"Simmons?"

Marshall turned to see a figure emerging from the shadows. As the man came closer, he could make him out more clearly. He was dressed incongruously for the time and any Roman seeing him would have puzzled over his strange clothing. The man was wearing a 20th-century three-piece charcoal-gray business suit, with a button-down white shirt and a red silk foulard tie. His hair was short, dark, and neatly styled. He had a closely trimmed beard that ran along his jawline and there was the faint bulge of a shoulder holster beneath his jacket on the right side.

"I hope this is important, Marshall," he said.

"Steiger's here," Marshall replied.

"Creed Steiger? He's in *Rome*? Are you sure?"

"Of course I'm sure. You think I'd have sent word to you if I wasn't certain?"

"Is he alone?"

"Yes and no. There's an adjustment team that's been clocked back here and he's technically working with them, but they don't know about it. He's undercover."

"Undercover?" Simmons frowned. "You mean working on his own, independent of the team? That's impossible. Forrester disbanded the old covert field section."

"Yes, that's true, but Steiger's trying to convince him to reinstate it. He's running this one on his own, to prove his point that there's a need for the covert field section. And that it can operate without corruption," he added wryly. "He even wanted me to come back in."

"He still doesn't know you're in the Network?"

"No, he thinks I've simply skipped out to join the Underground and get away from it all. He used some of our old contacts in the Underground to track me down. He wanted me to help him on his mission."

"That's interesting. It could be very useful. What is the mission?"

"A temporal anomaly involving Caesar. There's a chance he may not be assassinated on schedule. They think the S.O.G. might be involved."

"What do you think?"

"I think it's very possible."

"That could make things difficult. We can't afford any disruptions."

"Tell me about it. But I also can't afford being busted."

"Is that what he intends to do?"

"He says no, but I don't trust him. He's still playing cowboy, like he always did. Him and his psychotic mentor, Carnehan. He's not convinced the adjustment team can insure that Caesar will get killed on schedule, so he's

managed to buddy up to Caesar and get offered a tribuneship with the legions Caesar's planning to take on a
campaign to Parthia. That way, if Caesar doesn't die when
he's supposed to, Steiger's going to take him out himself
during the campaign, just to prove to Forrester that it
couldn't have been done without a covert wetwork specialist
on the scene. If he decided to bring me in, as well, it would
be an added bonus for him. They'd interrogate me about my
contacts in the Underground and my involvement with the
Network would be exposed."

"We can't have that, can we? Where is he?"

"Not so fast. About the contract. It's still on, isn't it?"

"You think we'd cancel it after all that son of a bitch cost
us with his damned Internal Security Division? Not bloody
likely. You take him out for us and you'll get the money,
any way you want it."

"Not me," said Marshall. "No way I'm going up against
Steiger by myself. Why do you think I called you?"

"You want to set him up for the hit, that's fine, too."

"I'll still get the money?"

"You'll still get the money. Provided Steiger's dead."

"That adjustment team might complicate things," Marshall said.

"Who are they?"

"Priest, Delaney, and Cross," said Marshall.

"That can't be. Col. Priest is dead."

"Well, he's a pretty lively looking corpse, if you ask
me."

"You actually *saw* him?"

"Only several hours ago."

"You're certain it was Priest?"

"Well, that's who Steiger said it was. I don't know the
man, myself, so I suppose it could be someone else. But
why would he tell me it was Priest?"

"I don't know. Unless he suspects you and he's planning
something."

"I'm sure he doesn't suspect me," Marshall said. "If he
knew I was tied up with the Network, you think I'd be here
talking to you?"

Simmons hesitated. "I don't know." He glanced around cautiously, and his hand went toward his shoulder holster. "You're certain you weren't followed?"

"I had his wine laced with a sleeping draught," said Marshall. "He'll be out like a light till dawn. You think I'd take any chances with him around?"

"I just don't understand why they'd try to pass someone else off as Col. Priest," Simmons said. "It doesn't make any sense. If he doesn't suspect you, then why would he lie to you?"

"Maybe Col. Priest didn't really die," said Marshall.

"They inscribed his name on the Wall of Honor. Why would they fake his death? Unless. . . ."

"Unless what?"

"Unless Forrester or Steiger are running their own covert operation."

"Then why would they tell me it was Priest? I mean, if they wanted to make it look like he was dead. It makes no sense."

"You're right, it doesn't. At least, not yet. But they're obviously up to something. You're absolutely certain that they don't suspect you?"

Marshall hesitated. "If they did, why wouldn't they have brought me in already?"

"Perhaps to smoke us out."

"Why would they need to? If they knew about me, they could arrest me, clock me back to Plus Time, put me through the wringer, and find out everything I know before the Network even realized that I'd been busted. Then they could simply pick up all my contacts one at a time."

Simmons nodded. "Yes, that makes sense. But the rest of it doesn't. We'll have to be very careful. There's obviously something going on here we don't know about. We'll have to bring some people in."

"What do you want me to do?"

"For the time being, play along. For your sake, Marshall, I hope you're right about their not suspecting you. Because we can't afford to have you taken in."

Marshall tensed. "You're saying that if they arrest me, I'm a dead man? You'll have me hit?"

"If they try to arrest you, you know what to do."

"And if I don't, you'll do it for me, is that it?"

"You know how the game is played, Marshall."

Marshall sighed. "Shit. So I'm stuck right in the fucking middle."

"It's your own fault for not covering your tracks better. If Steiger knew about your old contacts in the Underground, you should have broken off with them. You have only yourself to blame for allowing him to find you. Incidentally, if you're entertaining any thoughts about taking off again, I wouldn't advise it. Then you'd have both us *and* the T.I.A. looking for you."

"Hey, I've always done my part, haven't I?" said Marshall. "If I was thinking of going on the lam, would I have sent for you?"

"No, I suppose you wouldn't have."

"Damn right. You guys tried to take Steiger out in Plus Time and you couldn't do it. Well, I'm giving you a chance to hit him where he won't expect it and I intend to collect on that contract."

"You do your part and I'll see to it you get the money. But be careful, Marshall. Don't tip him off."

"Don't worry. I know what's at stake."

"Where is Steiger now?"

"Asleep at my house. It would be the perfect time to do it."

Simmons shook his head. "No, not with a potential temporal disruption going down. We simply can't take the chance."

"So what the hell am I supposed to do?"

"Hang tight and don't lose your cool. I'll bring some people in to cover you. In fact, I'll take charge of this myself. I'd like to see this so-called Col. Priest."

"You know him?"

"We've met. We'll move in close and keep an eye on things. Let Steiger and the adjustment team do what they have to do. Then once the temporal threat is over with, we'll take care of Steiger."

"What about the adjustment team?"

"Do they know about you?"

"I don't think so. Steiger's playing his own game, close to the vest, as usual."

"Then they may not be a problem. With any luck, we might be able to pull it off without them catching on. But if they get in the way, it'll be just too bad for them."

"So what you're saying is that I'm supposed to hang out in the breeze until Caesar's been assassinated, one way or the other."

"Or until they've neutralized the S.O.G."

Marshall grimaced. "Terrific. So we've got Steiger, the adjustment team, the fucking S.O.G., and me right in the middle of it all, out in the open. Damn it, I want some protection!"

"Take it easy. I said we'd cover you. If they don't suspect you, then all you've got to do is continue to cooperate with them. Long as you don't lose your nerve, you should be okay."

Marshall moistened his lips and nodded. "All right. But if they make a move on me, someone had better be there."

"Don't worry. They will be. I'll be in touch."

Simmons clocked out and disappeared.

Marshall reached into the folds of his toga and took out a pack of cigarettes. Normally, he never took the chance of taking them outside his room, where he could smoke with the door bolted and the wood brazier masking the smell, but his nerves were on edge and he really needed one. As he lit up, carefully hiding the flame with his hand and holding the cigarette with his palm cupped around it, he thought about the laser pistol he had hidden in a secret drawer in his room.

The trouble with Roman clothing was that it wouldn't hide it very well. A tunic wouldn't hide it at all, the bulge would be easily detectable beneath the drape of his toga and he couldn't very well walk around wearing a cloak all the time. He'd have to leave it where it was and count on his dagger to protect him, which any Roman male could wear openly without arousing any suspicion. But the thought of going up against Steiger with nothing but a dagger made his stomach churn. He had no doubt what the outcome of that would be. He wouldn't stand a chance unless he took Steiger completely by surprise. Get him while he's asleep, thought Marshall, and drive the son of a bitch up to the hilt into his kidney. Either that or cut his throat.

He looked out over the rippling, moonlit surface of the Tiber and exhaled heavily. He wished there was another way, but there simply wasn't. Steiger had him backed into a corner. Damn cowboy, he thought. This wouldn't have happened if he'd just gone along with the others in the organization. Or if he'd simply kept his mouth shut. But no, he had to get up on his white horse and take on the Network. Had to form the I.S.D. just to clean out all of the so-called "corruption." As if there was any harm in people trying to make a little money on the side.

The agency expected you to risk your life and all you got for your trouble was a lousy government pension. So what was wrong with trying to salt a little away for your retirement? All right, it was illegal, but so what? Everybody always looked the other way. Even the old director had been in on it. But then old man Forrester came in and got all tight-assed about it. Decided to put the Network out of business and bust everyone who was involved, right up to the old director. Jesus. It was his own fault the Network put a contract out on him. People were only trying to protect themselves.

Steiger should have stayed out of it, thought Marshall. He should have just kept his damn mouth shut and stayed out of it. It's not my fault, thought Marshall. He's left me no other choice. It was too bad that Steiger had to die, but there was just no way around it. And if it had to happen, why not collect on the contract, so at least some good would come of it? If not him, somebody else would get it. It might as well be him. You just do the best you can and take what comes, thought Marshall. That's how the game was played.

7 ⸻

Drummond and Andell had both hated the idea, as had
Travers. They thought it was much too dangerous, but
Andre had overruled them, and to their surprise, Priest and
Delaney had backed her up. The timing, they had said, was
too good to pass up. They thought it was a chance worth
taking. As Drummond and Andell were conducted into
Cleopatra's presence, each of them tried to keep his
nervousness from showing. If this goes wrong, Andell
thought, we could all be dead in the next few minutes.

"Stop! What have you there?"

"A gift from Caesar," said Andell, trying to keep his
voice steady. "For Queen Cleopatra."

A tall, well-built man approached them. His head and
face were both shaved and he was dressed in Roman style,
in an immaculate white toga worn over a gold-embroidered
tunic. He was slim, but his muscular definition spoke of a
man who was given to sport and exercise rather than luxury.
He had, thought Andell, the bearing of a soldier. He
frowned as he met Andell's gaze. Andell tried to keep his
expression neutral. He lowered his eyes, as a slave would
be expected to do.

"Have you examined it?" the man asked the two guards who had conducted them inside.

The guard hesitated. "No, Apollodorus. But if it is from Caesar . . ."

"Fool!" Apollodorus said. "Set it down at once!"

Suddenly Andell heard a throaty, feminine laugh.

"Apollodorus, do you not recall what day this is?"

Andell glanced up and sucked in his breath sharply. It was his first close glimpse of Cleopatra. Her hair was jet-black, worn in the Egyptian style, long and straight down to her shoulders on the back and sides, in bangs over her forehead. She was a small woman, delicately framed, with a narrow waist, full breasts, and long, shapely legs. The thin, silky white shift she wore was diaphanous and it clearly outlined the lush curves of her body. Her face was sharp-featured, with a graceful, Macedonian beauty and her eyes were dark and striking, outlined in kohl and heavily shadowed.

"He remembered," she said with a smile.

"Caesar?" said Apollodorus, frowning. "Remembered what?"

"Do you not recall, Apollodorus?" she said. "It was on this very day that you first brought me secretly into Caesar's presence, concealed within a carpet. And now he sends me one, to commemorate the occasion of our first meeting."

"It should still have been carefully examined," said Apollodorus, still frowning. "We do not know it came from Caesar. You have many enemies in Rome, my Queen. We cannot be too careful."

"You worry too much, Apollodorus," she replied. "Do you really think that some assassin would dare attempt to murder me here in this very house, with all your guards? And with Caesar's soldiers outside? I am as safe here as I would be in my own palace." She turned to Drummond and Andell. "Unroll it. Let me see."

Andell bent down and untied the fastenings, then he and Drummond unrolled the carpet. The guards gasped and reached for their swords as Andre was revealed, rolled up inside the rug. Cleopatra stared in astonishment.

"What is the meaning of this?" said Apollodorus angrily.

Then Cleopatra laughed and clapped her hands. "Oh, it is wonderful! Do you not see? How witty of him! Caesar has sent me a slave girl as a gift! And he has presented her in the same manner in which I arrived to him!"

"I hope that you will not take offense, Your Highness," Andre said, rising to her feet, "but I am not a gift from Caesar. Nor am I a slave."

Cleopatra frowned. "I do not understand."

"Who are you?" Apollodorus said. "Explain yourself this instant!"

"I am Antonia, wife to Marcus Septimus," said Andre.

"Septimus?" said Cleopatra. "You mean Caesar's friend?"

"That is Lucius Septimus," said Andre. "My husband, Marcus, is his brother. These two men are his slaves. To be truthful, my husband knows nothing of this. I fear that he would not approve. But I had heard so much about you and I wanted so very much to meet you! I had heard it said that you first came to Caesar in this manner when you met in Egypt and I struck upon it as a way to meet you. I thought that you might be amused, but I had no idea that your first meeting with Caesar took place on this very day. I apologize if my little ruse had made you angry. Such was not my intent."

"This is insufferable!" said Apollodorus. "You must leave this house at once!"

"She shall do no such thing," said Cleopatra.

"But, my Queen . . ."

Cleopatra smiled. "Do you not see, Apollodorus? It is an omen. Since I first came to Rome, I have had no one save yourself, my guards, and my female slaves for company. Except when Caesar comes, I am always lonely. And, unlike other Romans, who merely suffer my presence, this woman has sought out to meet me. The manner in which she chose to do it shows cleverness and wit. No, Apollodorus, she shall stay and dine with me this evening."

"But, my Queen," protested Apollodorus, "we know nothing of this woman!"

"We know she is the wife of the brother of Caesar's

closest friend," said Cleopatra. "Septimus has always treated me with courtesy, deference, and kindness. Caesar's regard for him speaks for his quality. I would expect no less from his brother."

"But we do not know his brother," Apollodorus persisted.

"Then we shall arrange to meet him," Cleopatra said. She smiled mockingly. "Or do you believe that he has sent his wife to murder me? I do not know what has come over you, Apollodorus. You see conspiracies everywhere. Come, Antonia. Pay no mind to my servant. He is merely overzealous in his duties."

"Perhaps he would like to search me, to make certain that I have no weapons," Andre said.

Cleopatra laughed. "Your wit appears to be a ready weapon," she said. "Come, sit with me. Apollodorus, we shall have some wine."

"As you wish, my Queen," Apollodorus said, though he was obviously displeased.

Cleopatra led Andre over to a couple of couches and a small table.

"I must admit," said Cleopatra, "that I am disappointed that Caesar did not choose to commemorate our meeting with this gesture, but doubtless, he has much on his mind now that he is preparing to leave on new campaigns. I fear he has forgotten. Still, I am pleased you came to see me in this fashion. It has added spice to a most dreary day."

"I was afraid that you might be angry at such an intrusion," Andre said.

"I might have been," said Cleopatra with a smile, "but I have too many other things to occupy my emotions these days."

"What things?"

"My son, Caesarion, who is growing up more Roman than Egyptian; my servants and my guards, who bore me; Apollodorus, who stifles me; Romans, who despise me . . . and Caesar, who maddens me when he is absent, but whose presence fills my heart with lightness. But tell me about yourself, Antonia. What made you want to come and see me?"

"I was curious," said Andre. "My husband says that it is my worst trait. I had heard that you were very beautiful and that your beauty had made Caesar your captive. Ever since I had arrived in Rome, I have heard of little else but you and I was seized with a compulsion to meet you."

"You do not live in Rome, then?" Cleopatra asked.

"We live in Cumae," Andre explained, reciting her cover. "I had never before visited Rome. Marcus came to visit Lucius, as they had not seen each other since Lucius left for the wars. We came with our friend Fabius Quintullus. Marcus, Lucius, and Fabius have been friends since childhood. Marcus is very interested in Caesar's Gallic campaigns. He thinks that Caesar is a great general. Perhaps even greater than Alexander."

Cleopatra smiled. "Caesar would love to hear that," she said, "only do not say 'perhaps.' Tell him that he has eclipsed the fame of Alexander and you will make a friend for life."

"What is he like?"

"Caesar? You have not met him?"

"Not yet, but Lucius had promised to introduce us. I do not know what to expect."

"You may expect to find him very charming," Cleopatra said. "He is not the handsomest of men, but there is much about him that is appealing. His wit, his strength of character, his self-possession, his intelligence. . . . He is a most unusual man. When I was still in Egypt, before we had met, and I received word that Caesar wished to see me, I was prepared to meet an arrogant Roman. I expected a man full of his own self-importance and disdainful of all others. Yet Caesar was none of those things. He had an easy manner and a confidence that required no boasts to support it. I was very taken with him right from the beginning. I know they say in Rome that I am some great seductress who has used her wiles to ensnare the Emperor, but the truth is that I was myself seduced. Caesar is a most compelling man."

"You must love him very much," said Andre.

Cleopatra smiled a bit sadly. "He is the first man I have ever truly loved. I left Egypt at his bidding to be in Rome with him, both because I wanted to be with him and because it is here, in Rome and not in Egypt, that I can best serve the interests of my subjects. I have borne Caesar's son, though I know that there are many here in Rome who denounce my claim as false, despite the fact that one can see his father's features in his own. Yet, unlike you, Antonia, I may not marry the man I love. Caesar will not divorce Calpurnia and he cannot marry me. He is Emperor of Rome and I am Queen of Egypt, by his own decree. Egypt is little more than Rome's possession now. And as Caesar is Rome, so I am Egypt. A mere possession."

Perhaps it was her loneliness that had made her vulnerable, perhaps she had caught her at an unguarded moment, but Andre found Cleopatra to be nothing like what she had expected. Instead of the cruel and imperious daughter of the pharaohs, the cold and calculating seductress that history had painted her as, here was a woman of warmth, candor, and perception. A woman who cared about her subjects, a woman of passion. As Andre sat listening to her, it seemed difficult for her to believe that this was a woman who had coldly ordered the murder of her own husband, who was also her brother, and yet history had reported that as fact. Although there had been many times when Andre had discovered that history had been in error. According to history, there had never been any love lost among the Ptolemy family. They intermarried, they quarreled, they fought and intrigued and killed each other, and yet Cleopatra was regarded by her subjects with affection. Though she was portrayed as one of the great seductresses of history, there was never any evidence that she was ever sexually involved with anyone but Caesar and Marc Antony. What Andre saw before her was not some Machiavellian female bent on manipulation, but a woman who seemed earthy, lonely, and very much in love.

"I fear for him," Cleopatra continued. "Between Caesar himself and Apollodorus, as well as my slaves who run my errands for me, I hear much of what goes on in Rome. Caesar has made many enemies. They say that it is I who have fed his lust for power, but the truth is that I have only tried to feed his caution, which has but little appetite. He says that the republic can no longer function, that the nobles have grown decadent and cannot rule. Without him, he says, the government would collapse and there would once more be civil war. He cannot believe that Rome would wish that. Perhaps Rome does not, but I fear that there are many Romans, men who seek influence and power, who do. Caesar is a great man, Antonia, and great men inspire jealousy in lesser men."

"But Caesar is well protected, is he not?" asked Andre. "Does he not have the Egyptian guard that you presented to him?"

"Yes, he does," said Cleopatra, "but he keeps them only because I begged him to take them for my sake. He begrudges their presence. He says that they make him look afraid, distrustful of his fellow Romans. He says that no man can truly guard against assassins who are determined. Must one live in constant fear, he says, trusting no one, afraid to eat without a taster, afraid to set foot outside his rooms without a dozen guards? I have changed my destiny, he says. I have set my feet upon a new path. I know not what he means when he says such things. He believes that Rome cannot do without him and so there is little risk to him. But I am happy that he keeps the guards, even if he does it just to please me. It was Apollodorus who suggested it. He picked the men himself, knowing my concern for Caesar. He promises that they will keep him safe, but I fear for him just the same. Even now, there are doubtless those who plot against him. Frightened, desperate men. I have learned," she added with a look of grave concern, "that desperate men do desperate things."

The *thermae*, or the Roman baths, had not yet reached their zenith. In the 2nd century B.C., Roman baths were little more than small wash houses, reserved for men, but in time, they grew to tremendous size, becoming luxurious in

their appointments, a place where Romans could spend the
entire day bathing or taking steam or fortifying themselves
against the cold with brisk baths in the *frigidarium*. They
were places where Romans could engage in impromptu
wrestling bouts or be massaged by slaves or simply relax
and gossip with their friends. For the price of one *quadrans*,
the smallest Roman coin, a citizen could gain admission to
the baths for the entire day. It was a place where one could
get away from the cramped, noisy, and often smoky
tenements to relax in splendid surroundings of marble and
gold and exquisite tiled mosaics. The baths were not only a
place to bathe, they were also recreation centers, equipped
with gymnasia, gardens, libraries, and reading rooms. No
expense was spared in making the baths a palatial and
comfortable community resource.

In the coming years, when the empire reached its zenith,
the baths would become architectural marvels. The Baths of
Caracalla, which would be constructed in A.D. 211, would
have a height of over 100 feet and the main block would
cover over 270,000 square feet, an area greater than the
modern houses of the British Parliament. The Baths of
Diocletian would be even larger, capable of accommodating
over 3,000 bathers at one time. The first baths built on a
truly palatial scale would by constructed during the time of
Agrippa, in A.D. 20, and they would be followed by the
baths of Nero, Trajan, Trajanus Decius, and Constantine.
But at the time of Caesar, the public baths in Rome were
still relatively small and nowhere near as spacious and
luxurious as they would become in the coming years.

Delaney paid his admission and entered the baths where
he had agreed to meet with Cassius and his friends. He
entered the small anteroom, where he removed his tunic,
toga, sandals, and loincloth and hung them up where they
would be watched by a slave attendant. As the baths would
grow larger in the coming years, the theft of clothing would
become more and more of a problem, so that most Romans
would wear only their oldest and most threadbare togas and
tunics to the baths in anticipation of losing them and having

to go home in thief's clothing or of having to send a slave home to bring them something to wear.

Delaney went into the main room, which was far smaller than the larger baths that would eventually be built. It consisted mainly of a pool with a tiled floor, considerably smaller than an Olympic-sized pool, the water in it kept warm by the hot air circulating beneath the floor, from the fire stoked in the basement. Off to one side was the smaller *frigidarium*, essentially a cold plunge, and through an arched doorway in the back was the *calidarium*, a small room that was similar to modern Turkish baths, except that the steam came from heated water, not from pipes. He passed a small area where several men lay naked upon tables, being scraped by slaves. There was no soap in Rome at this time and the bodily impurities released by perspiration were scraped off with a metal, bone, or wooden scraper called a *strigilis*, which had a curved blade, similar to the scrapers used on modern polo ponies after they had lathered up.

Several of the men were being anointed with oils and perfumes; others were being carefully depilated. A few of them made little grunts as their body hair was carefully pulled out with tweezers. On the opposite side of the pool was a lavatory, essentially a small, square-shaped room with benches running around all four walls. The toilets were merely holes cut in the benches with the waste dropping down into running water underneath. Instead of toilet paper, Romans used sponges on short sticks, which could be rinsed off. It was not the most sanitary of arrangements, but the practice was much more hygenic than what was known to most of the rest of the world at this time.

Cassius and the others were in the steam room, seated upon marble benches. All of them were nude, of course, as was Delaney. Romans had a healthy attitude about nudity, though mixed bathing was not practiced until the time of Nero. Men worked out and wrestled in the nude, and athletic competitions on the Campus Martius were engaged in with only the bare minimum of clothing, often nothing more than a simple loincloth.

"Ah, Quintullus!" said Cassius. "We were just talking about you. Come, sit with us."

Delaney joined them on the bench. They all stared at his physique. His muscular development was on a level that was virtually unknown in Rome and it predictably took them by surprise.

"By the gods!" said Trebonius. "Look at the size of him!"

"If I did not know better, Quintullus," Brutus said admiringly, "I would swear that you had once been a gladiator. Truly, you possess the physique of a Hercules!"

"I come from a family of large men," said Delaney. "And life in the country entails considerable physical labor."

"But do you not have slaves for that?" asked Albinus, frowning.

"My family is not as wealthy as that of Septimus," Delaney said. "We do have slaves, but their number is far smaller than most of the estates around us. But, to tell the truth, I enjoy physical labor. It may be unfashionable, but I find that it keeps me strong and healthy."

"A sound mind in a sound body," Trebonius said. "Truly, that is the Roman ideal. But you, Quintullus, have carried it much further than any man that I have ever seen. Aside from labor, it is clear that you engage in sport. Am I correct in guessing that you are a wrestler?"

"I do enjoy wrestling," said Delaney with a smile. "I find that it relaxes me."

"I will wager that you do not often lose," Trebonius said with a grin.

"That is true. I have not been bested since I was a boy."

"My friends, I see an opportunity for us to make some money here," said Trebonius.

"We did not come here today to speak of making wagers," Casca snapped. "We have matters of much more import to discuss."

"Patience, Casca," Cassius said. "Let us not rush into things. Let us take a little time and get to know our new friend, Fabius Quintullus." He turned to Delaney. "Casca is always fervent in his opinions, especially when it concerns politics."

"Politics often make for fervent opinions," said Delaney. "My friend Marcus and his brother, Lucius, both find mine a bit too fervent on occasion."

"I had that impression," Cassius said with a smile. "Our discussion at dinner last night became somewhat impassioned. I had the feeling that they did not entirely approve of our opinions. But we were, after all, merely expressing our concerns about Rome's welfare."

"Do not mind Marcus Septimus," Delaney said. "You must understand that he has led a quiet, uneventful life in Cumae. His brother, Lucius, went off to the wars and it fell to Marcus to remain behind and manage the estate. He always wished that he could go and experience some adventure for himself, win some glory, share in the booty of war, but that was not to be. So he had to content himself with the letters that Lucius sent home. Lucius painted such a picture that Marcus became enthralled with Caesar. He would read those letters over and over again, playing out the battles in his mind, as if he were there himself."

"That is not uncommon," Cassius said understandingly. "There are many Romans who followed Caesar's campaigns in such a manner, wishing that they could have been there with him. But as one who has been to war himself, I can tell you that the imagining is always much better than the actual experience. Much safer, too."

"No doubt," Delaney agreed. "For my part, I do not think that Marcus would have made much of a soldier. He has too soft a disposition. But who is to say? Men who fear a battle have often proved themselves the bravest soldiers, while those who swagger and boast of fearlessness often turn coward in the thick of the fighting."

"Yes, that's very true," said Casca. "I see you speak from some experience, Quintullus."

"I have had my share," said Delaney, "but Marcus has always known only the quiet life. And Lucius has always had a gift for writing. We often thought he should have been a poet. He described his experiences in Gaul so vividly that

Marcus came to idolize Caesar from afar. To speak against Caesar in his presence is like a personal affront. I can understand the way he feels, but in certain ways, Marcus can be blind to what is happening around him. In Cumae, he is removed from the politics of Rome. They affect him only slightly. Whereas I, who plan to settle down and live in Rome, have concerns that are considerably stronger."

"We had started discussing some of your concerns last night," said Cassius. "I would be curious to hear more of your thoughts on the matter."

Delaney shrugged. "Like you, I have certain opinions when it comes to Caesar." He glanced around, as if with some discomfort. "But perhaps they are opinions best kept to myself. I had a little too much wine last night and spoke a bit too freely. In such troubled times, one should be careful what one says in public."

"Come now, Quintullus," Casca said. "You are among friends here. And from what you said last night, it would seem that your thoughts and your concerns echo our own."

"Indeed?" Delaney said warily.

"Casca speaks for us all," said Cassius. "Men of intelligence can see that there is danger in one man having absolute power to rule in Rome. Especially a man like Caesar. In some ways, he is like another Sulla. Only Sulla was never made dictator for life."

"And he never took the title of *Imperator*," said Trebonius, "nor had so many honors and privileges been heaped upon him."

"What is the difference between emperor and king?" asked Casca angrily. "They are but different names for the same thing."

"It would seem so," said Delaney.

"Rome was done with kings ages ago," said Cassius. "Under the republic, we enjoyed freedom and democracy, a life such as no nation in the world had ever known. Through the Senate, the citizens of Rome all had a voice in how they were governed. Yet what have we now? A Senate that is little more than Caesar's tool. Look at the new men whom he has elevated. Are there any Ciceros among them? No.

They are all merely acolytes to Caesar, bowing to his every whim. Hardly anyone in the Senate dares to dispute with him. His word is law. His every action is unquestioned. And now he plans to leave on yet another campaign, to play at being Alexander, while we suffer his surrogates, mere secretaries, not even members of the House, to dictate to us in his absence! Is this not a mark of the contempt in which he holds the Senate?"

"I cannot disagree," Delaney said, nodding. "Since he became Emperor, Caesar has become more and more the autocrat. It is not in the tradition of Rome's institutions. Only what can anyone do? He has the support of the people."

"Perhaps he has the support of the plebeians," Brutus said, "who know only not to bite the hand that feeds them, but there are many men in Rome, men such as ourselves, who perceive the growing danger of his rule. Caesar has always catered to the masses, with his corn dole and his public feasts and entertainments, but in his ascent to power, he had made more than his share of enemies."

"Such as yourself, Brutus?" asked Delaney. "I have heard that there are intimate bonds between yourself and Caesar."

Brutus flashed him an angry look. "I am not his bastard, if that is what you imply!"

"I imply nothing," said Delaney. "I only repeat what I have heard. Did he not pardon you after you took Pompey's side during the civil war?"

"He pardoned Cassius, too," said Brutus. "And Casca and many others. It was all his way of showing himself to be magnanimous, the great general who was gracious in his victory. It was but another way to curry favor with the mob. It was no different from when he ordered Pompey's statues put back up after the mobs had torn them down. You think that he had any love for Pompey? If so, then why did he pursue him into Egypt? Why did he destroy his sons? Did he make a great show of remorse for having done so, as if he had had no other choice? No. He returned to Rome to celebrate a triumph. A triumph celebrating the destruction of one of the greatest families of Rome! There was your *true* Caesar, not the one who gave out pardons and ordered Pompey's statues put back up!"

"That was nothing but a show," said Casca derisively. "Another entertainment. It was as if to say, 'Let us have the statues put back up, to celebrate the greatness of the man I have defeated, thereby proving I am greater still.' His ambition seems to know no bounds. For the good of Rome, that ambition must somehow be curtailed."

"Strong words," Delaney said, "but then what good are words without acts to back them up?"

"We do not merely speak words, Quintullus," said Casca intently. "We plan to act as well!"

"Indeed?" Delaney said, raising his eyebrows. "What is it that you plan to do?"

"Peace, Casca," Cassius said, laying a hand on his arm. "Perhaps now is not the time."

Delaney smiled. "Yes, I have heard such talk before," he said wryly. "It is the wine-fueled courage of the dinner table, the whispered conspiracy of the baths. Men talk boldly, but when it comes time to act, they hesitate and say, 'Now is not the time.' And somehow, the right time never comes."

"What if it *were* to come?" asked Cassius. "Where would you stand, Quintullus?"

"Where I have always stood, with the strength and purpose of my convictions," said Delaney. "If there was something to be done and if there was a way to do it, and if Rome stood to benefit from the act that I was contemplating, then I would stand for Rome, of course." He shrugged. "But then, we speak only impassioned words. Impassioned *acts* are what is needed. Yet, as you say, Cassius, there are no more Ciceros. Even Cicero himself has retired from public life. No one opposes Caesar openly. There is nothing to be done."

"Perhaps there is," said Casca. "If, as you say, you are indeed a man who stands for the strength and purpose of his convictions. A man who stands for Rome."

Delaney gave him a steady stare. "So far, all I have heard

is talk," he said. "To oppose Caesar in the baths is one thing. To take a stand against him publicly is quite another. As you say, Caesar controls the Senate. What can a few men do?"

"Perhaps we are not quite so few as you suspect," said Brutus. "There are many others who share our feelings and concerns."

"I do not doubt that," said Delaney, "but I repeat, Caesar controls the Senate. When the House belongs to Caesar, what can anyone do?"

"We could remove Caesar from the House," said Casca.

There was a moment of tense silence.

"There is only one way to do that. You speak of murder, Casca," said Delaney softly.

"Not murder," Casca replied. "Tyrannicide! That is the only way to stop a man like Caesar! Or does the thought disturb you, Quintullus?"

"It is a disturbing thought," Delaney said.

"What happened to the man who spoke of the strength of his convictions?" Casca asked snidely. "A moment ago, you spoke of the need for action. Yet now, it is you who hesitates."

They were all watching him carefully.

"To hesitate is not the same as to weigh a course of action carefully," said Delaney. "It is one thing to huddle together in the baths and whisper boldly. It is another to plan a course of action. Such things should be entered into with great care. There have been others in the past who acted rashly. They did not live long to regret their choice."

"No one speaks of acting rashly," Cassius said.

"Then you have a plan?"

"We have considered it," said Brutus. "But we must be certain that those to whom we speak of it stand with us. You seem to be of a like mind with us, Quintullus. We spoke of that last night. The question is, have you the courage to stand with us?"

"Do I look to you like the sort of man who lacks the courage to stand for that which he believes in?" asked Delaney.

"No," said Brutus, "you do not seem like such a man. Yet that is not an answer."

"Before I give you one," Delaney said warily, "first tell me why you have chosen me, a stranger to you all, to reveal your thoughts to. That meant taking a great risk. How do you know that I will not denounce you?"

"A fair question," Cassius said. "And one deserving of an answer. First, we were favorably impressed with what you said last night. You spoke boldly and frankly, expressing thoughts similar to ours. A man such as yourself, strong, clear-thinking, forthright, did not seem to us like someone who would be afraid to follow words with deeds."

"There was a risk, of course, in sharing our thoughts with you," said Brutus, "but the risk was not so great as you imagine. You are, as you have said, a stranger and a newcomer to Rome, whereas we are all men of position and influence. There are no witnesses to testify to what has transpired here just now save for ourselves. If you were to inform on us—"

"Which would be rash, indeed," interrupted Casca.

"If you were to inform on us," continued Brutus, "it would be merely your word against ours. And we are all in a position to make certain that you could not pose a threat to us."

"Make no mistake, Quintullus," said Cassius, "we do not intend to threaten you. Brutus merely seeks to explain our reasoning."

"Your reasoning seems sound, so far," Delaney said.

"There is yet one more thing," Cassius said. "Your friendship with Lucius Septimus, and the fact that you are staying in his house, means that you could be very useful to us. Septimus is close to Caesar, a frequent visitor to the palace. He has Caesar's confidence. And you seem to have his."

"I see," Delaney said. "And Trebonius is friends with Antony, who is also close to Caesar. I begin to understand your methods."

"Yes, as you can see, Quintullus, we are careful men," said Cassius. "We must see to it that not a thing is left to chance. There is much at stake. The very fate of the republic, to say nothing of our lives."

"Indeed," Delaney said thoughtfully.

"So. What is your answer?" Cassius asked. "Do you stand with us, or against us?"

"I stand for the republic," said Delaney.

"Then you are with us?" Casca asked.

"If I am to be asked to risk my life," Delaney said, "then I would be a fool to undertake that risk for nothing."

Brutus frowned. "Is it payment that you seek?"

"I am not some assassin who works for hire, Brutus," said Delaney with an affronted tone. "I believe in the republic and I have come to Rome to build a life. But if I am to be instrumental in saving the republic, then I would like to have a hand in restoring it, as well."

"And so you shall," said Cassius. "We will need men of ability when the time comes, to prevent Rome from falling into chaos. Never fear, Quintullus, you shall not fall by the wayside. At the very least, a tribuneship could be arranged. What say you to that?"

"I think that I would like being a tribune," Delaney said with a smile.

"Then it is settled," said Cassius. "We shall meet again at my home an hour before sunset. And we shall drink to the future of Rome!"

8

"This will do," said Steiger, looking around at the small apartment in the tenement block that Marshall owned.

"Are you sure about this, Creed?" Marshall asked. "You don't have to stay here, you know. You're perfectly welcome to remain at my place."

"Am I?" Steiger said, giving him a hard look. His pale, blue-gray eyes were like cracked ice.

"Look, Creed, if it's about last night—"

"Yeah, that's what it's about," said Steiger, an edge in his voice. "Why didn't you kill me last night, John? What's the matter, lose your nerve?"

Marshall hesitated only a fraction of a second. "What the hell are you talking about?"

"Come on, John, you think I can't tell when I've been drugged? You must've slipped me a Mickey in the wine. You had your chance. Why didn't you take it?"

Marshall looked as if he were going to protest again, but then his shoulders sagged and he exhaled heavily. "All right. Look . . . I admit I thought about it, but when push came to shove, I—I simply couldn't do it. I just couldn't. You gotta understand, Creed, it wasn't because I *wanted* to, it's . . . I was just afraid."

"I must be slowing down," said Steiger flatly. "I suppose I should've seen it coming. I just never expected it from you."

There was an awkward pause. Marshall felt fear knotting his stomach. He wanted to run, but he was afraid that if he did, he'd never make it to the door. Sweat stood out on his forehead.

"What are you going to do?" he asked anxiously.

"Nothing, John," said Steiger, turning away from him. He stood at the window, looking out into the street. He sounded suddenly weary. "You caught me with my guard down and you had me, but you didn't do it. I guess that counts for something."

"Creed, I . . . Hell, I wish . . ." His voice trailed off. "I simply don't know what to say."

"There's nothing to be said," Steiger replied in the same flat tone. He shook his head. "You've changed, John. You used to be one of the best. Now you've become a frightened little man."

"Creed . . . try to understand. I didn't *want* to do it. And when it came right down to it, I—"

"Spare me, John, all right? Look, I appreciate the help you've given me, but I don't really need you anymore. Go back to your house and your teenaged female slaves. Go live your fantasy. Don't worry, I won't turn you in. I don't really give a damn about the Underground. Besides, you're just not worth the trouble."

Marshall looked down at the floor. "Creed, look . . . I was just scared, that's all. I didn't know if you were going to—"

"I don't really want to hear it, John, all right?"

Marshall sighed. "Okay. Look . . . you can stay here as long as you like. Do what you have to do. I won't come around and bother you. But if there's anything you need, money or—"

"Get out, John," said Steiger, without looking at him. "Just go away. I don't want to see you anymore. The minute you walk out that door, I'm going to forget that you exist."

Marshall moistened his lips nervously and nodded. "All right." He felt enormously relieved. "For whatever it's worth, Creed, I'm truly sorry things had to turn out this way."

"So am I, John. So am I."

"We're making good progress," Travers said, coming into the room. "That was a messenger from Caesar. We've been invited to dine with him and Cleopatra at her house tomorrow night." He glanced at Andre and grinned. "Cleopatra must have told him about how you managed to gain entry to her house. He said to be sure my brother brings his clever and audacious wife."

"Great," said Lucas. "I've been wanting to have a look inside that house. Good work, Andre. You got us in."

"The invitation did not include you, I'm afraid," Travers told Delaney.

"That's just as well," Delaney said. "I'm supposed to meet with the conspirators again tomorrow night."

"So then you're in?" asked Travers.

"For what it's worth, I guess I am," Delaney replied. "But if I didn't know that these guys actually pulled it off, I'd say they were a pretty sorry bunch of assassins. They seem to be all talk and no action. Less than two weeks to go before the Ides of March and they still haven't really got a plan."

"Disorganized?" asked Lucas.

"You'd have to see it to believe it," said Delaney with a derisive snort. "They're like a damn sorority trying to decide what decorations to put up for the dance. The leaders get together during the day, usually at the baths, where they huddle in a corner in a little group and whisper, then at night, they meet at Cassius' house for a long, leisurely dinner and gallons of mulsum. I don't know how they stomach the damn stuff. They just sit around drinking and trying to psych one another up. They say they have a plan and they're refining it, but there isn't any plan that I can see. It's just a bunch of guys tossing around wild ideas. And all during the night, other conspirators keep drifting in and wandering out, as if they were dropping into some lodge meeting. I can believe that there were about sixty people in on this thing. It's like a damned convention. These people are rank amateurs. They haven't got any security to speak of, just a couple of guards at the door who pass people in and out. The way they're going about it, if Caesar hasn't heard about this so-called conspiracy by now, he must be off in some other world."

"Well, according to history, there were many rumors of conspiracies against his life," said Travers, "but Caesar simply discounted them. There have always been conspiracies in Rome of one sort or another, but few of them ever came to anything. Caesar was even involved in several aborted conspiracies himself, such as the one with Crassus. He knows there's opposition against him, but the people support him and he's got the Senate cowed. If word has reached him about this conspiracy, maybe he feels the same way about it as you do. That they're all talk and no action."

"But would he just ignore them like that?" Andre asked with surprise.

"If he were anybody else, he probably wouldn't," Travers replied. "But he's Caesar. He's survived more bloody wars than any other general in Rome. The man simply has no fear. Maybe he really believes that he's invulnerable."

"According to your report, he didn't seem to believe it the night he heard the oracle's prophecy," said Lucas.

"A lot's happened since that night," Travers replied. "The Caesar who was about to cross the Rubicon was full of doubt and indecision. He'd always bucked the odds before, but for the first time in his life, he really wasn't sure. No Roman general had ever marched on Rome before. Even for Caesar, it seemed like going much too far. But he pulled it off. And he hasn't looked back since. After he defeated the great Pompey, he didn't think that there was anything he couldn't do." Travers paused. "After his death, Caesar was deified, but in his own mind, he's halfway there already."

"You mean he actually thinks of himself as a god?" asked Andre.

"No, I doubt that. I'm sure he doesn't, not in the literal sense. But with all he's managed to accomplish, it's clearly gone to his head. You know the old saying. Absolute power corrupts absolutely. Caesar hasn't really been corrupted, at least not in the same sense as Tiberius, Caligula, and Nero were, but he really does believe that he's infallible. Besides, his mind isn't really on what's happening in Rome. Being emperor doesn't seem to interest him anymore. He's bored."

"Bored?" said Lucas, raising his eyebrows.

"He's run out of challenges. Since he became emperor, Rome has been at peace. And peace is not Caesar's mileu. He's a soldier. He's not really alive unless he's in the field with his troops. It's what he does best. He can't wait to leave on that campaign. The old war dog wants one last taste of battle. He's not a young man anymore. This is his last chance to go down in history as the greatest general who ever lived, the man who surpassed even Hannibal and Alexander. There's a world to conquer out there." Travers shook his head. "He's not going to concern himself about a few malcontented senators."

"I wonder what would have happened if he wasn't murdered," Lucas said, musing out loud. "You think there's a chance he would have pulled it off?"

"I don't think there's much chance he wouldn't have," said Travers. "Jesus, wouldn't that be something? Rome's empire would have extended all the way from western Europe to the Far East. Caesar would have become the most powerful ruler who ever lived. History would have taken a very different course. Who knows how things would have turned out!"

"Let's hope we don't have to find out," Delaney said.

Travers glanced at him, as if suddenly remembering what they were here to do. "Yes," he said quietly. He sighed. "What's our next move?"

"Well, tomorrow we'll have a good chance to take stock of the situation at Cleopatra's house," said Lucas. "I'd like to look around and see if there's a good place I can drop in unexpected sometime."

"Probably the gardens," Andre said. "It looked like there were a few places where you could clock in unobserved. But I still can't believe that Cleopatra could be a ringer. She just seems so . . . genuine. It's Apollodorus I have my doubts about."

"You know how long he's been with her?" asked Delaney.

"Since she was sent into exile," Andre said. "She says he's served her loyally ever since. He was the one who smuggled her in to see Caesar." She looked at Travers. "You were there, you must remember him."

"Yes, I do," said Travers, "and I've seen him a number of times since then, but I've never really spoken with him."

"What's their relationship like?" asked Lucas.

"He seems to be a bit more than just a servant or a slave," said Andre. "He defers to her, of course, but I noticed that he does try to manipulate her, though that can't be easy. He's clearly in charge of the household. Cleopatra said something that I found very interesting. She's concerned about Caesar's safety, but she said it was Apollodorus who suggested she present him with a bodyguard. And he picked the men himself."

"That *is* interesting," said Lucas. "We'll have to keep a careful watch on him."

"We've got Castelli and Corwin watching Marcian and Sabinus," Delaney said. "That leaves Andell and Drummond free. We could assign them to work shifts on Apollodorus. Watch the house while he's inside, follow him when he leaves."

"Hell, I almost forgot to tell you," Travers said. "When Corwin relieved Castelli early this morning and Castelli came in to get some sleep, he reported that Sabinus has apparently moved out of Marcian's house and into a small apartment in the Argiletum."

"Isn't that sort of a working-class district?" Lucas asked, frowning.

"It's not one of Rome's best neighborhoods," Travers replied.

"Odd place to live for a man who just won a bundle at the races," said Delaney.

"That's exactly what I was thinking," Lucas said.

"I can't shake the feeling that there's something very familiar about Sabinus," Andre said. "I don't know what it is. I don't forget faces and I'm sure I've never seen his before, but there's still something. . . . I don't know. It's just a feeling."

Lucas glanced at Delaney. "Finn?"

Delaney shook his head. "He rang no bells with me, but then I didn't get a chance to talk to him. I was concentrating on Cassius and the others."

Andre shrugged. "Maybe I'm wrong. I don't know, it's just sort of a hunch. . . ."

"I've learned to respect your hunches," Lucas said. "We'll leave Corwin on Marcian and have Castelli stay on Sabinus. We'll need to bring in some more people to relieve them."

"I'll go wake up Castelli," Travers said.

"No, let him sleep," said Lucas. "There's time. When he wakes up, tell him we'll need a couple more T.O.'s transferred in."

"Just two?" asked Travers.

"For now," Lucas replied. "I'd like to keep the numbers manageable. The more people we bring in, the more chances we're taking of disrupting the timestream. We're taking enough chances as it is, interacting with the most pivotal characters in this temporal scenario. Let's walk softly, okay?"

Travers nodded. "That makes good sense to me."

"All right," said Lucas. "In the meantime, there are several things we'll need to do. First, we need to set up safe transition points for each of us somewhere in this house. Someplace where we'll be able to clock in or out, any time of day or night, without alarming any of the household slaves and with no chance of two people clocking in at the same time."

"I've already anticipated you," said Travers. "I keep only a few slaves and they've all got strict instructions not to enter my private rooms unless they're told to." He grimaced. "I would have liked to dispense with slaves altogether, but I have to keep at least a few to maintain appearances. I've got a personal transition point with coordinates in my bedroom, in case of emergency, and you can set up your transition points either in there or in the library. Those would probably be the best places."

"Good. We'll get those programmed in right away," said Lucas. "What about outside the house?"

"You want to set up transition points outside the house?" asked Travers, puzzled.

"Suppose we've got hostiles inside the house?" said Lucas. "We've got to consider worst case scenarios, such as if we blow our cover to the S.O.G."

Travers nodded. "Good point. What about the gardens down by the riverbank? Or the roof?"

"We'll use both," said Lucas. "The other thing we'll need is an arms cache. If we have to take on soldiers of the S.O.G., we'll need lasers and disruptors. Where can we keep them safely?"

"I've got that taken care of, too," said Travers. "I've got some concealed storage places underneath the floor in the library."

"Excellent," said Lucas. He glanced at the others. "Have I forgotten anything?"

"What about a safehouse?" asked Delaney.

Lucas snapped his fingers. "Right. We'll require a house or apartment somewhere in the city where we can hole up in case this place is compromised."

"I'll see to it," said Travers.

"Anything else?" asked Lucas.

Delaney shook his head. "I think we've got it covered."

"I hope so," Lucas said. He made a tight-lipped grimace. "I have a feeling this is going to be a tough one. God knows, we've had a lot more dangerous missions before, but I don't think we've ever had one with so many variables. How the hell are we going to take out a dozen people who are constantly in the public eye without having anybody notice?"

"The answer to that one's simple," said Delaney. "We can't. Unless we can figure out some way to separate Caesar from his bodyguards on March fifteenth, it's going to get messy."

"Maybe we'll get lucky," Andre said.

They simply stared at her.

"On the other hand," she said wryly, "maybe not."

Marshall jumped about a foot when Simmons suddenly materialized in his bedroom. He'd been sitting on his bed, with his door bolted, nervously smoking a cigarette, when the Network cell chief suddenly appeared before him.

"Christ, Simmons, you gave me a start!" said Marshall, exhaling heavily. "You should be more careful. What if I'd had a girl in here?"

"That would've been too bad for her," said Simmons flatly. He was dressed in black commando fatigues and there was a laser pistol in a tanker-style holster at his shoulder. "I'd suggest you curtail your sexual diversions for the time being. You've got more important things to worry about. Did you know you're being watched?"

"I'm being *watched*?" said Marshall, stunned.

"That's right," said Simmons. "I thought you said they didn't suspect you."

"But . . . I don't see how they could!" protested Marshall. "I haven't done anything to alert them or give myself away! I swear!"

"You must have done something," Simmons said. He looked at Marshall's cigarette with distaste. "Those filthy things are going to kill you."

"If I don't die of a damn heart attack first, from you popping in here like that," Marshall said. "I need these. They're my only remaining connection with the world I came from. An Underground connection picks them up for me. They help steady my nerves."

"Well, you'd better lay in a good supply, then," Simmons said. "You'll need your nerves steady. I see Steiger's left the house."

"You've got him under surveillance?"

"Of course. You think we're playing games here? Snap

out of it, Marshall, for Christ's sake. Start thinking straight. What happened? Why did he leave?"

Marshall glanced down at the floor and took a nervous drag off his unfiltered cigarette. "He wanted me to provide him with a separate safehouse."

Simmons regarded him steadily. "That's not all of it. What aren't you telling me?"

Marshall hesitated.

Simmons suddenly stepped forward and grabbed him by his tunic, lifting him up off the bed. There was a sound of ripping cloth. "Don't fuck with *me*, Marshall," he said in a low voice, through clenched teeth. "I could do this just as easily without you. Get my drift?"

"All right, all right! Let go of me!"

Simmons released him and stepped back. "Let's hear it," he said. "*All* of it."

"He found out I drugged him the other night."

"How? I thought you said he wouldn't suspect a thing?"

"I don't *know* how!" Marshall said. He took a deep breath and let it out slowly. "That stuff wasn't supposed to have any aftereffects and I know he couldn't have tasted it in the wine. But he figured it out somehow. He's good. He always was."

"So you gave yourself away," said Simmons with contempt. "How come you're still alive?"

Marshall shook his head. "When he confronted me with it, I was sure he was going to kill me. But he hasn't put it all together. He thought I'd gotten paranoid and drugged him so that I could kill him while he was out, because I was afraid he'd turn me in. I let him think that and convinced him I couldn't go through with it. That I'd lost my nerve. Since I hadn't gone through with it, I guess he felt he owed me something. So he said he'd stay in the apartment and he wasn't going to contact me again. As soon as I walked out the door, he'd forget I existed." Marshall sighed. "He said I didn't have to worry about him coming after me. I wasn't worth it."

"That's it?" asked Simmons skeptically.

"That's it."

"He must be getting soft."

"That's funny," Marshall replied dryly. "That's almost the same thing he said."

"You're lucky. It looks as if no real damage was done. All we've got to do is keep him under surveillance and take him out at the appropriate time."

"You'd better tell your people to be careful," Marshall said. "I wouldn't count on Steiger getting soft. He just let me slide for old times' sake. He's still the best damn field agent the T.I.A. ever had. If they get too close, he'll spot them."

"Don't worry," Simmons said. "I'm not about to under-estimate him. What concerns me now is that surveillance on you. They must have caught on to you somehow."

"Unless Steiger told them about me, I can't see how," said Marshall. "Even after what's happened, I don't believe he'd do that. He'd have to break his cover to blow the whistle on me."

"So what? I don't see how it would jeopardize his mission if he revealed himself to the adjustment team."

Marshall shook his head. "No, he wouldn't do that. I know Steiger. He's never been a team player. His whole purpose in being here is to prove to Forrester that the agency still needs the covert field section. He won't let the adjustment team know he's here unless it's absolutely necessary. You have to understand what drives him. He wants to go back to covert field work. Alone, in deep cover. Just the way his old mentor, Carnehan, always used to do it. The Mongoose and Steiger were cut from the same cloth. Both mavericks. Both in it for the thrill. Steiger's going to do things his own way. If the adjustment team stays in control of the situation, he'll hold off and cover them. If they blow it, he'll take Caesar out himself."

"Well, if Steiger hasn't told them about you, then obviously something you've done has put them on to you."

"I tell you, I haven't done anything that would make them suspect I'm part of the Underground, much less the Network," Marshall insisted.

"Maybe not," said Simmons, "otherwise I can't see any

reason why they wouldn't simply move in and apprehend you. But you must have done something to arouse their suspicion. *Think*. What have you done recently that might have drawn their attention to you?"

Marshall shook his head. "I tell you, I can't think of anything!"

"You had to have done *something*."

Marshall shrugged helplessly.

"Have you done anything different lately? Anything that was out of your ordinary pattern of existence? Anything at all?"

Marshall frowned. "The only thing I've done recently that I've never done before was fix a chariot race."

Simmons frowned. "When?"

"A couple of days ago. But I can't see how they could possibly know about that."

"Why did you do that?"

"It was Steiger's idea. He knows I've had contact with Marc Antony and he wanted to use that contact to get next to Caesar. So he had me fix the race so he could take Antony for a bundle, which would give him the chance to play the gracious winner and entertain Antony and his friends on his winnings."

"And you haven't done anything else out of the ordinary?"

"Nothing."

"Then that must have been it. Somehow they figured out the race was fixed and that you fixed it."

"I don't get it," Marshall said. "Even if they found that out, and I don't see how the hell they could have, why should that make them suspect me of anything other than being a crook?"

"You're not thinking, Marshall. They're on the lookout for any pattern of events that could connect to Caesar. If you arranged for Steiger to win a conspicuous amount of money from Marc Antony and that led to Antony introducing him to Caesar, it was something that would obviously attract their attention. Especially since Steiger came out of nowhere and suddenly he's interacting with key figures in this scenario."

"So that's what that invitation from Septimus was all about!" said Marshall with sudden realization. "That's why they asked me to bring the charioteers! They wanted to have a chance to look us over!"

"Who's Septimus?"

"He's an L.T.O. named Travers, who's been assigned to Caesar," Marshall explained. "Steiger warned me about him at the party. He wanted to make sure I kept my distance from him and the adjustment team."

"Oh, that's nice. Any other little details you conveniently forgot to mention?" Simmons asked dryly.

"I'm sorry. I meant to tell you about him, but—"

"But you were too busy worrying about your own skin."

"Okay, so I've been under a lot of pressure. You think it's been easy for me? Anyway, that must explain it. Septimus . . . that is, Travers, knows who I am. I don't mean who I *really* am, I mean he knows who Marcian is. If they somehow tumbled to the fact that the race was fixed, Travers probably figured out that I was the only one in a position to do it. That must be why they're having me watched. They can't really know anything; they're just not taking any chances. They'd never recognize Steiger with his new face and they don't realize he's here undercover, backing them up."

"Then it follows that they'd have him under surveillance, too," said Simmons. "For all they know, he could be S.O.G. This is turning into a regular Chinese fire drill. If he's not careful, he's only going to wind up interfering with their mission."

"We can't allow that to happen," Marshall said. "A temporal disruption would affect us all."

"You think I don't know that?" Simmons snapped. "If he spots the surveillance they've put on him, he's either going to figure out they're working at cross-purposes and break cover, or he'll think it's the S.O.G. and take out whoever they've got watching him. Then they'll be convinced that he's the opposition, and by the time they get everything straightened out, it could be too late."

"So what are we going to do?" asked Marshall.

"I'm almost tempted to play them off against each other," Simmons said. "It would really be something to make Steiger's plan backfire on him and have his own friends take him out for us. But with the S.O.G. around, that would be taking too much of a chance. We're just going to have to get Steiger to break cover and start working with the others before he screws everything up."

"But then he won't be on his own anymore," said Marshall. "He won't be as vulnerable. If you try to move against him then, he'll have the adjustment team to back him up."

"So we'll simply wait until they've completed their adjustment," Simmons said. "Then, if necessary, we'll take them all out."

"You must be crazy," Marshall said. "Going up against Steiger's bad enough, but I'm not about to try to take on a whole adjustment team!"

"No one's asking you to," said Simmons. "You let me worry about that."

"Yeah? And suppose you blow it? They'll be coming after me! Unh-unh. There's no way I'm going to take that kind of chance. I'm the one who's got the most to lose here. You want to take out Steiger, fine, but you stay away from that adjustment team!"

"Or else what?" asked Simmons softly.

"You just stay away from them, that's all. I'm not about to risk everything that I've built up here just because you want to be a cowboy, Simmons. Remember, I'm the one who called you in. I'm the one who gave you Steiger on a platter. And I'm going to be the one to call the shots."

"I don't think so," Simmons said.

He drew his laser and shot Marshall in the chest.

9 _____

It was one of the most fascinating evenings Lucas had ever spent. It was an intimate party, himself and Andre, Travers, Caesar and Cleopatra. The Queen of Egypt had provided a sumptuous repast, seven courses served with excellent Greek wines. A trio of musicians played softly and unobtrusively throughout the meal on cithara, lyre, and pan pipe. There were no jugglers or acrobats or midget wrestlers, merely silent and attentive slaves who brought them food and kept their goblets filled, under the watchful eye of Apollodorus.

Caesar was relaxed and loquacious in Cleopatra's presence. He was delighted to discover that "Marcus" was a student of his campaigns and they spent long hours discussing his wars against the Helvetii and the Nervii, the invasion of Gaul by the German tribes, the campaigns against Vercingetorix and the Aedui and the civil war against Pompey. Lucas quickly realized why Travers had such affection for the man and why Caesar's soldiers had always felt such a fierce loyalty toward him. Caesar had an enormous amount of charisma. He was a man of strong personality. He was quick-witted, with a sense of humor, an unintimidating manner, and a way of knowing how to make people feel comfortable around him. He was a fascinating and compelling conversationalist, but he also knew how to listen, an ability rarely found in men with large egos. He conveyed a sense of tremendous forcefulness and drive that was restrained, yet capable of being unleashed at any time. As Andre put it later, he was, quite simply, a very sexy man.

Lucas was constantly aware of Apollodorus throughout the evening. And of Caesar's Egyptian bodyguard. Most of them were stationed outside, but there were four of them present during the meal, two on either side of each entrance to the room. Their eyes never left the party at the table. Several times, Lucas caught Apollodorus staring at him intently. He smiled at him, but got no response. Apollodorus remained impassive. Caesar noticed Lucas glancing at the guards and gave Lucas and Travers the opening that they'd been waiting for.

"A grim-looking bunch, are they not?" said Caesar. "I am sorry if they make you feel uncomfortable. Apollodorus, tell them to take their posts outside. I very much doubt that I will be set upon in here."

Apollodorus hesitated a fraction of a second, then moved to comply with Caesar's order.

"Do they go with you everywhere?" asked Lucas.

"Everywhere," said Caesar wearily. "If I would let them, I think they would sleep at the foot of my bed. Cleopatra means to protect my imperial person from murderous shopkeepers and senators."

"You joke," said Cleopatra somberly, "but you have many enemies. There are men in Rome who resent your power over them. You should not treat such things so lightly."

"Should I concern myself with a handful of malcontented senators when all the rest of Rome supports me?" Caesar replied.

"It takes but one determined man armed with a sword or dagger to end a life," said Cleopatra.

"I have survived many determined men armed with swords and daggers," Caesar replied. He turned to the others. "You see, we have had this argument before. Cleopatra acts as if we are still in the palace of the Ptolemys, where assassins lurk in every shadowed corner and intrigues abound."

"There are intrigues in Rome, as well," she said. "I only want to keep you safe."

Caesar smiled. "I am as safe in Rome as I would be in the midst of my legions. The people love me."

"The people are cattle," Cleopatra replied scornfully. "They always have been. Their affections can be bought, as you well know, since you have spent so much to purchase them yourself. It is not the people you should fear, but those who stand to gain the most if you were to be removed from power."

"If I were to be removed from power, who is there who could take my place?" asked Caesar. "Antony? Perhaps, if he were to settle down and be more serious. But he is one of my dearest and most trusted friends and he does not wish to become serious. He would require a guiding influence, most probably a woman, but there is no woman in Rome strong enough to hold him in his traces. Save yourself, perhaps," added Caesar with a smile. "Antony would be no match for you. But I hardly think we need to worry about Antony. He is my staunch supporter. Who else, then? Cicero? He is an old man and much more suited to making speeches criticizing those who are in power than to rule himself. And though Cicero might still cherish dreams of the republic, he has no real ambition. Cassius, perhaps? An oracle once warned me to beware of men named Cassius, Casca, and Brutus. You remember, Lucius, you were there."

"I remember that night well," said Travers, nodding.

"Then you will remember the oracle also said that a man could change his destiny," said Caesar. "I took his words to heart and I have taken firm control of mine. I know that Cassius and his friends bear me no love. I do not underestimate them, but they would be incapable of ruling in my place. They would only fall to arguing amongst themselves. I have heard rumors that they plot against me, but these are but the idle whisperings of malcontented men. They would be fools to think the people would forgive them if they moved against me."

"With your bodyguard around you," Cleopatra said, "they would never dare."

"They would not dare in any case," said Caesar. "But with your Egyptians at my side, it makes my enemies believe I fear them and that only serves to bolster their opinion of their own importance."

"Caesar has a point," said Travers. "Though we know it is not true, there are those in Rome who believe that Caesar has become distanced from the people. An Egyptian bodyguard cannot help but contribute to that feeling."

"There, you see?" said Caesar. "Have I not said the same myself?"

"My concern is only for your safety," Cleopatra said. "I merely wish to keep you out of danger."

"Perhaps you overestimate the danger," Lucas said. "I, for one, find it difficult to believe that a general who was victorious in so many battles and who defeated no less a commander than Pompey the Great need fear for his safety in the streets of Rome."

Cleopatra shot him an angry look. "In battle, Caesar was surrounded by his legions. In Rome, he is surrounded only by bitter, jealous, and ambitious men. Is the Emperor not entitled to protection? Does he not have the right, the privilege, to maintain a bodyguard? Or would you have him travel about the city without a retinue, like any common citizen?"

"No one expects the Emperor to act like a common citizen," said Travers placatingly, "but perhaps the common citizens would take it better if the Emperor's retinue was Roman, rather than Egyptian. Please understand, I mean no insult, but there has been talk that Egypt has far too much influence with Caesar."

"You mean to say that *I* have too much influence," said Cleopatra angrily. "You disappoint me, Lucius. I should have thought that you, of all people, would be above listening to common gossip."

"I am sorry, I did not intend to make you angry," Travers said, "but the truth is that it is more than common gossip. You should know that I would be the last to speak ill of you in any way, but there are those in Rome who do not know you as I do and who believe you have little respect for Roman freedoms and traditions. They see an Egyptian guard protecting Caesar and it makes them feel uneasy that their Emperor chooses to surround himself with the soldiers of a foreign queen. It is a matter of appearances."

"Why should Caesar care about appearances?" she replied hotly. "He is the Emperor! It is not for common men to question his decisions!"

"It is not for common men to question kings," said Travers gently, "but Rome will not be governed by a king."

"Enough," said Caesar, who had been listening to their exchange with a frown. "Let us not end this evening with an argument. I have always valued your opinion, Lucius, and I have had similar thoughts myself. But I am not convinced most Romans feel this way. The people of Rome know that my concern is only for their welfare. Still, I do not wish to give the appearance that I am fearful for my safety." He held up his hand, forestalling Cleopatra's response. "I will give the matter careful thought. But we shall speak no more of this tonight."

The streets were dark when they left Cleopatra's house and started on their walk back to Travers' villa, a short distance away. Their way was lit by two slaves bearing torches and another five slaves accompanied them as their armed retinue. The streets of Rome were dangerous at night. They spoke in Greek, a language that would not be unusual for educated Romans to converse in and one which none of Travers' household slaves would understand.

"What did you think of Cleopatra?" Andre asked.

"If she's a fake, then she's a good one," Lucas replied. "I'm inclined to believe she's genuine. I think Apollodorus is definitely the one to watch."

"Caesar's guards all looked very capable to me," Delaney said. "Alert, high level of fitness, taller than average . . . they could easily be our men."

"Caesar seemed very ambivalent about having them around," said Lucas. "What do think, Travers?"

Travers sighed. "I think there's a good chance he may dismiss them, unless Cleopatra manages to change his mind. The question is, what will we do if he doesn't?"

"We'll have to make sure he does," said Lucas. "An attempt on Cleopatra's life would convince him that there are people in Rome who fear her influence on him and conspire to assassinate her. He'd believe the threat to her was greater than any threat to himself and assign his Egyptian guard to protect her. That would get them out of our way."

"It might work, but it would be dangerous," said Travers.

"We knew that going in," Delaney said. "But we've only got a little over a week left. We can't afford to waste any more time."

They turned into a quiet side street.

"The best way to get inside would be through the gardens at the back of the house," said Lucas. "We go in wearing masks and we knock out the guards. We don't want to kill any of them, at least not until we're sure about them. The thing is, we want to get close, but not too close. We need to make enough of a commotion to arouse the guards inside the house, so that—"

Travers suddenly cried out as a bright beam of laser light penetrated through his left shoulder. It all happened very fast. The two slaves ahead of them dropped their torches and fell as laser beams stabbed through them. Two of their armed guard dropped before any of them had a chance to react.

"It's an ambush!" Delaney cried out, dropping to the ground as the street became a crisscross latticework of light. The three remaining slaves took off in fright. One of them ran directly into a beam, screaming as he fell. Lucas vanished as he translocated and a second later, Delaney also disappeared as he clocked out.

"Get back to the house!" Andre shouted to Travers as he fumbled for the controls of his warp disc. Then, suddenly, it was all over. It had all taken no more than twenty seconds.

Travers vanished, clocking back to the transition coordinates inside his house about three quarters of a mile away. Andre stayed put, stretched out behind the body of one of the fallen slaves. She had pulled the laser pistol, which she had strapped to her lower thigh, beneath the loose, ankle-length, pleated tunic she wore. She lay very still, staring intently into the darkness. The street was deserted. A moment later, she heard Lucas.

"Andre, it's me."

"Are you all right?"

"Get back to the house. Right now."

She reached for her warp disc, which was disguised as a heavy bracelet, and punched in the preprogrammed transition code for Travers' house. Moments later, they were all together in the library. Travers was in some pain, but fortunately, his wound wasn't very serious. The beam had penetrated the shoulder bone and gone straight through, cauterizing the wound.

"Well, it looks like the cards are on the table," Andre said as she examined his wound. "Did you see any of them?"

"Yeah," said Lucas, frowning as he opened up the hidden weapons cache beneath the floor. "We found them."

She paused and glanced up at him. "You found them?"

"They were dead," Delaney said, taking a laser pistol from Lucas and checking its power pack. "We found six bodies. I recognized two of them from Cleopatra's house. One of them served us dinner. They'd been shot with lasers."

"What the hell?" said Andre. "But . . . *who*?"

"We don't know," Delaney said. "But whoever it was saved our asses."

"It was probably the Underground," someone said from behind them. They spun around to see Sabinus standing casually in the entrance to the library. Only he had spoken to them in English. There was something very familiar about his voice. Castelli suddenly came up behind him, putting a laser pistol to the back of his head.

"Don't move," he said.

Steiger froze.

"I'm sorry about what I said back at the penthouse, Priest," he said evenly, "but as you can see, I had my reasons."

"Steiger!"

"Jesus Christ," said Andre. "I *knew* there was something familiar about him!"

"It's all right, Castelli," Delaney said. "He's one of us. Capt. Castelli, Col. Steiger."

"I'll be damned. Sorry about that, Colonel," Castelli said, putting away his gun.

"That's perfectly all right, Captain," Steiger said. "You did pretty good back there."

"I should have guessed," said Lucas. "That was you back there."

"No, actually, it wasn't me," Steiger said, coming into the room with Castelli following him.

Delaney frowned. "But I thought you just said—"

Steiger sat down in an ornate, ivory-inlaid chair. "I was talking about the hit they tried to put on Castelli, here. He handled himself real well."

"What?" said Lucas.

"I'm afraid I'm not following any of this," said Travers as Andre sprayed a medicated sealant on his wound from a first-aid kit. "Who *is* this person?"

"Col. Creed Steiger, Capt. Jonathan Travers," Lucas said, introducing them. "Col. Steiger's T.I.A. He used to be the senior agent in the covert field section. He's also head of the Internal Security Division for the agency."

"And he was also supposed to be back in Plus Time," said Delaney wryly, "because he asked to be relieved of duty on this mission."

"Up to your old tricks again, I see," said Andre.

"I'm sorry about that," Steiger said. "The idea was to back you up, just in case your covers got blown. Which is apparently what's happened."

"Terrific," Lucas said with a grimace. "We thought you might be the opposition. Damn it, Steiger, you could have screwed up this whole mission. Where the hell does Marcian fit in?"

"Marcian was really John Marshall, a former field agent who went over to the Underground," said Steiger.

"Was?" said Andre.

"Yeah, was. He's dead. Looks like the S.O.G. got him. Like they almost got Castelli and you. I came to warn you that this place is no longer safe. I suggest we move elsewhere, quickly."

"We've got a safehouse set up," Lucas said. "But we'd probably be safer here. This place is more easily defended."

"Will someone please explain to me what's going on?" asked Travers with a confused expression on his face.

"It's pretty simple, actually," said Steiger. "I was officially relieved of duty in Plus Time so that I could clock back here undercover and back up the team. They didn't know I was here and they didn't recognize me because I'd had cosmetic surgery."

"Was this Forrester's decision?" Lucas asked.

"Yes and no," Steiger replied. "The truth is, I had my own agenda. I wanted to demonstrate to him that there's still a place for covert operations. I'd been bugging him for a chance to prove my point, so he decided to go along with it, only unofficially. Officially, I'm still on leave. That way, it's just my ass that would be hanging in the wind if I screwed up."

"You almost did just that, God damn it," said Lucas. "You realize we wasted valuable time and manpower keeping you under surveillance?"

"Like I said, I'm sorry about that. But I had no idea I'd done anything to give myself away. What put you on to me?"

"The chariot race," said Delaney. "While we were watching it, Andre figured out that it was fixed and that all the drivers were in on it. Travers said that the only one in a position to put in that kind of fix was Marcian, so we checked and found out that a man named Sabinus, who came out of nowhere, was the big winner that day and that he was connected to Marcian."

"So you had someone watching Marshall, as well?"

"Lt. Donovan," said Castelli. "He's one of the new T.O.'s I just had brought in to help with the surveillance. Him and Sgt. Hall. Hall's asleep upstairs. He was due to relieve Donovan in about an hour."

"Well, you can tell him not to bother," Steiger said. "And you'd better check on Donovan, as well. They might've gotten him, too."

"Shit," said Castelli. "I'd better clock over there right now."

"Wake up Hall and Corwin and take them with you," Lucas said. "Make sure they're both armed. Then go check on Andell. If Donovan and Andell are both all right, bring them back here and leave Hall and Corwin on surveillance duty at Cleopatra's house. But tell them to be very careful. They're on to us."

"I'll get right on it," said Castelli, hurrying out of the room.

"What the hell happened, Creed?" asked Delaney.

"I'm not exactly sure," said Steiger. "But we've all been blown somehow. Like I said, your man Castelli was pretty good. I never spotted him until tonight, but I had this prickly feeling at the back of my neck and I knew something wasn't right, so I started looking. I went out for a walk to see if I could flush my tail, if there was one, and sure enough, after about five blocks, I spotted him. Just about the same time, they tried to hit him. There were three of them and by rights, they should've got him, but he was pretty fast. They missed their first shot at him and he clocked out right away. Didn't waste a second. I didn't know the players without a scorecard, so I didn't waste any time doing the same thing. I clocked over to Marshall's place, because I thought he might've had something to do with it. Only when I got there, he was already dead. Shot with a laser."

"Why did you think Marshall was behind it?" Lucas asked.

"Because Marshall's a deserter," Steiger replied, "or *was* a deserter, and he was scared. We went back a long way together. He used to be in the covert field section. I guess it got too much for him. He started slowing down and he decided to opt out. He just disappeared one day. But we'd both maintained contacts with the Underground, so it wasn't too hard to figure out what he'd done. Only I didn't know he was in Rome. When this mission came down, I started checking with my old contacts to find out if they had anyone back here and bingo, Marshall's name came up."

"Did I understand you correctly?" Travers asked with astonishment. "You maintain contacts in the Underground?"

"Occasionally, they can be very useful," Steiger said.

"But . . . but that's against the law! Those people are criminals!"

"Those criminals probably saved your life tonight," said Steiger.

"I still don't understand," said Travers.

"Marshall must've been holding out on me," said Steiger. "There's apparently a bunch of them back here. I didn't know that, but it's the only explanation that makes sense."

"But you said you thought he was behind what happened tonight," said Andre.

"That's what I thought at first," said Steiger, "until I overheard you just now, before I came in. Which reminds me, your security stinks. Why haven't you got guards posted?"

"Because we didn't know that we'd been blown," said Lucas, "and because we couldn't spare the people, no thanks to you." He glanced up as Castelli came back in with Donovan and Andell.

"I need a report, fast," he said.

"I didn't see anything tonight, sir," Donovan said.

"Me, neither," said Andell. "Nobody left Cleopatra's house after you'd gone."

"They must have clocked out to set up the ambush," said

Lucas. "We'll fill you in later, but right now, we need some security around here in case they try again."

"Right," said Castelli. "Andell, you take the roof. Donovan, watch the back. I'll take the front."

They hurried to their posts.

"All right, get back to Marshall," Lucas said to Steiger.

"He wasn't thrilled when I suddenly popped in on him," Steiger said. "He was worried that I might turn him in when this was over. He should've known better, but he wasn't the man he used to be. He caught me off guard and drugged me the other night. I guess he meant to kill me, but he lost his nerve. He said he couldn't bring himself to do it. But after what happened tonight, I thought maybe he'd changed his mind. Only when I clocked back to his place, he'd been dead for hours. In his room, with the door bolted from the inside."

"Suicide?" asked Andre.

Steiger shook his head. "No, his laser was still in its hiding place. He'd been murdered. My guess is the S.O.G. caught on to him somehow and took him out. His conscience must have bothered him, so he got his buddies in the Underground to keep an eye on us. Maybe that's what tipped the opposition, I don't know, but it's the only explanation I can think of for what's happened tonight."

"It would make sense," said Lucas, nodding. "The Underground doesn't want a temporal disruption any more than we do, so they're backing us up, only the paranoid bastards are staying out of sight so we won't know who they are." He sighed. "Unfortunately, with Marshall dead, unless they contact us, there's no way we can get in touch with them."

"Sure looks that way," said Steiger.

"Well, at least we know one thing," said Delaney. "There's no question anymore that our so-called Egyptians are really S.O.G. Unless Cleopatra issues lasers to her troops."

"I'd just like to know what the hell gave us away," said Andre. "I can't think of anything we've done that should have aroused their suspicions."

"Maybe it wasn't anything you did," said Steiger. "Maybe it was something I did, or something Marshall did. Or maybe they've already been through this before."

"What do you mean?" asked Travers.

"It's just an idea, of course," said Steiger, "but maybe they sent in Observers of their own in advance of the mission, to document the scenario as thoroughly as possible, figure out who all the players were and so forth. Then they could have simply clocked in their Special Operations Group back to the beginning, after they already knew as much as possible about the way things went down. If that's the case, then we obviously would've stood out like sore thumbs, because we weren't around the first time."

"Wait a minute," Travers said with a frown. "That doesn't make any sense. It would be impossible."

"Why?" asked Steiger, raising his eyebrows.

"Because it would violate temporal physics," Travers said. "This scenario occupies a particular temporal location in the timestream. If they clocked in Observers in advance, and then tried to clock in their S.O.G. team back to the initial point of the scenario they were observing *after* the Observers had finished their task and made their report, then they would have altered the very scenario they were attempting to observe in its unaltered state."

"You want to give me that again?" said Steiger, looking puzzled.

"It violates the Principal of Temporal Uncertainty," explained Travers. "Assume they clocked in their Observers first, say to the temporal locus of the night before Caesar crossed the Rubicon. The Observers have strict instructions only to *observe*, to do absolutely nothing that would in any way interfere with the scenario. In effect, functioning as a Temporal Pathfinder unit. We will leave aside for the moment the question of Heisenberg's Principle and assume that they did not significantly alter the scenario by being here to observe it. So they complete their period of observation, say up to the time that Caesar is assassinated, go back through the confluence point they're using, wherever the hell it may be, and make their detailed report. So then the S.O.G. team is clocked in to effect the disruption, going back to whatever optimum temporal locus point they have selected. Let's say it's the same point, the night before Caesar crossed the Rubicon. Only their Observers are already *there*. And what they will wind up observing would no longer be the original scenario, but the scenario as it's affected by the presence of the S.O.G. team! It's a temporal paradox."

"Not necessarily," said Steiger. "They would've had to receive a report of the original unaltered scenario *before* they sent in their S.O.G. team, so there would have to exist a space of time in which what their Observers saw was an unaltered scenario."

"No, you're wrong, Creed," said Delaney, who'd had much more training in the complexities of temporal physics. "Logic would seem to dictate that you're right, but logic breaks down when it comes to zen physics. If we're to assume that's what they did, then the moment their Observers clocked back to this scenario, they became a *part* of it, just as we are now. They altered it to the extent of their presence here. And maybe what they first observed was the scenario as it had occurred before their S.O.G. team was clocked in, but the moment the S.O.G. team was brought in, then *they* became a part of the scenario and changed whatever their Observers had originally observed. Travers is right. They would've created a temporal paradox. They would've changed their own past. That would have meant risking a timestream split."

"Only they would have risked it in *our* timeline," Lucas said with a thoughtful expression upon his face.

It suddenly got very quiet.

"Ooops," said Delaney.

For a moment, no one said anything. Then Steiger broke the silence.

"Of course, it was only an idea. We don't *know* that's what they did."

"Ah, but that's exactly what they *did* do, my boy," said a new voice.

Travers jerked around, startled, and found himself looking at a tall, gaunt, dark-hired man with a neatly trimmed moustache, deep-set dark eyes, and a sharp, aquiline nose. He was dressed in a gray herringbone Harris tweed sport coat shot through with fine threads of blue and peach; light gray flannel slacks; black kidskin loafers and gray silk socks; a button-down collar white shirt of raw silk, open at the neck, and a light blue silk ascot with a gold paisley pattern. He was holding a blackthorn walking stick and there was a gray, Irish tweed walking hat set at a jaunty angle on his head. Travers blinked. He could see the rolls of books right through him in their cubbyholes on the shelves.

"Oh, dear," he said weakly. "I'm almost afraid to ask."

"Capt. Travers, meet Dr. Robert Darkness," Lucas said, "the man who's faster than light. And who is, unless I miss my guess, about to make our lives utterly miserable."

Suddenly Darkness wasn't there anymore. One moment, Travers was staring at him and the next, he was simply gone. Only to reappear an instant later standing directly in front of him.

"How do you do?" said Darkness, offering his hand.

Travers flinched. "Hello," he said uncertainly, taking the man's hand. It felt solid enough, but he could see his own palm through it as they shook. The man seemed to flicker faintly. "I—I've heard of you," said Travers. "But I also heard that you were dead."

"Reports of my death have been greatly exaggerated, to quote Mark Twain," said Darkness. "I've read your book on Caesar. An outstanding piece of work. Highly illuminating."

"But . . . I haven't even written it yet!" said Travers, thoroughly confused.

"Ah, but you will," said Darkness. "Assuming, of course, that things proceed on schedule."

Travers stared at him as it finally sank in. "My God. You're from the future!"

"I am from *a* future, Mr. Travers. About which, for an entire plethora of reasons, the less said, the better."

"Then if he wrote the book, the mission was . . . *is* going to be . . . successful," Lucas said.

"That will be entirely up to you," said Darkness. "I did not say how the book ends, did I?"

Delaney exhaled heavily. "Jesus, this is it, isn't it? The key point in time. The reason you came back. This is where it's all going to hit the fan."

"Only partially correct, Mr. Delaney," Darkness said. "This is *one* of the key points in time, but it is, or it is about to be, a highly significant one."

"You're saying we blew it the first time around?" asked Steiger.

"The first time?" Darkness said. "There is no *first* time. As Delaney was just saying, quite correctly, there is only time. A nebulous commodity that can be disturbingly fluid and unstable. This moment, right now, is in fact a temporal disruption. *I* am a temporal disruption. And if the time-stream has become a sea of instability, we are about to enter into the eye of the storm. What you are about to do, one way or another, will change the course of history. That you will effect a change is unavoidable. That you will effect the right change is conjectural. But you *will* effect a change."

They all remained very silent.

"I see I have your attention," Darkness said with a slight smile. But it was a smile that had no amusement in it whatsoever. "In the past," he said, "I have interfered, in one way or another, in each of your lives. Except, of course, for you, Mr. Travers, as we have never met before. Your role in what is about to happen will be minimal. Whereas theirs"—he indicated the others with a sweeping motion of his walking stick—"will be pivotal and crucial. You doubtless have questions that you'd like to ask, but I'm afraid that I have neither the time nor the liberty to answer them right now. However," he continued, addressing his comments to the others, "everything that I have done up to this point has had a purpose.

"There is a great deal that I simply cannot tell you," he went on, "but I can tell you this—something has occurred in the time period from which I came that has resulted from a series of pivotal events that took place in the past. Not all of those events involve you, but some of the most significant ones do. And this one is, perhaps, the most significant."

"Will it be the last?" asked Andre softly.

"That all depends, Miss Cross," Darkness replied. "If we pass this test—and it is very much a test, for you as well as me—then there will be at least one more challenge that we shall have to face together. But if we fail here and now, then it will all be moot, for I will have only one chance to attempt to set things right. Because, as you were saying just a few moments ago, to risk attempting it a second time would create a temporal paradox and the consequences of that would be dire, indeed. For we are already involved in one, you see. In a manner of speaking."

"What do you mean, in a manner of speaking?" asked Delaney.

"I cannot tell you all the details of what is about to happen," Darkness said, "but Steiger has guessed correctly. The Special Operations Group from the parallel universe has indeed created a temporal paradox by their actions in this scenario. Had they done so in their own timeline, they would have risked bringing about a timestream split. But they have done it in *our* timeline, which changes the situation considerably."

"I'm not sure I see how," said Travers. "If they sent in Observers through the confluence point who then returned and made their report, then by sending through an S.O.G. team and having them clock back and interfere with temporal continuity during the same period their Observers had reported on, then the minute their Observers return, they will have altered their own past."

"Not necessarily," said Darkness. "Not if the Observers do not return."

"What?" said Lucas. "You've lost me. They would have *had* to have returned in order to make their report, so the S.O.G. team could come through and act on it. Because if they *didn't* return and make their report, then how could the S.O.G. team have received it in the first place? It's the Grandfather Paradox."

"Precisely," Darkness said. "So let us use that as an example. Assume that you clock back into the past in an attempt to kill your grandfather before he ever met your grandmother and you succeed in doing so. Your grandfather has now died before he could sire your father, which would have made it impossible for you to have been born. If you had not been born, then how could you possibly have gone back into the past to kill your grandfather? The most basic problem in temporal physics. Seemingly insoluble. Only Mensinger had solved it. His solution, of course, was the timestream split. However, Mensinger had not anticipated a Grandfather Paradox that could involve *two* separate universes. And this is precisely what we are confronted with.

"Let us now take our particular example of the Grandfather Paradox and follow it through using the two separate timelines," Darkness continued. "Step one: the people in the parallel universe locate a confluence point and send Observers through in order to research as thoroughly as possible the temporal scenario they wish to disrupt. Step two: the Observers complete their task, go back through the confluence point to their own timeline, and make their report. Step three: a team is assembled from your counterparts in the parallel universe, the Special Operations Group, and sent through the confluence back to the scenario the Observers had already reported on. Of course, since they are going back into a past scenario into which they had already sent Observers, those Observers are still going to be here when they arrive, because they will not yet have finished their task and made their report. And if at that point the S.O.G. team does anything to disrupt the original scenario, then obviously that will affect the scenario, changing it from what the Observers had originally reported on. You with me so far?"

"Right," said Lucas.

The others mumbled their assent or nodded.

"All right, then," Darkness said, "we understand that the moment the S.O.G. team arrives here, then the moment they do anything that affects this scenario, they change the past. They change what their Observers had originally seen. And at that point, they create a temporal paradox. So in order to avoid that, they proceed immediately upon arrival to step four. They kill their own Observers."

"Wait a minute," Travers said, frowning. "That wouldn't work. Then they'd still be faced with a paradox. Their Observers *had* to have made their report in the first place in order for the S.O.G. to receive and act on it."

"You're absolutely right," said Darkness. "Now they're faced with the hypothetical dead grandfather. Only in this case, he's been killed in another timeline. So what they've done has not affected their timeline at all."

"But it would still affect *them*," insisted Travers. "The ones who did the killing, I mean. The paradox still exists."

"You're quite right," Darkness replied. "And it centers around them. Only they are no longer in their own time-line."

"I can't see what difference that makes," said Travers.

"Can't you? Follow it through. What has actually occurred in their own timeline? They sent Observers through a confluence point. That doesn't change. Their Observers completed the task they were sent out to do and came back to make their report."

"That *does* change," Travers said. "The team went back and killed them, so now they never come back."

"Correct," said Darkness. "But let's get back to their original scenario. After the Observers made their report, the team went through the confluence point to effect their disruption. So what do we have so far? Observers leave on their mission. They come back and report. The S.O.G. team leaves on its assignment. Only part of their assignment is to kill the Observers, so now they can't come back. The grandfather has been killed. So now the grandson can't possibly exist. Only he does exist. Not in his own timeline, but in ours, where he doesn't really constitute a paradox. The temporal paradox would only come into play when he went home again, back to his own timeline. Because then we'd have an S.O.G. team that would be returning to a universe where their actions in ours had changed the past in theirs. As a result of what they'd done, their Observers never returned. And since their Observers never returned, the S.O.G. team never would have left. So *they* can't return, either."

"I'll be damned," said Travers slowly. He moistened his lips nervously and nodded. "It works. So long as they don't go back, there's no temporal paradox in their own timeline." He shook his head with awe. "It's positively brilliant. They came here on a suicide mission!"

"No, they didn't," Lucas said quietly.

Travers glanced at him. "But then, how . . ."

"They just came here on a one-way trip," said Lucas. "They can never go back. But they can go anywhere they want to in *our* timeline."

"A guerrilla disruption team," Steiger said. "They can spend the rest of their lives clocking through our timeline, disrupting our history everywhere they go. And since they can never go home again, they've got nothing left to lose."

"Which means that we not only have to stop them from preventing Caesar's assassination," added Delaney, "we've got to make sure we find every single one of them. And kill them all."

"You'll need to do much more than that," said Darkness. "Keep in mind that they're in a position to affect the lives of at least *two* pivotal figures in this scenario. Any well-planned mission has both a primary *and* a secondary objective."

"Cleopatra," Andre said.

"Precisely. If they fail in their objective to prevent Caesar's murder, they can still affect the course of history by killing Cleopatra. Or Marc Antony, for that matter. Or even Octavian, who will become Caesar Augustus."

"Hell, I knew I was going to hate this mission," said Delaney.

"We can have Antony and Octavian covered," Lucas said, a worried look on his face, "but they've already got Cleopatra."

"Which is why I'll have to kidnap her," said Darkness.

10 ⸻⸻⸻⸻⸻⸻⸻

Capt. Zeke Hollister of the Special Operations Group sat on a couch in his room at Cleopatra's house, scowling and smoking a cigar. He was scowling at the men standing before him, dressed in white cotton tunics and sandals. They were all standing at attention, their eyes firmly fixed on a point somewhere above his head.

"At ease," said Hollister in a voice that was quiet, yet laced with barely suppressed fury.

The men assumed a position of parade rest, their eyes still focused on a point somewhere above him. They did not look at all at ease.

Hollister looked up at his platoon sergeant. "All right, Maselli," he said, around his cigar, "what the hell went wrong?"

Sgt. Robert Maselli's jaw muscles tightened for a moment before he replied. "We got hit, sir."

"I know you got hit, God damn it, what I want to know is *how*? And by *whom*?"

Maselli swallowed nervously. "We don't know, sir."

Hollister stared at him for a long moment. He took a deep breath and let it out slowly in an effort to control his temper. "Tell me what happened."

"We took three squads," Maselli said. "Petrone led the first, Morton the second, I took the third. I figured we had plenty of time to conduct the operation. I knew we had at least a couple of hours once they went into the bedroom and I figured half an hour at most would be enough, plenty of time to get the A team back before Caesar was ready to leave."

Their platoon was divided into three squads—A team, B team, and C team. The A team was Caesar's bodyguard, with Sgt. Morton in charge. B team, under Cpl. Petrone, remained stationed at the house with Hollister. C team, under Maselli, was recon and surveillance.

"It was going to be a fast operation," Maselli continued, "hit and run and get out quick. Petrone led the detachment from B team against Septimus and the others. They set up an ambush on a quiet side street a short distance from their baseops. Morton led the group from A team against that Sabinus character and I went in with four men from C team to get Marcian. I know the idea was to take him alive for interrogation, but he was already dead when we got there."

"Dead how?"

"Shot through the heart with a laser," said Maselli. "And there's one more thing. A guy was watching his house."

"What guy?"

"I don't know, sir, I never saw him before. He was taking good cover and we almost didn't spot him. We took a risk and clocked straight in from the coordinates I picked up when we were at that orgy Marcian had a couple of weeks back. We found him dead in his room, with the door locked from the inside."

"Suicide?"

"No chance," Maselli said. "Whoever killed him had to have clocked out."

Hollister frowned. It wasn't making any sense. "Go on."

"We decided not to do anything about the guy keeping Marcian's place under surveillance. Apparently, he didn't know Marcian was already dead, so I doubt he was involved. For all we know, maybe he was just a burglar, casing the damn place."

"You should have taken him," said Hollister.

"I'm sorry, sir, I guess I made the wrong decision. It's just that finding Marcian dead really threw me. It simply didn't make sense and I didn't want to take any unnecessary chances."

"All right," said Hollister, chewing on his cigar. "What the hell happened with the other two assault teams?"

"After we found Marcian dead, we clocked over to back up Petrone's team," said Maselli. "Only we were too late. They'd already been hit. No survivors. I left Church behind to take their discs and clock the bodies out and the rest of us clocked over to check on Morton's group. They'd been hit, as well."

"I don't believe it," said Hollister. "All right, Morton, let's hear it."

Sgt. Morton picked up where Maselli had left off. "We clocked over to the Argiletum, where Sabinus had just moved into a small apartment. We figured he was only one guy, we'd have no trouble. We could probably take him alive for interrogation. Only there was someone keeping him under surveillance. We held back and while I was trying to figure out what the hell that meant, Sabinus came out and started walking down the street."

"Alone?"

"Alone. And this guy started tailing him. So we started tailing them both. I didn't know what the fuck was going on. But after a couple of blocks, I was pretty sure that Sabinus or whoever the hell he really is spotted the guy who was tailing him so we decided to move in. Only before we could, somebody opened up on our tail with lasers."

Hollister frowned. "What the hell . . .?"

"That's just what I thought, sir. And right about the same time, we got hit, as well. I don't know where the hell they were. I never even saw them. Randall and Biers were down before we knew what hit us. Sabinus and the guy tailing him both clocked out to who knows where. Then we got the hell out of there ourselves before we all got wasted. That's all there is, sir."

"Son of a *bitch*!" said Hollister, through gritted teeth.

"What the fuck is going on? How many sides *are* there to this thing?"

"The only explanation I can think of is that it's their Underground," said Maselli. "They must have an entire cell back here. They've caught on to us and started backing up the T.I.A. team to prevent a disruption on their home turf."

Hollister nodded. "That would fit," he said. "They could be covering the T.I.A. people, but that doesn't explain the hit on Marcian. We're pretty sure that he was either in their Underground or another L.T.O. In either case, why take him out? It doesn't make any goddamn sense!"

"There's obviously something going on that our Observers weren't aware of," said Maselli.

"We allowed for the possibility of a T.I.A. adjustment team being clocked in," said Hollister, "but we didn't count on members of the Underground coming to their aid. We should have foreseen that possibility. But it's still not necessarily a problem." He got up and started pacing back and forth. "Marcian's murder bothers me. It simply doesn't fit. Why would they want to take out one of their own people?"

"Maybe he wasn't one of their own people," Morton suggested. "Maybe we were wrong about him. Maybe he was just an ordinary Roman whom they used."

"Then explain the cigarettes we found in his room," said Maselli. "And the warp disc and the laser he had hidden away. No, Marcian or whoever he really was had to be either T.I.A. or Underground. We know their Temporal Intelligence agents used contacts in the Underground from time to time. Hell, we've done the same thing. So either way, it doesn't make any sense that they should kill him. There's got to be a part of the picture we're not seeing. In any case, it probably doesn't matter anymore. If they had any doubts about us before, they don't after tonight. I think it's time we considered aborting the mission."

Hollister spun around to face him. "We're not aborting anything, Maselli! We've come too far and we're too close to give up now! Besides, we're still holding all the cards. So long as we stick close to Caesar and Cleopatra, they can't touch us. Not without risking a temporal disruption. They can bring in as many people as they want, an entire fucking army, and it still wouldn't do them any good. Caesar's got to die on the fifteenth and he's got to be murdered by Brutus, Cassius, and the other conspirators. Anything they do to change that would play right into our hands. Even if they figured out some way to get the conspirators past A team and take out Caesar, we've still got Cleopatra. And we can still shift our objective to Antony or Octavian. Their hands are tied by their own temporal continuity. We don't have to worry about that, do we?"

"No, sir, I guess we don't," said Maselli.

"You're damn right, we don't. Just about anything we do here can constitute a disruption, so we stick to the original objective. Morton, you get back to the rest of A team. If Caesar asks about the missing men, tell him that you sent them out for wine or something and they were set upon and killed. That should make Caesar think twice about discounting the rumors of a conspiracy against him. Maselli, I want you to bring the rest of C team in. From now on, A team sticks to Caesar like glue, B and C teams remain right here at baseops. If Cleopatra decides to go out, B team stays as close to her as possible. She's our insurance. In the meantime, we'll double the guard here, just in case they're crazy enough to try anything. And nobody, *nobody*, gets inside unless they've been cleared through me first. Got that?"

"Yes, sir."

"Any questions?"

"No, sir."

"Right. Dismissed."

They all snapped to attention. Morton and Maselli both clocked out and the others went back to take their posts. Hollister took his cigar out of his mouth, spat out a soggy piece of tobacco, and crushed the butt out in a small dish he was using as an ashtray.

Merely a minor setback, Hollister told himself. So they'd lost a few people. They had expected that. They had all volunteered for this assignment, this mission from which there would be no return, and they had all expected to die, if not in this temporal scenario, then in some other one they'd clock to after they were finished in Rome. The plan was simple. Cross over and research one temporal scenario early in their history as thoroughly as possible, create a disruption that would have maximum impact, then immediately clock ahead to another time period and try to pull off another one. Keep doing that, building on the domino effect of temporal disruptions in their timeline until they were either all killed or until there was no possible chance of the T.I.A. being able to reverse their actions. Then, thought Hollister, their one remaining chance for survival would be to find some time period that was still relatively safe, while the damage escalated of its own momentum elsewhere in the timestream.

Until tonight, everything had gone off like clockwork. The one part he hadn't liked was killing their own Observers, but there was no avoiding it. It had to be done. The poor bastards hadn't known what was coming, of course. They had thought that they were just sent through to scout a temporal location for a baseops that would serve as a jumping-off point for temporal assault missions further down the enemy timestream. But at least they were able to make it quick and painless.

The rest of it was easy. Killing the real Apollodorus and taking his place had proved no problem. Hollister had been carefully selected for the mission so that his body type would correspond with that of Apollodorus and the rest had been accomplished by cosmetic surgery. Cleopatra had never suspected a thing. The rest of it, getting the others into place, had all been easy once he had assumed the identity of Apollodorus. Cleopatra trusted him. Even now, she was sleeping soundly in her bedroom, having had her bones jumped by the Emperor of Rome, never suspecting that anything was amiss in her household. So long as she was there, she was the perfect hostage. There were guards outside her door and all around the building and the grounds. Even on the roof. They still had a firm lock on the situation.

Hollister poured himself some wine and walked over to the window. The shutters were open to let in the cool night breeze. He looked out at the dark surface of the Tiber, and along its banks, toward the house where Travers lived.

"Come ahead, you bastards," he said softly. "Take your best shot."

The scene inside the library of the handsome Roman villa of Lucius Septimus was highly incongruous, to say the least. It was three o'clock in the morning. The library door was bolted, just in case any of the household slaves felt restless in the middle of the night, heard voices in the library and decided to investigate. Travers had given strict orders to his household slaves and they knew that certain rooms in the house were off limits to them, especially the library, but had they glanced inside, what they would have seen would have astonished them.

Reinforcements had arrived. Finn Delaney, Creed Steiger, Andre Cross, and Lucas Priest had all doffed their Roman tunics and were now dressed in black combat fatigues, with lasers holstered at their sides. They had spare charge packs attached to their belts and combat bowies strapped to their calves, above their boots. They wore extremely lightweight, black nylon, Balaclava-type hoods over their heads, leaving only the area from the mouth to the eyebrows exposed, and those parts of their faces had been blackened with camo stick. There were two dozen other people in the room, all similarly dressed for night fighting. Some of them, in addition to their laser pistols, were armed with night-scoped laser rifles, others with the ugly, mean-looking disruptors designed by Dr. Darkness, which looked incredibly innocuous for what they were. They resembled a cross between a small riot gun and an antique blunderbuss, but they were considerably more sophisticated than either, capable of firing a pulsed neutron beam on either tight focus beam or wide spray. Their inventor sat comfortably in a carved ivory chair, observing the proceedings.

Lucas and Finn stood over a couple of hastily drawn interior maps of both Cleopatra's house and the imperial palace. Seeing Lucas had been a shock for those who had arrived, because they had all believed him dead. But it was a mark of their professionalism that, stunned as they were, they simply accepted his remark that there would be time for explanations later. They were all bursting with questions, but those questions would have to wait. They had a mission to perform.

"All right, let's go over it again," said Lucas. "Bryant, you'll take your team into the palace. Where are the guards' quarters?"

"Right here," said Major Bryant. He pointed to the drawing with his bowie knife. "There will probably be at least a couple of them posted in the corridor. We're going to have to get in fast, clocking directly to the transition points that Capt. Travers has supplied, which will put us here, here, here, and here."

"Good," said Lucas. "Now remember, we don't want any accidents, so be sure that everyone clocks in no closer than three feet away from each other. Check your final coordinates now."

He waited while they did so.

"All right. Caesar's chambers are right here." He pointed to the diagram. "He sleeps there with his wife. Be sure to take out the guards at his door right away. And you've got to do it without making any noise. Now, these areas marked off here, with stars, are where Roman legionaries are usually stationed. Stay the hell away from them, whatever you do."

"What if something goes wrong and we accidentally alert any of the Roman guards?" asked Bryant.

"Make sure you don't," Delaney said, staring at him hard. "If you have to, knock them out, but under no circumstances are any of them to be fired upon. We can't afford to raise an alarm in the palace. You've got one thing going for you. None of the S.O.G. people will be wearing Roman uniforms. As part of their cover, they'll be dressed as Egyptian soldiers. Either that, or they'll be in their quarters, asleep. I doubt they'd expect us to try anything this desperate. So with any luck, you'll get most of them in bed. I hope."

"Yeah, so do I," said Bryant.

"Use disruptors on all the bodies," Lucas said. "I want them all to disappear without a trace."

"How are you going to explain that?" asked Sgt. Neilson, who'd worked with them before on a mission in 19th-century London.

"It's not your job to worry about that, Scott," Lucas said. "Leave that part to me. I've got it covered."

"Yes, sir. Sorry, sir."

"No need to apologize. You just do your part, we'll take care of ours. You'll have more than enough to worry about. You guys are going to have to move fast and there won't be any room for mistakes."

"That's what I've always liked about you, Lucas," said Bryant with a smile. "You always give me the easy jobs."

"You'll have the Doc here for backup," said Lucas, "in case anything goes wrong. But don't count on him for everything. He can't be everywhere at once, even though it sometimes seems that way."

"Glad to have you along, Doctor," Bryant said.

"Just try not to trip over one another and wake up the whole palace," Darkness said.

"We'll take our shoes off and walk on tippy-toe," Bryant replied, deadpan.

"Okay, Cooper, let's go over your end of it," Lucas said.

Col. Cooper was the commander of the Temporal Counter-Insurgency strike force headquartered in Galveston. The T.C.I. troops were elite combat commandos, specially formed by General Forrester to deal with S.O.G. infiltrations. They were on constant standby, in combat readiness, and for this operation, Cooper had clocked in with a dozen picked men.

"We'll be going in with Delaney, Cross, and Steiger to hit Cleopatra's house," Cooper said. "There are some Roman soldiers stationed outside, here at the front gates." He pointed to the second diagram. "We trank them with stun darts. I have three men clock in here, here, and here. That should give them a good shot at the guards. What about traffic in the street?"

"There isn't any traffic on that street this time of night, so

the risk should be minimal," said Lucas. "But if any
pedestrians happen to get in the way, trank them, too."

"Got it," Cooper replied with a curt nod. "The rest of my
people clock in here, here, and here. Three on the roof,
three in the back garden, three in the atrium."

"Right," Lucas said. "Now here's where it gets unpleasant. Some of the people in there could be Egyptian slaves,
or they could all be S.O.G. Unfortunately, we haven't got
any way of telling that for sure. That puts your people in a
pretty tricky situation. Except for the legionaries at the front
gate, anyone stationed on guard duty will be S.O.G. for
sure, so don't take any chances with them. Take them out
right away. But the moment you get inside the house, you
run the risk of killing innocent civilians, so use your
stunners. Unless you see someone carrying any weapon
other than a dagger or a sword. In that case, take 'em out.
But we need to get at least one or two of them alive for
interrogation, just to make sure we've got them all. Now
there's going to be a risk factor involved in doing it that
way. Anyone you trank, you got maybe a second or two
before they go down, and if they've got a concealed weapon
on them, they just might have enough time to get off a shot
before the drug takes effect, so watch yourselves. Stay in
your teams of three. Two men carrying stunners, the third
ready with a laser or disruptor. Again, speed's going to be
critical, but remember that these people are all pros. All
right, Finn, let's go over your part."

"Creed, Andre, and I are clocking in directly to the
peristylum, right here," Delaney said, pointing to the
drawing. "Our objective is to try to take Apollodorus alive,
if possible. As soon as the house has been secured, we
conduct a thorough search, remove anything that doesn't
belong there, then get right back here."

"Right," Lucas said. He looked around at them. "Any
questions?"

Cooper shook his head. "No. My people are ready."

"None here," said Bryant.

"I guess we're set," Delaney said.

Lucas took a deep breath. "All right, then. Everyone stand by. Doc, you want to go get our guest of honor?"

"I'd be delighted," Darkness said. He disappeared.

Simmons listened on the headphones as he aimed the dish mike at Travers' house.

"What's going on?" asked one of the Network men beside him. They were concealed behind a clump of bushes near the riverbank.

"They've clocked in reinforcements," Simmons said. "From the sound of it, some of them are old First Division commandos and some are T.C.I. troops."

"T.C.I.?" one of the others said. "Jesus, they brought in the fucking strike force?"

"Yeah. Cooper's in there. I can't tell exactly how many of his people he's brought with him, but I'd say at least a dozen, plus the T.I.A. assault team. Bryant's in command, so it sounds like they brought in some of the old First Division people."

"Shit. This just became a brand-new ballgame."

"It's still the same game, Rick. There's just a few more players, that's all," Simmons replied.

"The hell you say! Taking on First Division commandos is bad enough, but Cooper's a stone-cold killer. Some of his strike force recruits don't even survive the training. What the hell are they planning in there, a goddamn war?"

"That's about the size of it," said Simmons. "They're about to launch a simultaneous two-pronged assault against the S.O.G., in the palace and at Cleopatra's house."

"Fuck. They *are* crazy. No way do I want any part of this!"

"We came here to do a job, Warren," said Simmons.

"Yeah, against Steiger and maybe the adjustment team, but not a whole assault force. There's only eight of us, for Christ's sake!"

"We don't have to take on the whole assault force," Simmons said. "All we have to do is pick the right moment, take out Steiger in all the confusion and we're gone."

"Forget it! I don't know about the rest of you, but I'm not about to take my chances against those kind of odds. You want that bounty on Steiger so bad, Simmons, you're welcome to it. I'm outta here."

"Warren . . ." Simmons began, but Warren had already clocked out. "Warren? Son of a *bitch*!"

"Warren's right," one of the others said. "This whole thing just became too hot to handle. Let's get the hell out of here. It's not worth it."

"It's worth it to me," insisted Simmons. "That bastard busted up some of our best operations and he cost me my career. And he did the same thing to every one of you."

"So there'll be other opportunities to square accounts," the man named Rick said. "This one just went sour. It's just too risky. I'm out."

"So am I," one of the others said.

"Me, too. I didn't bargain for this."

"Fine," said Simmons coldly. "If you gutless wonders want to tuck your tails between your legs and run, then go. I don't need you. I'll do it myself."

"Don't be a fool. Why take the chance? There'll be another time."

"No," said Simmons firmly. "It's gonna be this time. Right *here*. Right *now*."

"Suit yourself," said Rick, shaking his head. "It's your funeral."

"Oh, there'll be a funeral, all right," said Simmons. "Only it ain't gonna be mine."

There were two guards standing on either side of the doorway to Cleopatra's bedroom. Neither of them heard a thing as Darkness suddenly materialized beside the Queen of Egypt's bed. He reached out and flung the bedclothes off her and as she jerked awake with a gasp, he pulled her into his tachyon field and translocated. Before Cleopatra could even react to what was happening, she had reappeared with Darkness a nanosecond later in the library of Travers' home. Corwin held her while Castelli fired a stun dart into her upper arm.

"Sorry about that, Your Highness," said Castelli. "But it'll be okay, you won't remember a damn thing."

She collapsed in Corwin's arms with a small moan.

Lucas gave the order. "Okay, people. *Move out!*"

Bryant's team clocked out to the palace. Simultaneously, Cooper's strike force unit clocked to Cleopatra's house.

"Okay," Lucas said to Castelli and Corwin. "You know what to do. Move."

Castelli and Corwin snapped a preprogrammed warp disc around Cleopatra's wrist and clocked out to the future.

"Andell, you ready?" Lucas said.

"Ready," said Sgt. Andell.

"Okay, Finn, get going," Lucas said.

"Good luck, Lucas," said Delaney.

"You, too."

"Travers, if we're not back in ten minutes, get the hell out of here," Delaney said.

"You'll be back," said Travers.

"Okay," said Lucas. "Let's go for broke."

They all clocked out together, leaving Travers alone in the library. He crossed his fingers.

There were two S.O.G. men standing guard outside the door of Caesar's chambers. Two more were stationed in front of the sleeping quarters of the guards. There was a sudden *whoosh*, followed by a loud *thwaack*! One of the guards at Caesar's door crumpled unconscious to the ground. The other guard jerked around, startled, but he didn't see a thing except the unconscious form of his companion. Suddenly a disembodied hand appeared floating in midair, about a foot and a half in front of him. It was holding a blackthorn walking stick. The guard's jaw dropped as he stared at it with astonishment. *Whoosh, thwaack!* Two down.

Major Bryant materialized in front of the two fallen guards, holding his disruptor. He glanced down quickly at their unconscious forms, then looked up to see Dr. Darkness leaning back against the wall, blowing an imaginary speck of dust from the head of his walking stick. Bryant tossed him a casual salute. Darkness touched his walking stick to the brim of his hat.

At the same time, the other commandos of Bryant's team clocked in to their transition points. They fired their disruptors and the guards were briefly wreathed in the blue glow of Cherenkov radiation as the neutron beams struck them, then they disintegrated. They never even had a chance to scream.

Bryant aimed his disruptor down at the unconscious guards and quickly disposed of them, then moved quickly and silently toward the sleeping quarters of the other S.O.G. men. Moving softly, the commandos fanned out throughout the room, covering the sleeping guards. One of them, either feeling the call of nature or reacting subconsciously to their presence, woke up. He had only an instant in which to register the black-clad men spread out throughout the room. He opened his mouth to shout out a warning, but at that precise instant, they all fired. The room became bathed in the bright blue glow of Cherenkov radiation as the S.O.G. men, their bedclothes, and their beds all disintegrated. It was over in a matter of seconds.

As Bryant and his team coped with the guards, Lucas and Andell clocked directly into Caesar's bedroom. Calpurnia was sound asleep, but Caesar, a light sleeper with instincts honed by years of battle, awoke as they started to move toward his bed. He sat up suddenly as Lucas quickly raised his stunner and fired a dart into his chest. Caesar jerked and fell back onto the bed. At the same time, Andell fired a dart into Calpurnia. She jerked slightly and moaned, then lay perfectly motionless.

"A trifle late, there," Darkness said as he appeared standing against the wall, toying with his walking stick.

"How are the others doing?" Lucas said as he and Andell quickly started strapping preprogrammed warp discs around the wrists of Caesar and his wife.

"Surprisingly, they seem to have the situation well in hand," said Darkness. "I'd better go check on that great clod, Delaney, and see if he's managed to do his part without shooting himself in the foot."

He disappeared.

"If you ask me, that man's a few cards short of a full deck," Andell said.

"Maybe," Lucas replied, "but what cards he does have are all marked. You ready?"

"Ready," said Andell.

"Okay, check your time. I want them both clocked back here exactly one minute from now. Ready?"

"Mark!" Andell said.

"Go!"

Andell activated the warp disc on Calpurnia's wrist while Lucas simultaneously clocked out Caesar. They both vanished.

"All right, I'm on my way," Andell said. "Good luck, Lucas."

"You, too."

Andell clocked out.

Now came the tough part. Lucas held his laser pistol in one hand and his stunner in the other. He stood back against the wall, out of immediate sight of anyone who might be coming through the doorway, but in a position where he could clearly see them. Now all he had to do was keep the room secure and wait for the longest minute in the world.

Cooper's strike force troops started moving the second they clocked in. Three of them took down the legionaries posted at the front gates, aiming carefully and firing their stun darts into the exposed flesh at the upper arms and thighs of the soldiers, where their breastplates could not deflect them. Then they immediately started moving onto the grounds. Three more men clocked in on the roof and that was where they sustained their first casualty.

One of the S.O.G. guards on the rooftop just happened to move to the same spot where one of Cooper's men was clocking in. Two objects could not occupy the same time and space simultaneously. There was a brief, agonized scream, and then a hideous, misshapen mass of bloody, writhing flesh that was barely recognizable as being human fell to the rooftop. For an instant, the other rooftop guards were too shocked to move and in that instant, Cooper's men fired their disruptors. The S.O.G. men were briefly wreathed in a blue aura, then they disappeared.

"Oh, God," one of Cooper's men said, staring at the horror lying at his feet.

The other one fired his disruptor at it, disintegrating the

sickening remains of two fused human bodies. "Come on, snap out of it! The whole house must've heard that scream!"

Indeed, the whole house had. In that moment, the element of surprise so necessary to the speedy conclusion of the raid was lost. Hollister heard the scream and came awake instantly, rolling out of bed and lunging for his weapon. He was already shouting out a warning at the top of his lungs as his fingers closed around it and he went running out into the hall barefoot, dressed only in his tunic.

The guards outside Cleopatra's bedroom immediately ran inside to seize their hostage and were dismayed to see the bed empty. They wasted valuable seconds looking for her around the room. By the time they heard the sounds behind them, it was already too late. The stun darts struck them as they turned and collapsed to the floor.

Outside on the grounds, laser beams crisscrossed in the darkness as the firefight erupted between the S.O.G. men on security duty and the men of Cooper's unit. As Delaney, Steiger, and Andre clocked into the *peristylum*, they could already hear the sounds of shouting and running feet.

"God *damn* it!" said Delaney. "Come on, let's *move*!"

They ran across the open space of the courtyard, heading toward the servants' quarters.

"Watch it!" Andre shouted.

She dove to the ground and rolled as a laser beam stabbed through the air above her and fired as she came up. One of the S.O.G. men fell. Delaney dropped another one and they kept going, moving as quickly as they could, the adrenaline pounding through their systems.

Hollister spotted three men moving down the corridor and fired without hesitation. Two of Cooper's men fell dead, one of them the man armed with the disruptor. The third man brought up his stunner and fired, but Hollister quickly ducked behind a column and fired. The third man went down.

Laser beams made a webwork of light in the atrium as the two opposing forces met in the central hall. Cooper's team had taken casualties, but the S.O.G. men in the grounds had all been dealt with and the fight now moved entirely indoors. Several of the household slaves ran screaming in terror down the corridors and were dropped by stun darts, though a few ran directly into the path of laser and disruptor beams and ceased to exist. Others cowered fearfully in their quarters, convinced the world was coming to an end, while a few simply dropped down to their knees in supplication before the invading demons and were quickly tranked.

Outside, Simmons moved carefully across the grounds, crouching low and taking advantage of the darkness, holding his laser pistol ready. His warp disc was already preprogrammed with his escape coordinates. Screw the others, he thought. Who needs them? This was the perfect opportunity. In all the confusion, he could slip in and nail Steiger, then be gone before anybody realized what had happened. He bent over the body of one of Cooper's men. Perfect. He quickly stripped off his own clothes and started putting on the corpse's T.C.I. fatigues. He slipped the black Balaclava hood over his head, then smiled as he picked up the disruptor.

Hollister came bursting into Cleopatra's room, then stopped as he saw the unconscious bodies of his men lying on the floor. There was no sign of Cleopatra. Somehow, incredibly, they had managed to get her out. He couldn't believe it. He heard running footsteps coming down the hall. He quickly punched in a preprogrammed sequence of transition coordinates and clocked out just as Delaney came diving through the doorway, firing his stunner. The dart passed harmlessly through empty air.

Lucas waited tensely, glancing every couple of seconds at the readout on his warp disc. The time was almost up. Andell had clocked to Plus Time with Caesar and Calpurnia, as had Castelli and Corwin, with Cleopatra. It would take days for them to be properly conditioned by the psych teams at TAC-HQ, but then they would be clocked back to Minus Time so that only one minute would have passed since they'd been gone. They would reappear, sedated, safely in their own beds. They would wake up several hours later, completely oblivious of what had happened to them.

As soon as the operation at Cleopatra's house was concluded, assuming that it was concluded successfully, the survivors would be clocked to Plus Time and interrogated under drugs. The household slaves would then be separated from any surviving S.O.G. infiltrators. Castelli would take charge of a team that would clock out to ancient Egypt, where they would purchase slaves that would replace the S.O.G. men. Once those slaves had been acquired from the markets in Alexandria, they would then be tranked and clocked to Plus Time, where they would be conditioned to believe that they had been in the Queen of Egypt's service all along. Cleopatra herself would be conditioned to believe that they had come to Rome with her. Then Castelli and his team would clock back in with them, all before daybreak.

Cleopatra would remember nothing of what had happened to her. She would recall meeting Marcus Septimus and his wife, Antonia, though she would believe that they had left Rome. Both Caesar and Calpurnia would recall how he had dismissed his Egyptian bodyguard because he did not wish to give the appearance that he feared his enemies or that he was too much under the influence of a foreign queen.

In a matter of seconds, Lucas thought, if all goes well, Caesar and his wife would reappear in their bed and they would wake up in the morning as if nothing had ever happened. Cleopatra and her new slaves would be clocked back into her house.

They had put the plan together quickly, but it seemed to Lucas as if they'd covered every contingency. At least, he hoped they had. Everything hinged on the assault against the S.O.G. unit at Cleopatra's house being successful. Lucas checked the time again. Another few seconds. He swallowed nervously. *Had* they covered everything? All right, he thought, come on. What have we missed? What else can go wrong?

Hollister materialized inside the quarters assigned to his men at the imperial palace. And froze, absolutely stunned. He recovered quickly and glanced around, sweeping his weapon around the room, but Bryant and his team had already left. He had missed encountering them by scant seconds. He moved quickly to the door leading to the corridor and listened intently. Everything seemed quiet.

For a moment, he simply stood there, not moving. He risked a glance out into the corridor. There was no sign of his men. They were all gone, every last one of them. Jesus, Hollister thought, they must have hit the palace and the house at the same time! He was staggered by their audacity. They must have clocked into the palace, and while Caesar slept just a short distance down the hall, they had killed every one of his men and gotten out again, a lightning operation, brilliantly executed and devastatingly efficient. He had never dreamed they would dare take such a risk. He had vastly underestimated them and it had cost him. It had cost him everything.

His mind reeled as he realized that his operation was totally undone. All that work, all that preparation, wiped out in just one night. It was beyond belief. How in hell had they managed to snatch Cleopatra? And how could they cover everything that they had done without risking a temporal disruption? He had to think. He had to put himself in their shoes and imagine what he might have done if he were in their place. And if he were desperate enough to try something like this. Desperate, hell, he told himself, the bastards had actually pulled it off.

All right, he thought, if they snatched Cleopatra, they could do a wash job on her brain. Program her and she'd come out believing whatever they wanted her to believe. They'd have to do the same with Caesar. Make him believe that he'd dismissed the bodyguard. God damn it, it'll work, thought Hollister. They've beaten us.

His heart sank with the realization. But it wasn't over yet. He was still alive. And if any of his men got out, they'd clock to their escape coordinates and rendezvous as planned. He wasn't finished yet. Even if he was the only one left, he could still do some damage here.

Hollister, well trained in temporal terrorist tactics, had quickly and professionally sized up the situation. He was not the sort of man to panic when things fell apart. He was a pro and he kept his mind on his mission. The parameters had changed drastically and he had to adapt to the new situation without a moment's hesitation. He realized that the success of the T.I.A. strike was totally dependent on everything being accomplished during this one night. The activities of mission support teams back at headquarters in Plus Time would have to be completely governed by the timetable of the team in Rome. The timing would be close. If they'd taken Caesar when they killed his men, which would have been the only time when they could do it, they would have to return him by morning in order to minimize the danger of a temporal disruption. Then, with their teams in place to monitor events, they would remain to make sure that Caesar was killed by the conspirators on schedule.

Only what if he died a week early, murdered along with his wife in his own bedchamber?

There could then be no explanation for the sudden disappearance of the Egyptian bodyguard. The blame for Caesar's death would fall on Cleopatra, instead of on Brutus, Cassius, and the other conspirators. She would be arrested, tried, and executed. She would never live to join forces with Antony against Octavian. It would not be as great a disruption as they'd originally planned, but it would be a disruption nonetheless. It might even bring about a timestream split. Best of all, the T.I.A. wouldn't be expecting it. When they discovered that they'd missed "Apollodorus," they'd naturally assume that he'd escaped to some other time period. It would have been the logical thing for him to do. They'd never think he'd risk coming to the palace. It would be foolhardy. Almost as foolhardly as what they'd done tonight. Hollister smiled. Learn from your enemy, he thought. It was risky as hell, but it was worth a try.

Slowly, cautiously, holding his weapon ready, Hollister moved out into the corridor, heading toward Caesar's chambers.

11 ===============

They had counted on the element of surprise and they had lost it almost immediately. The scream from the rooftop had galvanized the opposition into action and even though they hadn't expected such a bold attack, they responded like the pros they were. They didn't run; they chose to stand and fight.

In spite of the swiftness of their attack, Cooper lost almost half his men in the first three or four minutes of the assault. Three more were wounded, two of them seriously. As Andre ran across the atrium, a laser beam lanced out and burned a hole right through the left side of her shirt, missing her kidney by scant millimeters. Steiger, running right behind her, took out the man who'd fired the shot, but another one they hadn't seen until it was almost too late fired at him as he was bringing up his stunner. The beam struck Steiger's forearm and burned a long furrow from his wrist up to his elbow. He cried out, but managed to hold on to his weapon long enough to fire a dart into his attacker, and Andre shot him with another one almost immediately. He crumpled to the floor.

"You all right?" asked Andre.

"I'm fine, go!" Steiger shifted his weapon to his left hand

and followed her as they moved quickly from room to room.

Cooper's men had rapelled down from the rooftop and as soon as they secured the upper floor, they ran down the stairs to join the battle in the main part of the house. Cooper heard the sounds of their booted feet coming down the stairs and turned his head to shout a warning to them so they wouldn't fire on their own men. In that instant, a laser beam burned its way through his left cheek and out the right. Cooper was so psyched, he didn't even feel the pain. He spun around and fired, dropping his attacker, then kept right on going. If he hadn't turned his head just at the right moment, the laser would probably have killed him.

Delaney found himself pinned down behind a column in the atrium, under fire from three directions at once. Three laser beams bracketed him, one passing to either side of the column, the third grazing the marble, inches from his head. He dropped down low and risked a glance around the column. In that instant, he saw a sight that made his jaw drop.

Darkness suddenly appeared out of thin air and, moving faster than the speed of light, plucked the weapon from the hand of one man while he knocked him senseless with his cane. Then he materialized behind the second gunman and clubbed him to the ground, before his afterimage had even faded from where he had first appeared. He repeated the same procedure with the third S.O.G. man, but at the speed with which he moved, it all happened in the same instant and Delaney actually saw *three* of him. He jumped about a foot when Darkness appeared standing right beside him.

"Somehow I knew I'd find you in a situation like this," Darkness said laconically.

"Jesus, Doc," Delaney said, exhaling heavily, "I wish you wouldn't *do* that!"

"If I hadn't done that, you lunkhead, you'd look like a Swiss cheese."

"How's Bryant doing at the palace?"

"Knocking them dead," said Darkness. "You, on the

other hand, seem to be having a few problems. Excuse me. . . ."

Suddenly he simply wasn't there anymore. Delaney heard a sickening crunch behind him and spun around in time to see Darkness dropping the limp form of an S.O.G. man whose head he'd smashed against a marble column. Then he jerked as he suddenly heard Darkness speaking beside him even as he saw his image disappear again.

"I'd move somewhere else, if I were you."

"Thanks, Doc."

"Don't mention it."

He vanished.

Delaney crossed the atrium and encountered Cooper and two of his men coming the other way. Andrew and Steiger came running up behind them. Several more strike force commandos came running into the atrium from the opposite side.

"Our wing's secured, sir."

"Second floor secured."

"Grounds secured, sir."

"How many did we lose?" asked Cooper, glancing around quickly.

"Kaufman bought it outside," one of the men said.

"Hockett's dead," another man said. "He clocked in right on top of one of the roof guards."

"Poor bastard," said Delaney.

"We lost Bishop and Grant."

"Campbell's wounded. We had to clock him out."

"How bad?" asked Cooper.

"Pretty bad. I don't know. He may not make it."

"Connors, you hit?"

"I'll make it."

"Where's Sharp?"

Silence.

"Damn it. Okay, you all know what to do. Find Sharp, see if he's alive. Search the house and grounds. All bodies, tranked or dead, get clocked to TAC-HQ. Make sure there aren't any weapons left lying around. Move it!"

"Well done, Colonel," said Delaney.

"You're hit."

"So are you."

"Yeah, but I'll be okay long as I don't drink any beer," said Cooper. "Did you get your man?"

"No, dammit," said Delaney. "I had a shot, but I was just a second too late. He clocked out on us."

"Well, we might get lucky and track him down through one of the prisoners, but he's probably long gone," said Steiger.

"We'll have some of Bryant's people on Octavian and Antony, just in case," said Andre.

"Where's Darkness?"

"Who the hell knows?" Delaney said. "He saved my ass back there and then just popped off, like he always does. But he said things at the palace were under control."

"We'd better get back to the house and check on how it went with Lucas," said Andre.

"Cooper, why don't you clock out with your wounded and get yourself and them some medical attention?" Steiger said. "I'll take over here."

"Thanks. I appreciate it."

"Okay, I'll meet you all back at the house," said Steiger. "Go tell Travers we pulled it off before he dies of an anxiety attack."

Andre and Finn clocked out while Cooper hurried to check on his wounded. Steiger stood alone in the atrium. He took a deep breath and let it out slowly. I'll be damned, he thought. We did it.

"Steiger. . . ."

He turned around. One of Cooper's men was standing by a marble column about twenty feet away, holding a disruptor.

"What is it, soldier?"

"It's payback time, you bastard."

"Simmons!"

As Simmons fired, Steiger made a flying dive to the left. The deadly blast from the disruptor barely missed him. He rolled and came up with his laser in his hand. Both men fired at the same time.

• • •

"Now," said Lucas, and Caesar and Calpurnia suddenly materialized beside each other on their bed. Lucas heaved a deep sigh of relief. Andell was right on schedule. He laid his weapons on the bed and bent to remove the warp disc from Calpurnia's wrist, then went around to the other side to get the one that Caesar wore.

As he started to remove it, he heard a voice say, "Freeze."

An invisible fist grabbed a handful of his insides and started squeezing. His laser and his stunner were both on the far side of the bed.

"Don't try it," Hollister said. "You'll be dead before you get your hands on 'em. Just straighten up slowly and keep your hands at your sides, where I can see them."

Lucas knew his only chance was his thought-controlled transponder. All he had to do was concentrate and . . .

"Move away from the bed."

Nothing! Lucas tried again, with the same result. It had finally decayed. He had hated the damn thing, but of all the times for it to go out. . . .

"What's your name?" asked Hollister.

Lucas swallowed hard. "Priest. Col. Lucas Priest."

"You in command?"

"That's right," said Lucas. His mind was racing, but there was no way out. The weapon in the S.O.G. man's hand was dead steady. And dead on target. "And what do I call you, Apollodorus?"

"Name's Hollister. Captain. That was some job your people pulled off tonight. Took a lot of fuckin' balls. My compliments, Colonel."

"Thank you, Captain," Lucas said. "I'm just sorry they missed you. Mind if I ask how it went?"

"First-class operation," Hollister replied. "Your people took some losses, but I'm afraid we lost. However, the war's not over yet."

Lucas moistened his lips nervously. There was no chance to rush him. He'd be dead before he got two steps.

"It's funny," Hollister said. "I came here to prevent

Caesar's assassination and instead, I'm going to be the one who kills him."

"Of course," said Lucas. "Caesar and his wife are murdered in their bed, the Egyptians turn up missing, and Cleopatra gets the blame. Very good, Captain. That'll change the whole scenario. For a piece of last-minute improvisation, that's not bad at all. I don't suppose there's any way that I could talk you out of it."

"I'm afraid not, Colonel. I've got my orders. Sorry."

"Hollister, wait," said Lucas quickly. "Listen to me. You can't ever go back again."

"I know that."

"I give you my word of honor as an officer and a gentleman that if you surrender to me, I'll see you're treated well. And I'll guarantee that the men we've taken prisoner from your unit will get the best of treatment."

Hollister smiled. "You know something, Colonel? I believe you. And because I believe you, I'll make you a deal. I know you'd be willing to die to stop me, but you'd never make it, so why die for nothing? You give me your word that you'll see my people are well treated and I'll let you live. Sorry, but that's the best I can do."

Lucas sighed. "Damn you," he said softly. "All right, you've got my word."

"Thank you, Colonel. Now, just to make sure you don't attempt any last-minute heroics, would you be so good as to lie facedown on the floor?"

Lucas hesitated.

"*Now*, Colonel," Hollister said. "Unless you want me to burn a hole in your kneecap."

If I dive across the bed, thought Lucas, he might not kill me with his first shot and I may have a chance to—

Hollister fired and Lucas screamed with pain as his leg buckled underneath him. He fell to the floor, clutching his kneecap and moaning in agony.

"If it's any consolation to you, Colonel, you never would've made it," Hollister said. "I'm a dead shot. Remember, sir, you gave your word."

He raised his laser and aimed it at Caesar's sleeping form.

Whoosh, thwaack!

Hollister cried out as the weapon was struck from his hand and clattered to the floor. The blackthorn walking stick whistled through the air once more and Hollister crumpled to the floor, unconscious.

Lucas looked up, grimacing with pain, and saw Dr. Darkness standing over him.

"Got yourself shot again, I see," said Darkness. "Well, cheer up. At least you didn't get killed this time."

EPILOGUE ══════════════

"Feel up to some visitors?" the nurse said, smiling.

Lucas looked up as Finn, Andre, and Travers walked into the room. Forrester came in behind them and the nurse left to give them some privacy.

"How's the knee?" asked Forrester.

"They tell me it'll be fine after I've had some therapy," said Lucas. He grimaced. "First a bionic eye, now a nysteel kneecap. If I keep this up, before too long I'll be a cyborg. How's Hollister?"

"He's busted up a bit, but he'll live," said Forrester. "Darkness fractured his skull and broke his wrist. He asked about you too, by the way."

Lucas smiled wryly. "He could easily have killed me."

"Why didn't he?" asked Andre.

"Because he was concerned about his men. He said he'd let me live if I gave my word as an officer and gentleman that they would be well treated."

"They will be," Forrester assured him.

"Hollister's a good man," said Lucas. "He just happens to be on the other side. In a way, I feel sorry for him. I trust the rest of the mission went all right?"

"The mission was totally successful," Forrester replied.

"Capt. Travers tells me that there weren't any problems with Cleopatra's reinsertion. Or with Caesar and Calpurnia. With the bodyguard out of the way, the conspirators were able to move against him and he died on schedule, in the Senate. Congratulations. You did a hell of a job."

"Thanks," said Lucas. He glanced at Travers. "How does it feel to be back?"

"A little strange," Travers replied. "It's going to take some getting used to, but I'll have plenty of time. I've already started working on my book. You've given me one hell of a final chapter. I'm going to dedicate it to Col. Steiger's memory, and the other men who fell in battle."

Lucas stared at him, stunned.

"Oh, hell," Travers said with a stricken look. "You didn't know?"

Silence. After a moment, it was broken by Delaney.

"Creed didn't make it, Lucas," he said softly. "He caught it during the assault."

"Oh, shit," said Lucas.

"Nobody saw it happen," Andre said, "but we know who did it. Creed took out his own killer. It was a man named Simmons, a former field agent who was involved with the Network. It's possible that he was involved with the Underground, as well, but if he was, the Underground probably didn't know about his Network connection. They don't knowingly cooperate with those people."

"Damn," said Lucas. "How did it happen?"

"We figure it had to be Marshall," Delaney said. "He's the only one who could have alerted the Network to our presence in Rome, so he must have been involved. Creed obviously never suspected that. He figured that Marshall had just deserted to the Underground because he was burned out, but he must have done it because he was afraid to be exposed. When Creed showed up, he must have panicked."

"So it was Network that intervened when the S.O.G. tried to ambush us?"

"We think so," Delaney said. "They couldn't afford to have a timestream split go down any more than we could. The only one we found was Simmons, so either the others got away or they pulled out when our reinforcements arrived."

"Simmons was a real hardcase," Forrester said. "After Steiger formed the I.S.D., he busted up several Network operations. One of the biggest ones he exposed was headed up by Simmons, only we never got him."

"We never found Creed's body," Andre said, "but we found Simmons. He'd been shot through the heart with a laser. There was a disruptor on the floor beside him. The way we reconstruct it, Simmons got onto the grounds when the assault was in progress. He was wearing Kaufman's uniform, so he must have taken it off Kaufman after he was killed, or maybe he killed Kaufman himself in the confusion and took his disruptor. Then he waited for the right moment and made his move. They must have both fired at the same time."

"So Steiger went down fighting," Lucas said. He sighed "I guess it's the way he would have wanted it."

"He was a good man," said Forrester. "His name's going to be added to the Wall of Honor. At the same time as we take yours off. Officially, you're back among the living."

"What about Darkness?" Lucas asked.

"He disappeared again after the assault," said Delaney. "We haven't seen or heard from him since."

"If it hadn't been for him, Hollister would have beaten us," said Lucas. "One more second and Caesar and his wife would have both been dead."

"Maybe there was a time in which that happened," said Delaney. "A scenario in which Hollister had won. If Darkness hadn't changed your destiny back in Afghanistan, somebody else would've been in that room with Caesar. That could have made all the difference. Maybe it would have been me or Andre, or maybe Steiger. Perhaps his death was the price we had to pay to get history back on the right track."

"But is it?" Lucas asked. "What *is* the right track I wonder if we'll ever know."

"All we can ever know about for sure is our own past," said Forrester. "To Darkness, his past is still our future.

And for all we know, there may well be other people from the future in our present, and our past, trying to influence our actions in an attempt to compensate for whatever disaster lies up ahead. Chances are we may not even live to see it."

"I remember something a Roman centurion once told me, about three thousand years ago," said Travers with a smile. "It was on the night before we crossed the Rubicon, when this whole thing started. He said, 'If it is my fate to die tomorrow, I would prefer not to know of it tonight.' And then he put his hand on his sword hilt and added, 'I would sooner trust my fate to this than to the prophecies of oracles and soothsayers.' He was just a simple soldier, but there was a lot of wisdom in his words."

"Whatever happened to that oracle?" asked Lucas. "What was his name, Lucan?"

"Interesting that you should ask," said Forrester. "We found him."

"You found him?" said Delaney with surprise. "You never mentioned that!"

"Because I'm still not certain what to make of it," said Forrester. He turned to Travers. "You remember how you said he seemed to simply disappear as soon as you passed him through the gate of Caesar's camp?"

"Yes," said Travers. "There was no sign of him. I figured he clocked out."

"He did," said Forrester. "Or, more accurately, he *was* clocked out. After we received your report, we went back a Search and Retrieve team to apprehend him. They got him just as he was coming through the gates."

"Then he disappeared because *you* clocked him out?" said Travers with astonishment.

"That's right," said Forrester. "The temporal anomaly had already occurred with the prophecy itself. But for all we know, perhaps it *wasn't* an anomaly. Because we interrogated all the prisoners extensively and none of them knew anything about the oracle. We also interrogated Lucan himself. As far as we've been able to determine, he was absolutely genuine. He grew up in a village not far from where Caesar made his camp that night."

"But . . . how is that possible?" asked Travers. "If he wasn't from the Special Operations Group, how could he have known about Caesar's assassination? He even knew the exact date, and the names of the assassins!"

"Apparently, he had precognitive powers since early childhood," said Forrester.

"You mean he could *really* see into the future?" Lucas asked.

"It would appear so," said Forrester. "It seems he really had the gift of 'second sight,' if you can call it a gift. He seemed to think of it more as a curse." He paused. "I suppose it must have been. I assigned an agent to keep him under surveillance after we clocked him back to his own time. It was a very short-term mission."

"Why?" asked Lucas. "What happened?"

"I suppose Lucan must have seen something again," said Forrester gravely. "The morning after we clocked him back to his own village, he committed suicide."

"My God," said Travers in a low voice. "He *knew*!"

"He knew what?" asked Forrester, puzzled.

"Just before we passed him through the gates that night, I asked him if he could look into my future," Travers said. "He told me that he couldn't, because he needed time to recover. . . . And he was leaving on a long journey in the morning."

AUTHOR'S NOTE ━━━━━

To those readers who might not be familiar with the history of Rome, I urge you to discover a fascinating subject. There is a wealth of information available, both in your library and in your local bookstore, but some books are more readable than others and for those who might be interested, I can make a few recommendations.

For an overall perspective, the *History of Rome* by Michael Grant is an excellent resource. In fact, anything at all written by Grant would be well worth your time. He has written extensively about Roman history and he has also penned biographies of Caesar, Nero, and Saint Paul. His book, *The Twelve Caesars*, based upon the work of Suetonius, is highly readable and eminently enjoyable. However, I urge you to discover the classical historians themselves, in particular Suetonius *(The Twelve Caesars)* and Plutarch *(Plutarch's Lives)*, as well as Tacitus *(Annals of Imperial Rome)*. For those who aren't afraid of a bit more heavy going, I can recommend Polybius, Livy, and Cassius Dio. Livy is, perhaps, the most readable of the latter three.

There are quite a few books available about daily life in Roman times. The most readable and my personal favorite is F. R. Cowell's *Life in Ancient Rome*. If you are technically oriented, you can consult J. G. Landels' *Engineering in the Ancient World*. For those interested in finding out more about Caesar's legions, I refer you to Harry Pratt Judson's *Caesar's Army: A Study of the Military Art of the Romans in the Last Days of the Republic*. Other references worth consulting are *The Oxford History of the Classical World* by John Boardman, Jasper Griffin, and Oswyn Murray, as well as *A History of Private Life, From Pagan Rome to Byzantium*, edited by Philippe Ariès and Georges Duby.

Also, surprisingly, a number of fine sources can be found in the children's section of your library or bookstore, many of them quite well illustrated. An excellent example is Giovanni Caselli's *The Roman Empire and the Dark Ages*, part of the "History of Everyday Things" series.

Finally, students of Latin will probably be well familiar with Caesar's *Commentaries*, which are briefly referred to in this book. I can well remember suffering through translating them from the Latin when I was in military school and, frankly, at that point, I would have gladly joined Cassius, Brutus, Casca, and the other conspirators in cutting old Julius to pieces. However, those of you who were spared sadistic Latin instructors will find Caesar much more enjoyable in English. Several excellent translations are available, notably Rex Warner's *War Commentaries of Caesar* and *Julius Caesar, The Battle for Gaul* by Anne and Peter Wiseman. These are not books about Caesar, they are actually the words of Caesar himself and it's quite an experience to read the personal chronicles of one of the greatest generals in history and a man who, if he was around today, would have made short work of Libya and Iran. Of course, if he was around today, the Senate would probably kill him all over again. . . .

Simon Hawke
Denver, Colorado